2

Winter Lake

S

Sky Blue Waters Press
http://www.skybluewaterspress.com/

2012

Winter Lake

Craig J. Hansen

Acknowledgements

I want to acknowledge the help of the people who shared their time and talent in reading various drafts. I am indebted to many, including Laurie Bibo, David Ruch, Kevin Giles (whose press is kind enough to publish my work), and Doug Hemer.

I want to express particular gratitude to Laura McLennan, for her eagle-eyed review and proofing, and Karen, my wife, for her reading, re-reading, proofing, wise advice, and unending encouragement. Finally, this is dedicated to the part-time musicians who fill the bars, festivals, coffee shops, and street corners with music, for little more than love of song.

Preface

Winter Lake continues the story that began in The Skeleton Train. Winter Lake can stand alone as a reading experience, but you might find it helpful to read the following synopsis to provide background on some of the characters and events you will encounter in Winter Lake.

Jason Audley narrates his story in The Skeleton Train. It begins when he is fourteen, living in a new suburban development in an industrial Illinois town. He meets a new neighbor, a boy his own age. Davey Miller is good looking and likable—everything that Jason is not. As Jason's family life spirals down, quickly followed by his school life, he finds himself a social pariah, someone Davey Miller ignores. But away from school, Davey and Jason have a quiet friendship, based on the one thing they have in common: a love of hopping freight trains.

Jason's world centers on weeks with his father in a broken-down trailer home, and weekends with his mother, who lives with her lover, the acerbic poet Anna Bella. The center of social life is the restaurant where he washes dishes, chugs leftover drinks and becomes the favorite of a combative waitress, Cherry. Jason—awkward, quiet, poorly dressed—spends much of his time reading. He's an indiscriminate reader, but, whatever it is, he absorbs it.

As the narrative progresses, Jason and Davey concoct increasingly audacious freight train travel. Along the way, they meet others, including a young woman who calls herself The Phaedra. She's both alluring and frightening and tells many conflicting stories about herself. They also meet Rommel, an explosive, ragged man who claims to be a member of the Freight Train Riders of America (a kind of Hell's Angels on the rails).

Jason, Davey, and Phaedra encounter Rommel as they ride a train back to Illinois after visiting Hannibal, Missouri. Rommel abducts Phaedra.

The boys set off to find and rescue Phaedra. It's a perilous quest, full of choices, twists, and sacrifice. In the end, Jason has to choose between Phaedra's strange but compelling world, or finding his own way to adulthood.

Winter Lake begins seven years later.

Chapter 1

"Your Uncle Karl says you play drums," Chess Chalmers says.

"Yup," I say.

"You any good? How long have you played?"

"I've been playing for seven, eight years," I say.

"Here's what I mean by are you any good. Them drummers that got their diddles and daddles and fills that go in circles until the band's lost in the woods, that ain't good. You know, those guys with twenty toms and bongos and whatnot, sit back there like the grand pasha?"

I nod.

"But a drummer who can keep a beat." Chess pounds a funereal rhythm on the table. "That's a drummer. That's what I'm talking about. Can you do that, or are you a diddle-daddler?"

"I can do that," I say.

"This ain't no picnic. We play for some demanding folks. They've come to expect a lot from Chess Chalmers. I'm kind of a celebrity on this circuit, kind of well-known. Respected. Had some hits, you know. Regional. Never made the charts. But these folks, they know me. They know my standards. And we play a whole lot of different stuff. A show band. You follow?"

"I do. You're talking about quality," I offer.

"You bet I am, young man." Chess leans back, pushes his half eaten sandwich away. He waves to the waitress.

"This here's on me," he says when he gets the bill. "I tell you what. I'm going to take a chance here. Your Uncle Karl, he's a stand-up guy. You don't exactly look like a drummer

9

to me. I'll be honest. You're kind of—tall, big. But I'm going to say, let's go for it. I'm going to say welcome from Chess Chalmers."

He offers his hand. It's a firm, brief shake.

"Great," I say. "Mr. Chalmers..."

"Chess," he says, "goddam it son, call me Chess."

"I thought you planted trees," I say.

"Well, yeah, I got a tree farm. But once I get 'em in the ground, I hire out the rest of it to the Mexicans and I tour."

"That's cool," I say. "Where exactly do you tour?"

"Didn't your Uncle Karl tell you anything? It's a big deal, Chess Chalmers and his band. We tour all throughout northern Wisconsin. All summer. Through all them resorts, clubs, casinos, biker bars, you name it."

"So I'm not planting trees?" I say. "You serious about drumming?"

"Hell, yes, son. Those trees are in the ground. That's done. Now it's up to the Mexicans."

Chess gets up, hitches up his jeans. He's a thin man, but he's got a little belly, like he swallowed a grapefruit. Chess looks at me, right in the eyes. "You finish up. I gotta run. What you say your name was?"

"Jason," I say.

"Okay, Jason. We'll meet you here, 6 AM tomorrow. Bring your drums. You got drums, right? Cases?"

"Nope," I say.

Chess nods. "Yeah, well, I got some drums for you to use then. They'll be in the truck. You just show up here, with your personal gear then."

"Tomorrow?" I say.

Chess nods. "I wanted to go this afternoon, but I got some things to take care of."

"Don't you rehearse or something first?"

"Hell, no," Chess smiles. "The boys know the tunes. You'll pick it up." He leans over and taps out the dirge again.

I nod.

Chess winks. "You gonna meet some ladies, ladies who like Chess Chalmers and his band."

"Great," I say.

Chess walks away, stopping to talk to everyone in the diner. They all know him. I guess that's because he's a celebrity.

I go back to Uncle Karl's.

"You get the job?" he asks.

"It was to be a drummer. To go on tour," I say.

"No shit," Uncle Karl says, and laughs. "Well, maybe we can find you something else tomorrow."

"I took it," I say. "I'm going on tour."

Next morning. I'm there, with a duffel. Rained last night and there's a mist close to the ground. Chess introduces me.

"This here's Jake," he says, pointing to me. "New drummer."

"Jason," I say.

"Rusty," says an Asian man about my age. He's smoking, palms his cigarette in his left hand, and shakes with his right. His hand is cold.

"Best goddam lead player north of Kenosha," Chess says. "And over here, these sorry looking sons of bitches, they're the Tierney boys, Bob and Miles. Bass and piano."

They are a few years older than me. "Jake," one says, "welcome, man."

"And here we got Lark," Chess says. "My niece."

Lark is small, skinny. She wears a sleeveless tee shirt. I'm chilly in a jean jacket. Her dark hair is short, kind of a Julius Caesar haircut. She's got a tattoo on one arm, but I can't see what it is.

"She plays trumpet and a little bit of sax," Chess says. "Helps out on the vocals. She brings the zing to the Chess Chalmers band."

Lark frowns at me.

"Me and Lark, we'll drive the truck." A white panel van, rusted, says Chess Chalmers Review in curly, red letters. "You boys, you follow in the Chess-mobile."

It's like an old airport van, with flat gray anti-rust paint. Inside is a split captain's chair for the driver and three tight rows of school bus seats. We toss our gear in the back. Bob drives. He fires it up and exhaust swirls into the cabin. Bob yells something back at us, but we can't hear him over the engine.

Bob turns, yells again. "Try not to breathe deep," he says.

Astrid died three years ago. She's my mother. Was. This is how it should have gone:

Astrid is out running. Tall, bony. Her hair just started to turn gray, and it's tied back. It's long, like a pioneer woman. It swings when she runs. Suddenly, she sees a kid. A blind kid, riding a bicycle. Nothing good can come of this, she thinks. And sure enough, he rides out into the street, right in front of a bus. Astrid reacts instantly, dashes out, snatches the boy off the bicycle just as the bus crushes it. The bus driver, horrified, jerks the wheel and crashes into a tank truck carrying something really volatile. The tank truck flies off the street and lands on a man mowing the grass. Volatile liquid spills, and the spark plug ignites it.

12

There's a thudding explosion and a ball of superheated plasma engulfs everything. The truck. The bus. The man and the lawnmower. The little blind boy. And Astrid, though she never knows what happened. It's too fast. She's aware only of a flash of light and then a sensation of falling. Falling apart, first in big pieces, then in small pieces, then in molecules, atoms, quarks, muons, gluons, and strings. She feels no pain, no fear, no surprise, no regret. She embraces dissolution unlike anything else in her life.

But it didn't happen that way. She got uterine cancer and despite the cuttings, the poisonings, the positive attitudes, it spread through her like kudzu until she was dead. I don't understand cancer's motives, its raison d'être. It exists to grow, to take over, to win. But what it conquers it kills, thereby killing itself. Is it stupid? Or does it have a tragic sense of destiny? Or is it martyrdom? Or does it feel cheated? Striving, growing, living, it all leads to oblivion.

The funny thing, the really funny thing, is that about one year after Astrid died, I got cancer. Miller Construction wanted to take me on full-time, instead of paying me under the table. I had to get a physical.

"Have you been sick?" the doc asks me.

"No," I say.

"Your glands are swollen," he says.

And so I find out, a bit down the line, that I have lymphoma. Hodgkin's disease. One of the most common cancers in young adults, and a good one to get, because, five years after treatment, 80% have not had a reoccurrence.

I had no symptoms, other than swollen lymph nodes. Never felt sick, or lethargic. No pain. Nothing. I felt fine. I felt fine until I went through the treatments. I lost a year to chemo, radiation, and more chemo. Lost my muscles and my hair. Lost contact with my life. What I gained was debt. I had no insurance. The Millers helped me out. Anna Bella helped me out. Lydia, my sister, helped me out. But I am 25 and I can't see that I will ever be able to pay this off. In two years, I've not dented it.

And two years after the treatment, more swollen glands. That's what I have now. No symptoms. Just swollen glands. I can't tell anyone about this. It's embarrassing. I want to be a winner, not a relapser. I can't lose another year. Not just yet. I decide, after sober reflection, to wait and see.

Most of the time, I live in Anna Bella's basement. Anna Bella Woolcott, Astrid's girlfriend. She cried like a baby when Astrid died, and didn't write poetry for six months. During this time, I emptied the dehumidifier, cut the grass, cooked, went to work, took some classes, and got drunk with Anna Bella.

Outside of the van, rain falls and we close the windows. Rusty chain-smokes and I feel queasy. I'm riding in the back, which jolts and bounces crazily, in three dimensions, maybe more. Bob strains to see through the foggy windshield. No A/C, so no real defrost. We lose Chess when one of our wipers flies off. We pull over. Rusty finds it in the ditch, his black hair plastered to his head, a soggy cigarette in his hand.

"Aha!" he says. Bob tries to reattach it, but something's missing, and it flies off again as soon as he turns it on, catapulting back into the ditch. Rusty and Bob think this is hilarious. They do it again, and once more, watch the wiper flip away. It just kills them. Then there's a simultaneous flash of lightning and gut-thumping thunder and we get back in the van.

Bob starts the motor and yells to Rusty, conferring about where to go. Rusty pulls out his cell phone. "Oops," he says. "Battery's dead." In this short time, Miles has fallen asleep. They wake him up because he also has a cell phone, but it's dead, too. He hasn't paid the bill in six months, he says, but he still likes to carry it around.

"Where are we going?" I shout to Rusty.

Rusty turns, grins. "Wherever Bob takes us, man," he says.

We find Chess and the panel truck at a gas station and follow it into Esquato. We aren't far from Green Bay. We pull into the gravel lot of a VFW hall.

"Wedding," Chess tells me. "Perfect place for your first gig. No one gives a shit at a wedding."

We unload equipment into a large, stale room. Card tables have white paper taped over them. Looks like it would seat about 100. There's a small riser for the band back in a dark corner. It's 3 o'clock. We have until 5 to set up. I can haul things, but I'm no help in plugging things in. So I set up the drums, which seem to be missing some important pieces. Like wing nuts to hold the cymbals on, stuff like that. The drum heads are loose and I can't find a drum key to tune them up. I borrow a vise grips from the bartender. Then I stand and watch the boys run cables.

Lark watches for a while, from the opposite side of the stage, and then goes outside. I follow.

"Hey," I say to her.

"I don't want to talk," Lark says. She's staring out at the highway, arms folded loosely. I can see that the tattoo on her arm is Thumper the rabbit.

"Nice tat," I say.

"Look," she says. "I don't want to talk. I don't want to answer questions. I don't want to know anything about you."

"Okay" I say. "Why?"

"Because you are a loser."

"I'm not a loser," I say, by reflex,

She looks at me. "How much are you getting paid for this?"

"For this particular gig, or the whole summer?" I ask.

"You don't know, do you," she says.

I guess I never asked Chess about that. "I play for art," I say.

She raises an eyebrow. "You're an artist," she says. "That's just another name for loser."

"So, it's trumpet you play?" I say. The obvious retort is to say she's a loser, too, if she's in the same band. But that seems like a conversational dead end.

Lark ignores me, looks at the highway. I do, too. It's mostly pickup trucks. After a while, I go inside.

"How much do I get paid?" I ask Chess.

"You better get your mind on the music, Jack," he says.

"No, really." I'm sitting at the drums. We are ready to play. I put my drumsticks down.

"Christ. Alright," Chess says. He's dressed in a white shirt and black jeans, as is the rest of the band. Except Lark. She wears black jeans and a black sleeveless top. Except me. I'm wearing jeans and a Lynwood Lions tee shirt. That's where I went to high school until I got kicked out.

"I told you what clothes to bring," Chess said.

"No you didn't," I say.

"We'll get some for you, though it's coming out of your pay."

"So, what do I get paid?" I say.

"It's complicated. Percentages and such. You know, bonuses, deductions. We'll talk about this later. Get your head into the music now."

"Song list?" I ask.

"Whatever I say we are going to play," Chess says. He turns to the mike, says hi to everyone. Hopes they are having a good time. Congratulates the bride and groom by name. Makes some lame wedding jokes. Miles, the bass player, sidles over. "Just let us start," he says. "Then join in, but make it sound like it's on purpose. You know, come in with--conviction."

"Got it," I say.

Chess introduces us as Chess Chalmers and the Mellowmen, then starts strumming his guitar and singing a sappy old song from the 60's. "Last night at the dance I met Laura..."

I start tapping along. "Isn't this song about a girl who dies and becomes a ghost?" I say to Miles.

He nods. "Makes me want to puke," he says.

Lark adds a little trumpet. Her cheeks puff out and her neck goes red. She looks way too small and skinny to play a horn. It's kind of hard to watch. Chess wiggles his butt as he sings. That's even worse. I search for somewhere safe to aim my eyes. Then a cymbal stand collapses in a ringing crash. Chess jumps a foot in the air.

"Jesus Christ!" he says in the middle of the song.

I learn to stare past Chess and his wiggling butt and watch the crowd. It's interesting watching the wedding party. The bride is chubby, drunk, beautiful. The groom has bushy sideburns and loves his new wife. I can tell. She dances with lots of people and he watches, grinning, happy. He goes under her skirt to get the garter belt and stays there for a while. People start to laugh. We on the riser start to laugh. The bride slaps at her skirt and tells him to get the hell out of there. He does, then throws the garter. A groomsman catches it, the boyfriend, I think, of the girl who caught the bouquet. Everyone's happy. Chess narrates from the microphone, announcing the throws, the dollar dance, the girls-ask-the-boys dance.

A little boy stands near me. He's somber, dressed in a shirt and tie like a little accountant. At the first break, he says, "How long have you been playing drums?"

"45 minutes," I say. I think that's kind of funny.

He nods. "Thought so," he says.

We sit at a table near the stage. Miles and Bob pound down beers. Rusty smokes and sips a rum and coke and watches the party. Chess is milling around in the crowd. Lark is somewhere else. I sit and rotate my plastic glass of beer in its little puddle of sweat. It's stuffy in the VFW.

Guests take turns at the mike. They are pretty drunk. Bridesmaids toast the bride and groom and wipe away tears.

A couple of groomsmen tell stories and end by praising Jesus.

"I didn't see that coming," I tell Rusty.

"What?"

"The Jesus part."

"Oh, beer and Jesus, you know. Kind of goes together up here."

"So you don't have a beer," I say.

"I'm a foreigner," he says. He leans over. "Asian," he says.

"Ah," I say.

The father of the bride is wasted. I think he's looked kind of down all night. Maybe it's money. Maybe it's the loss of his daughter. Maybe it's the gaining of a son. He wobbles to the mike, says a few things and ends by raising his glass and saying, "I just hope these kids are as happy as his mother and I have been." A moment of silence and then laughter. "What?" he says. "What did I say?"

By the third set, it's pretty empty. The bride's father comes over, says we can pack up, pays Chess, then walks to each member of the band, shaking hands and saying how goddam good we were.

"Let's tear down," Chess says. He looks tired and his shirt sticks to him.

Rusty says, "Catch you later boys. I'm going for bridesmaid."

They are standing at the back of the room, 4 of the 6 of them, dressed in tight lime green dresses.

"You are not, goddam it, Rusty," Chess says. "You gotta help us pack up first."

I peel duct tape of my cymbal stands. The screws are stripped and the stands slowly collapsed as I played. By the end of a set, my cymbals were knee high. When we are packed and loaded, we stand around the panel truck.

"Get some food, boys," Chess says, and gives us each $10. "I got us some rooms over at the Super 8. Don't stay out late. We got another gig tomorrow afternoon."

"Wedding?" Miles asks.

"Nope. Festival. Gooseberry Days," Chess says.

"Over at BERF?" Miles says. "Cool."

"Berf?" I say.

"Yes," Chess says. "Where else would it be?"

Chapter 2

We walk over to a little bar next to the VFW, me, Rusty, and the brothers. Lark goes with Chess.

It's dark inside, almost as dark as the parking lot. Smoky. Country music playing quietly. A TV on in a corner over the bar with no sound. Half a dozen guys turn in their barstools when we walk to a table, then they turn back.

Bob goes to the bar, orders a couple of pitchers, gets Rusty a rum and coke.

"You a beer drinker?" Bob asks me.

I nod. Bob pours. Miles starts talking to him and they sort of turn away, talking brother talk I guess. I find they do this a lot.

Rusty is looking at me.

"What are you doing?" he asks.

"Feeling my lymph nodes," I say. "Bad habit."

"It's creepy," Rusty says. Then we sit for a while.

"So," he says. "What do you think?"

"It's great," I say.

Rusty laughs, stubs his cigarette and slowly lights another. "We suck," he says.

"What's this with the Mellowmen?"

Rusty laughs again. "You'll see."

"You've done this before?"

"Yeah," Rusty says. "Last year. So, you got family?"

"Yeah," I say.

"You gotta Mom?" he asks.

"Dead," I say.

"Dad?"

"Dead."

"Brothers? Sisters?"

"All dead."

"Dog?" Rusty says.

"Ran off," I say.

"That's fucking bullshit, man," Rusty says, smiles a little.

"Well, my Mom's dead," I say.

"Don't be killing off your family," he says. "Christ, if I had some, last thing I'd do is say they're dead. Bad luck."

"Sorry," I say.

Rusty takes a long pull on his rum and coke. "I'm adopted," he says.

"Oh," I say. I pour myself another beer. Miles points his empty glass at me without even looking at me. I fill his and top off Bob's.

"What happened to your mother?" Rusty asks.

"Saved a kid from a truck and got blown up."

"Jesus."

"Blown to atoms," I say. "Or subatomic particles. No one knows for sure."

Rusty snorts.

"So I live with my Mom's girlfriend. A black poet named Anna Bella. She has a dog that used to belong to the guy my uncle shot," I say.

"You are so full of shit," Rusty says. "You have a mental condition or something?"

"I'd be the last to know," I say.

I pour another round of beers.

"So, who adopted you?" I ask Rusty.

"Some rich folks in Evanston. That's by Chicago. Jewish couple, nicer than crap," Rusty says. "You play pool?"

We play pool. Rusty is good. So am I. It's a competitive game and some people stand by the table and watch. Then Miles and Bob come over, say it's time to go.

A young woman works by herself at the motel counter. She looks at us a little nervously.

"We got some rooms," Bob says. "Probably under Chalmers."

She looks at us, looks down and flips through a book.

"Yup," she says. "I got it."

"How many?" Bob asks.

"One," she says quietly.

"Shit," Miles says. "He's doing it again."

"What?" I say.

"Nothing," Bob says. He fills in paperwork and grabs the key. "Bed dibs," he says.

The four of us crowd into the single room. The windows won't open and the A/C smells fungal. Bob and Miles say they'll share the only bed. We find a couple of extra pillows and blankets in the closet and Rusty and I sleep on the floor. The carpet smells like ashtray and dog pee.

"Lark," Chess says the next morning, "you ride with the boys. Jack, you ride with me."

"Jason," I mutter.

I get in the panel truck, sit on the bright red plastic seat.

Chess starts it up and slowly pulls away from the motel. He's a slow driver.

"BERF ain't too far," he says. "But we got to be ready to play by one o'clock."

"What is BERF," I ask.

"Black Eagle River Falls," Chess says. "But I didn't invite you in here to talk geography. No, we got some other things to talk about."

"Okay," I say.

"First, not bad on the drumming. A little diddle daddley, but not bad. Let's try not to knock over the gear, though. Scared the living crap out of me. I was in Nam you know and them loud noises, you just don't know what I'm going to do."

"I didn't knock the cymbal over. The screws are stripped..."

"And another thing," Chess says. He pauses, then turns to look at me. "Lark says you been chatting her up."

"Chatting her up? No, I..."

"Listen to me, Jack. That girl has had a world of hurt and she don't need any more trouble. She's a cutie, I know, and real fun to be around. But that's just hiding the pain. You hear what I'm saying. She's a good girl and she don't need any trouble."

"Got it," I say.

"I'm her uncle and if there's trouble, well, you just don't know what I might do."

"Got it."

"Good man," Chess says. "Now let's talk about more pleasant subjects. Number one, you got to grow your hair. Crew cut just doesn't say musician. Number two, we got to get you some stage clothes. It's all about image, about marketing."

"I'll start working on the hair," I say.

"Good man. Marketing. That's half the battle. You win the marketing, and they'll hear whatever you want them to.

See what I mean. If they expect The Beatles, they hear The Beatles."

I nod.

"Do you think my name is really Chess?"

I look at him, waiting.

He waits for me though and says, "Well, do you?"

"I don't know," I say.

"Well, it's not. Name is Chuck. Picked out Chess because of Chubby Checkers," he says.

I must look blank.

"You know, Chubby Checkers, 'Do the Twist' and such?" Chess says.

"So I play on people's minds. That's marketing. I'm Chess, and inside their heads, people are making this connection to Checkers and thinking, I know that name. This guy is famous."

"Makes sense," I say. "Though I thought your real name was Chess."

"That's the beauty of it. Don't matter. Still works. Whether you think it's my name de plume or my real name, you're still going to be thinking, I know this guy."

"So maybe I should change my name," I say.

"No, wouldn't work," Chess says emphatically. "First, you need a plan. Got to think this through. Second, you aren't a headliner."

"Got it," I say. "I'll stick with plain old Jack."

"Good man," Chess says. "To be a headliner, you got to have talent. You got to be an entertainer. You got to have some hits."

"Wish I had some hits," I say.

"Well, you don't. Not yet, anyways. Who knows? Maybe you'll come up with something. Me, I got several."

"We didn't play any last night, did we?" I ask.

"Nope, but we will today. But that's enough chatter. I got to focus on driving, start to get my head into the music. We're just going to listen to the radio now. And you think about all I said. All of it."

BERF is a pretty town. Big trees, nice old houses. A banner across the street says "Gooseberry Days." It's only 10 AM, but Chess frets about getting set up. But we can't set up. The band shell sits in a nice little park, the center of Gooseberry Days festivities. And there's a school band just getting started. They kick off with "On Wisconsin" and the crowd claps along. Chess is not happy, but he tells us to get some food and stay close, because when it's time for us to move, we'll be moving hard and fast.

I sit under a tree and listen to the concert. The kids in the band look really young. Might even be a junior high band. I buy some fried cheese curds and a lemonade from the Lion's Club food trailer. The old guys are friendly. The wind begins to pick up and some paper bags blow across the grass. Sun's out, but it's still cool. Early June in Wisconsin, I guess. I think of going to find a sweatshirt, but I don't know where the van is parked. So I sit in the sun, listen to the band play a Disney theme. Next to me is a playground. Faded timbers, ladders, and a yellow plastic slide—crawling with kids. In one area, kids swing from hand to hand, from ring to ring, graceful primates. Kids charge up the slide, playing tag. Parents watch, some absently, some like life and death. I hear a snuffy sound and turn to see a dog eat my cheese curds.

"Hey," I say. "How's life in BERF?"

Miles and Bob sit down by me. "We found the beer tent," Miles says.

"Where's the van?" I ask.

"Already lots of people in there. You buy tickets and then a beer is 2 tickets."

"I want to get my sweatshirt," I say.

"Here," Bob says, tosses me the keys. "Right behind the bandstand."

I walk past BERFians on blankets, benches, strollers, walkers, skateboards, bikes. As I move closer to the bandstand, the music is louder and I hear all the wrong notes. Rusty is standing next to the van, talking on a cell phone. He moves away as I approach. It's warm in the van and I take my time locating my sweatshirt.

I have an urge to get in and drive away. That's my nature, I suppose. Tom Audley, my father, isn't like that at all. He sticks things out until he fails totally. No half way for Tom. Find a crazy idea and then plumb it to the very depths of potential for disaster. Since he's been hanging with Cherry, though, she chooses the paths and they march toward doom together. That's how I see it anyway. I'm getting morose in the hot van, morose and tired. Maybe I should find the beer tent.

Rusty pulls a door open. "Jesus," he says. "Why don't you just run a hose in here and get it over with? You trying to bake yourself?"

"I got kind of cold," I say.

"Time to unload. You won't be cold for long," Rusty says.

No one is paying much attention to us as we set up and no one pays much attention to us when Chess steps up the mike.

"Testing, testing," he says. "Ho, anyone out there?"

Then a guy walks up, asks to use the mike.

He speaks in a booming voice. "Hey, everyone having fun at Gooseberry Days?" A couple of people clap.

"Well, we got the Miss Gooseberry coronation coming right up after these guys here play you some polka. Here's Chess Chalmers and the Heidelberg Boys."

"We're going to start with you know what!" Chess says, taking back the mike. "The song that made Chess famous."

The guys start playing and start tapping out the ridiculous polka beat—thump, tap, thump, tap. Chess begins to sing.

The Beer Fartin' Polka
By Chess Chalmers

Spend the day with my mother-in-law
Take her out for a drive
I drank way too much beer last night
And now I need somewhere to hide.

The old bat, she sees what's wrong
Why I'm looking tormented and meek.
She makes a face, rolls the window down
Says "I think that I smell rotten meat."

Well, I'm doing the beer fartin' polka
Too much brew did I sip
I'm squirming and dancing to keep it inside
Guess I'll just let her rip.

It can happen at Walmart, happen at church
Happen wherever it's rude
Your wife will avoid you, your dog run away
'Cause inside your guts have been brewed.

Well, I'm doing the beer fartin' polka
Too much brew did I sip
I'm squirming and dancing to keep it inside
Guess I'll just let her rip.

When the song's over, the crowd claps, whistles, and hoots, especially the women. I can't believe they liked it. Chess turns to me, "See kid? That's star power."

Chapter 3

When I was younger, I read all I could about the Romans. I don't like Romans like I used to. The past seems so distant. Yes, you can learn from history, and yes, part of being educated is knowing the past, especially of your own culture. Those are good reasons, except that a) I am not educated, nor am I likely to be and b) the Romans were very un-Audley-ish. They were perhaps western history's greatest overachievers. The Audleys are not historically significant, never will be, and achievement is unknown. You might say I am comparing apples and oranges, an entire classical civilization to a weak-minded branch of an obscure Welsh family. But who says equations have to balance? Why can't Audleys = civilization? I brought this up in a philosophy class, the arbitrary nature of logic, the capriciousness of syllogism. This was an introductory philosophy class at Middle Illinois Community College, taught by a moonlighting choir director. He didn't even know Latin. What kind of educated person doesn't know Latin? I may be distancing myself from Romans, it's true. Latin is another thing—a timeless language, a living language until the Renaissance killed it.

If not Romans, then what? Perhaps I should move further up in time, something more contemporary, like the Middle Ages. They had it all—whole wheat bread, mysticism, strong beer, an overwhelming fear of almost everything. Very Audley. We spent almost two weeks on the Middle Ages in the history class I took at MICC. It was a survey class, and medieval history was a particular passion of Ms. Natalie Boxer, M.A. The Reformation and

Renaissance shared a week. We skipped the Enlightenment altogether.

This is what I'm thinking as I lie in the van, listening to the snores of the Heidelberg Boys.

"Tough luck," Chess says when he finds us in the beer tent. We've been there since the conclusion of our all-polka performance, and I, for one, am drinking it away.

"Something got screwed up at the motel. Just a room for Lark and me. Sorry guys," Chess says. "I grabbed some blankets and such and they're in the van. One night sleeping in the van won't kill you." He laughs heartily. "See you all tomorrow."

Along with the snoring I hear the sound of an air compressor and nail guns. I sit up and see that they are reflooring the bandstand. Why do this after Gooseberry Days, I can't imagine. What if the school band had crashed through the old, presumably rotten floor, tubas, tympani, kids, tumbling, mixing like salad. Gooseberry Days would forever conjure dark memories in BERF.

So I'm sitting on the last seat, after a long night of sticky plastic, smelly feet, and mosquitoes. The compressor reminds me of Lark, of how she looks when she's playing the trumpet.

I crawl out through the van's back door and stand stiffly in the morning sunlight. I warm myself like a lizard, preparing to move.

My other deep thought of the night is that, so far, I have made minus $40 on the Chess Chalmers Tour.

Lark walks up to me.

"You are supposed to wake up and get ready to go," she says.

"How do you feel about the Romans?" I ask.

31

"We are playing at a church thing this afternoon. It's like four hours away. So you guys have to get moving," Lark says.

"Are we the Heidelberg Boys again?" I ask.

"Probably," she says.

"Then I'm going to fall on my drumsticks," I say.

"Last year, Rusty tried to plug himself into the amp. That was after three nights of polka," she says.

"Well, we should at least be the Heidelberg People, to be gender neutral," I say.

"The Romans suck," she says and leaves.

We're in the van. Rusty is hung over. He hit on a couple of BERF women in the beer tent. The BERF men didn't like it, though all they did was tell him knock it off. Still, Rusty took it hard and drank a lot of beer, then smoked a lot of dope with the women-defending BERFians.

I take a turn behind the wheel of the van. You have to steer like crazy to go straight. You have to press the brake pedal with both feet to get any stopping power.

Miles watches me. "It's not a real nice vehicle," he says.

"No, it's not," I say. My heart is pounding from trying to steer the van through a gentle curve. It's like a bad dream where you try to hold a curve, but your car just keeps sliding away under you. I take the next curve at 14 MPH and a hay truck passes me.

"I'd like to introduce," the minister says, "Chess Chalmers and the Bible Boys."

Chess strums his guitar and starts singing "We are climbing Jacob's Ladder..."

I look desperately at Miles, but he won't look at me. I feel my face turn red. I'm not sure of the reason for this, but suddenly I need air. Christians are closing in all around me.

Chess turns and mouths "Drums," and nods his head. Woodenly I begin to tap along.

I'd like to think I'm suffering from an acute awareness of public hypocrisy, on my part. I'm not Christian. I'm not anything. Let them pray, bless, praise, sing, obey, forgive, serve, celebrate, tithe, hope, hearken, and hold hands. Let them love one another, comfort the afflicted, aid the poor, spread the word, welcome the sinner, and climb Jacob's ladder higher and higher. It's all great. It's just not where I am, something I explained to my friend Davey's parents in my experimental youth, when I went with them to church. And even after Davey disappeared, they welcomed me, forgave me, hired me, for god's sake. They're good people, the Millers.

Or maybe it's because I'm backed up against a brick wall, at the edge of the church parking lot, I'm crowded in on all sides, sweating through my white shirt and black jeans we got at Walmart. It's gotten hotter than hell today. Bricks and blacktop radiate heat. I drop a drumstick. Slips right out of my hand. Grab the spare from beside me and the people crowded around me, they applaud. I smile weakly, tasting sweat. If Hieronymus Bosch grew up in northern Wisconsin, he would have painted a scene of torment like this. Here sits the sinner, surrounded by the faithful, roasting and tapping, up against the wall, for eternity.

We take a break. A teenaged girl, with red hair and a sun dress, brings me an ice cream cup.

"You look so hot," she says, ambiguously.

"Thanks," I say, taking the cup. "Do you have a spoon?"

"No," she says. "You're really good."

"Drumming?" I say. "Naw."

"Oh, yes you are. I'll get you a spoon."

She brings me a spoon and napkin. "What's your name?" she asks.

"Lars," I say.

"I'm Martha," she says.

I hold up my ice cream cup. "This was very nice of you, Martha," I say.

She smiles, blushes.

"Well, better get back to work," I say.

"Okay," she says and watches me.

We're actually not in Wisconsin. We are in the UP, the upper peninsula of Michigan, which I have never thought much about. I don't know if anyone thinks about it. How did a state get a satellite state. It should be West Michigan, like West Virginia, or maybe part of Canada. I bet I am seeing fifty per cent of the population.

The church faces Lake Michigan, and I'd guess we are about 3 hours north of Green Bay. I've asked Chess where we are going, an overview.

"Well, that's hard to say," Chess says, frowning. "We'll kind of go east to west, but it don't always work that way. I try to get these bookings in winter, but by the time we actually get out here, well, some places have closed and others opened, and people call me up with gigs. Yup, we'll do zigging and zagging. But July, August—those are the real peaches. Good gigs. Lots of tourists at the resorts, looking to party."

I survive two more sets. It starts to cool off. We throw in a couple of polkas and couples fly around the pavement.

"Folks, we are going to be winding up here," Chess says. "We're gonna finish up with a Chess Chalmers original, one you probably heard on the radio."

I cringe, but he doesn't kick off The Beer Fartin' Polka. He strums and sings softly.

Prayer
By Chess Chalmers

Lord, keep me tranquil
When the winds blowing mean
And keep my eyes skywards
Like a praying machine.

Lord, keep me well- rested
And when I'm troubled of heart
Keep me invested
To the love that thou art.

Lord, keep me devoted
To my loving wife
And these eight little children
That they'll keep quiet at night

And Lord, keep me faithful
And honest because
I'm proud to be humble
When I'm living your laws.

And bless this old guitar
For when I meet my end
I can play it in heaven
With other heavenly men.
Amen.

Martha walks up as we are tearing down equipment. Rusty nudges me and gives a sort of pirate laugh.

"Hi, Lars," Martha says. "Can I help?"

"Sure," Rusty says.

"No," I say. "Don't worry about it." I put down the cable I'm coiling. I am certified to coil cable now, after lessons from Bob. He was really serious about it. "Let each cable finds its own coil. Loose wrist. Just go with it."

"Martha," I say. "Is there like an internet café here, or something like that."

Martha frowns. "You need to use a computer?" she says.

"Yeah."

"Well, you can come to my house. My Mom wants to know if you've eaten dinner."

I glance at my watch. It's a little after 4 PM.

"Nope," I say.

Martha's father says grace. It takes a long time. He's the church president, he explains, and it's a pleasure to bring a Christian musician into this home.

Martha's mother says, "So, do you tour around, playing at churches?"

"Yes," I say.

"No other—gigs?" Martha's father says.

"Well, we do a few weddings."

"Lars is a really good drummer," Martha says. Her parents smile at her. She has two younger brothers who eat in silence.

"So," Martha's mother says, "are you earning money for college?"

"Yes, ma'am," I say. "My parents died. And my sister. So I'm kind of alone in the world. Just playing music to pay tuition."

Martha's eyes mist. Martha's Mom does not look so convinced. "All dead? How sad," she says.

Martha's father says, "What are you studying?"

"The law."

"That's great," Martha's father says. "What school?"

We're eating chicken in some kind of casserole with tater tots and mushrooms. It's good. I chew slowly, considering my options. What did I say, law?

"University of Illinois," I say finally.

"Excellent school," Martha's father says. "Martha is going to the University of Wisconsin this fall, in Marinette."

I nod at Martha. "Great choice," I say.

"Well, all the boys in your band got to eat with parishioners tonight, but Lars, I'm glad we got a chance to meet you," Martha's father says.

I want to send an email to Anna Bella, tell her to save me. Drive up, bring me home. When we go to the den, where I can use the computer, the whole family stands and watches me.

"Well, I could of told you the weather forecast," Martha's father says. "More of this hot streak, then a whole lot cooler and rainy by Wednesday."

"Thanks," I say, pushing back from the little computer desk.

"Want to watch a movie?" Martha asks.

"Sure," I say. I sink onto a couch. Martha sits next to me, not touching, but close enough. Martha's mother says, "I'll find you a movie. Maybe we have one about lawyers." She picks up a plastic folder.

"Dad alphabetizes all the movie titles," Martha explains.

The doorbell rings.

"It's for the guy," one of the little brothers says.

I go to the door. Miles and Rusty.

Miles speaks softly. "We got to rescue Bob. He's with this holy roller family."

"And then we'll get drunk," Rusty adds. "C'mon."

I make my excuses. The family walks me to the door.

"Goodbye, Lars," they say. "Stop again any time."

I turn to leave and Martha touches my arm. She hands me a slip of paper. "My email address," she says. She smiles and I feel myself turning red.

"Lars?" Miles says when we get to the street.

"Cute girl. Good work," Rusty says. "Nice little bod."

But I'm quiet. I've got a glowing little knot inside. It doesn't feel good and it doesn't feel bad. I'm not sure what it is. Maybe regret. Maybe longing.

Chapter 4

Lark seems dark and sullen compared to Martha. Lark frowns at me.

"Stop staring," she says.

I am, it's true. Lark has a strange build. Long legs, narrow shoulders, short torso. She's so thin you hardly notice the structure. Her eyes glitter in an unhappy way.

"We got a night off," Chess says. "But we're going to scoot back down to Wisconsin today. Take something off the drive tomorrow. Besides, I think I better get you boys out of town, between Romeo Jack here and Bob fighting with the people that fed him dinner."

"It's not what you think," I say.

"Oh, yes, Hell it was," Rusty says.

"Here's a little mad money," Chess says, handing each of us $10.

I use Rusty's phone and call Anna Bella.

"What's up?" she asks.

"Help," I say. "I'm playing polka and Jesus music."

"I thought you were planting trees," she says.

"Well, I joined the guy's band instead."

"How much are you getting paid?" she asks.

"I'm not sure. This might be costing me money."

"Jason, don't be a loser." Anna Bella sounds cross. "Look, I was just into writing some really good stuff. Now I'll have to go back in the shower."

Anna Bella gets her best poetry ideas in the shower. She's in there a lot.

"Okay, sorry," I say.

"Suck it up," she says. "Make lemonade. Turn your frown upside down. Put on your big boy pants. Does that help?"

"I feel so much better," I say.

"Good," Anna Bella says. "Let me know if something is really wrong and then I'll do—something."

"Okay," I say.

Of course, I could just quit. I could grab my duffel and walk back to Illinois. Or hop a train. I'm good at that.

Instead, I spend the day at a bar in Peshtiqua. It's called Tavern. It's the only one in this tiny town, so it doesn't need to offer any more marketing enticement. Miles, Bob, Rusty, and I are the only ones in it through the early afternoon. We play a lot of pool on a strangely sagging table. Our shots defy the laws of physics. Every once in a while, I go outside to watch it rain. The rain came on Monday instead of Wednesday.

A couple of locals come in, eye us, start talking to us. Bob tells them we're with Chess Chalmers.

"Didn't he write some song about pudding wrasslin'? A country song?" one of the guys asks.

"God, I hope not," I say.

Bob buys them a round of Pabst and they get really friendly, tell us what a shithole their town is, and how all the women are mean.

"Mean?" Rusty says. "Like how?"

"I don't know," one guy says. "You know, just plain mean."

"Well, there's kind of sexy mean, and then there's just bitchy," Rusty says.

"I can't say that it's either of those," the guy says.

"More like certain looks and noises," another guy offers.

"What kind of noises?" Rusty asks.

The man demonstrates, clucking his tongue and sighing deeply while eyes rolling.

"Shit, that's bad," Rusty says.

We all lapse into a reflective silence.

"Let's do shots," Bob says.

I started drinking young. I could cut back any time. Quit, I don't know. I worked in a restaurant where we dishwashers poured every leftover drink into a pitcher and drank it at the end of night. After training like that, all normal alcohol tastes pretty good.

"In the Middle Ages," I say, "people drank beer for breakfast." I know this really needs more explanation, but I'm just making conversation.

"No shit," Rusty says, and we lapse into silence again.

We watch a Brewer's game, eat some bratwurst and barbecue potato chips. Chess and Lark said they'd meet us at the Tavern, but they never show. No motel in Peshtiqua, so we sleep in the van again.

Miles doesn't sleep well. He's restless all night. I notice he sleeps a lot during the day—sleeps through every car ride, sleeps between set up and the gig, if he has a chance. Bob and Miles, they were both in the Army. Bob worked in communications and never left the States. Miles saw action in the Middle East. We've talked about this. Mostly Bob tells stories and Miles listens. He tells stories for Miles, who nods his head and Bob speaks. Bob is using the GI bill to study hotel management at UW Stout. He says it's a slow process because he works. Miles hasn't decided what to do with his life.

"I don't know," he says.

"What interests you?" I ask.

"Nothing," Miles says. He and Bob both look younger than they are. Bob is 28, Miles 26.

"How long have you had no interests?" I ask.

"About six years," Miles says.

Miles has sandy hair, curly and clumped, so that he looks like a mushroom. He smiles a lot and he's a good bass player.

"Did you do music in the service?" I ask.

"No."

"Do you want to go into music, professionally?"

"No."

"Do you want to be an astronaut?"

'No."

"A podiatrist?"

"No."

"A race car driver? A forest ranger?"

"No."

"How about a hit man?" Rusty asks.

"Maybe," Miles says.

Bob tells me that Miles spends most of his day playing video games. He delivered pizzas in the evening, for six years. He lives with Bob in Menomonie, Wisconsin, in a rented house.

"Landlord was putting on a new roof. Fell off. Now he's a vegetable. Hope we don't lose our lease," Bob says.

"So what did you communicate in the Army?" I ask Bob.

"Well, the usual. I write super good," Bob says. Bob is taller than Miles, wider, more substantial.

"You know, it's not fair that you guys had to sleep in the van," Chess says when he comes by the next day. "So I stopped up at the Walmart and got these." He holds up two fat nylon bags. "Tents," he says. "For when somebody screws up the motel reservation and such." He smiles. "Hey, you guys gonna like this. We got a four-night stand over at a bar in Three Ladies. Wednesday through Saturday. We'll drive on over today because it's most the way to Madison. Check the place out. Ain't played there before."

In the van, I try not to think about the steering. Bob is driving and he looks comfortable behind the wheel. I'm afraid to go to sleep because I might not ever wake up, with all the exhaust that circulates around us. That and cigarette smoke from Rusty. And the bumps. I've taken to sipping water from a plastic bottle to keep the nausea under control.

I kind of want to call my sister. I watch Rusty play a game on his cell phone. He twitches, squirms in his seat, and cusses a lot. I'd like to use that phone, call Lydia.

She's in med school, doing rounds last I heard. Working in the ER. She wants to be an oncologist. This came about after Astrid died. Before then, she wanted to be a kid doctor. Her boyfriend, Barrett, is in med school, too. They share an apartment, but I bet it's more like roommates. Lydia is just not the boyfriend type. Too ambitious. And she's seen too much of our family life.

Three Ladies is a little town north of Madison. The Bible Boys get to share a room at the Pocket Motel. It's a tiny room with cheap wood paneling and cowboy decorations. They have probably been on the wall for forty years or more.

Miles uses the bathroom and can't get out. For a while, we laugh.

"C'mon guys," Miles says. "Let me out."

"You got yourself in. You can get yourself out," Rusty says.

"That's the American way," Bob says. "Self-reliance."

"I can't get the door handle to turn at all," Miles says.

I get up from the bed. I've been sitting in front of the TV, watching some kind of talk show full of angry people. I try the doorknob, and it pulls off.

"I've got bad news, Miles," I say.

The other guys stir and we try to muscle the door open. It's an old door, solid as a rock. It won't move.

"Is there a window?" Bob asks.

"No," Miles says. "I'm getting claustrophobic."

"Good," Rusty says. "Panic is good. It'll give you super strength."

"Do you have something you can pop the hinge pins with?" Bob asks.

"No," Miles says. "There's some kind of liquid coming up through the bathtub drain," he adds.

"Try flushing the toilet," Bob says.

"That made it worse," Miles says. "It's really gross."

I find the proprietor. After a cross lecture about "shutting bathroom doors too damn tight," he pries the door open with a tire iron. He tells us the bathtub fluid happens if too many people flush at the same time.

"There are like two rooms with people in them," Bob says.

"That's too many," the man says.

We spend the evening at the bar where we'll be playing. It's big, looks like a pole barn from the outside. It's called The Three Ladies Bar.

"We get an older crowd mostly," the manager tells us. "Local folks. Come out here to do a little dancing, a little drinking. Darts, pool. That kind of thing." He looks at Chess. "Now you said you weren't too loud, right?"

"Right," Chess says. "You will be telling us to turn it up."

"I doubt that," the manager says. He's a big, wide man with a long, drooping moustache. "Most of these bands now, just too damn loud. And you play rock n' roll, like 50's and 60's?"

"That's what we do and no one does it better," Chess says.

After Chess leaves, we just sit around the bar and drink beer.

"So, tell me about Lark and Chess," I say.

The other three look at each other.

"What?" I say. "Is there some big secret?"

"Sort of," Bob says. He looks serious. "Lark has had a tough time."

"Like what?" I can't help asking.

"Like maybe she'll tell you," Bob says. "It's her business."

"But, you know, they share a room and all..." I say.

"Hey, that don't mean a thing," Miles says. "Chess done a lot to help that girl."

Rusty is smoking, looking the other way. I'll try him later.

Rusty turns to us. "Let's get drunk before we play tomorrow," he says. "Really drunk."

"Can't get drunk," Miles says. "I can drink and drink. Never get drunk."

"Ever since the Army," Bob says, nodding at Miles.

Next day, we dig deep into the panel truck, haul out lights, big PA speakers—much more equipment than we've been using. "Got to walk the walk," Chess says.

"Good evening," Chess says to the crowd of one, a bored barmaid. "We're here to rock the night away. So just strap in and take a ride with the Chess Chalmers and the Flamin' Rocketmen." There's a quiet moment before we begin playing and I can hear a train rattling by. It's a siren's call, and if I were Odysseus, I'd answer.

It's a long and dreadful night, four hours of playing to almost no one. Four hours of stumbling through songs that were old and tired before I was born. Chuck Berry tunes. Buddy Holly, Chubby Checkers. They're catchy at first, but when nobody's listening, their forced cheerfulness is trivial and depressing.

Lark looks how I feel. She stands with shoulders slumped, hardly bothering to blow her trumpet, singing slightly flat back-up to Chess' enthusiastic vocals. Once, Lark catches me watching her and stares back at me. I smile. I didn't mean to. It just comes out. Lark looks at me, shakes her head, and turns back to the empty room.

Back at the Pocket Motel, we have two single beds in our room. We draw straws. Bob and Miles get the beds.

We spend the next day watching TV, sleeping, and timing flushes so we can shower in an uncontaminated tub.

It's cloudy and cool outside. I take a short walk around Three Ladies but drizzle drives me back indoors.

Thursday night is almost the same as Wednesday, except the regulars show up, a group of men and a few women who sit at the bar and stay there all night.

I go to the bar to get some water.

"What you drinking?" a woman asks me. She sits sideways on the stool, holds a glass with maybe a gin and tonic.

"Just getting water," I say.

"Water?" she says. "That stuff will kill you. Bill, get this guy a drink. Put it on me."

"Thanks," I say and ask for a beer.

The woman continues to look at me.

"How old do you think I am?" she asks. I look. Blond hair, probably dyed. White sandals. Red toenails that match her fingernails. A stretchy top over big boobs and a bit of a belly. Shorts. Decent legs.

"The eyes," she says. "Look at the eyes. That's how you tell how old someone is." She takes a drink. "You like playing this old shit?"

"No," I say, ready to move on.

"Then why do you play it?" she asks. When I don't answer, she says, "So, what's your name?"

I sigh. Finally I say, "Trevor."

She nods. "Yeah, I figured you guys for gay, especially the skinny one."

"She's a girl," I say.

"No shit? Well you can't tell, know what I mean? And what are you guys called, the flamin' cock men or something?" A couple of guys next her laugh. They turn to hear more.

"So, gay band in Three Ladies. Makes sense," the woman says.

"I have to get back to the band," I say.

"Hell, your break just started. Don't you like me? I bought you a beer, for Christ's sake. Talk to me. Tell me what it's like to be gay."

"It's great," I say.

"Why? I'm curious." The woman leans forward.

"What's your name?" I ask.

"Melody," she says. "Melody Schmutz. You're in Schmutz territory here. Did you know that? We own half the goddam county."

"They do not," a man says.

"Used to," Melody says.

"Like a thousand years ago," the man says.

"I've got Indian blood in me," Melody says. "That's how far back we go. Can you see it?"

"Nope," I say and start to go.

"You guys are here until Saturday, right? Hey, we can talk again. We can do girl talk." The men laugh.

"Who is that?" Rusty asks when I get back.

"That lady? Her name is Melody. Real nice. Sweet. A little bit shy. You'd like her. I think she's kind of on the prowl," I say. "You should check it out."

"I Schmutz'd Rusty," I tell Lark.

"What does that mean?"

"I'm not sure," I say.

I encounter Lark while I'm out walking. It's a beautiful day. Sunny, cool. No bugs out. When you walk out of Three Ladies, you find yourself on the edge of the Dells, an area of water and rocks and woods around the Wisconsin River. Lark is standing on a bridge looking down.

"You going to jump?" I ask.

"It's like five feet to the water. Why would I jump?" Lark says.

"So, what are you going to do with all the money you make?"

"What do you mean? From playing this summer?" she says, sounding almost conversational.

"Yeah."

She shrugs. "There are some relatives I'd like to put contracts on, but that would be too expensive."

"You need a beginner hit man, someone who wants to break into the field," I say.

"Like I would know how to find them. No, I'll probably just save my money, if we actually see any."

"But who in your family..."

"Would I take out?" Lark says. "A certain uncle would be a good start."

"Chess?"

"No, Jesus, why would I do that? A different uncle. A step-uncle."

"I hear Miles wants to be a hit man."

"Yeah, well I think he's already done enough of that," Lark says and starts to walk away. I follow.

"What did your step-uncle do?" I ask.

"None of your business. Forget it."

"This music is killing me," I say. "That's how you could do it. Hire Chess?"

"If you don't like the music, then fucking quit," Lark snaps.

But I'm not a quitter. I didn't really drop out of high school. It was a mutual decision by me and the high school administration, a thing that was better for all concerned. I finished high school by taking tests. And I'm making darn good progress in college. Seven years on and off at Middle Illinois Community College. I need 30 classes to get my associates degree in general studies. And in 28 classes, I have 6 A's, 4 C's, 1 D, and 17 withdrawals. I didn't like the instructors. Or the textbooks. Or the syllabus. Or the classroom. Some are really ugly. And there was the cancer thing.

Lark has walked off without me. I start to walk back, hear a chainsaw, watch a man felling a tree. He sees me.

"Hey," he says, waving me over. "I'll pay you twenty bucks if you help me with this. My back is killing **me**."

So many ways to die.

"Sure," I say."

Chapter 5

"Jake, if you ever do that again," Chess tells me, "you're fired."

I was late. Gig started at 8 and I got there a little late, just before 10. The chainsaw guy, Dennis, he's very interesting. That's what he does, chainsaw trees. A modern lumberjack.

"People got all these woods and all these dreams of heating their cabins with woodstoves," Dennis says, "But they don't know shit about cutting trees down, cutting, splitting, drying. Or managing their woodlots. When to thin. What to thin. That's what I do."

"Kind of a summer thing?" I ask.

"Hell, no. Winter is the best time for this work. I hate summer. Hot. Buggy. That's how I hurt my back. Twisting around to swat a deerfly. Just a little twist, and zap, my back spasms."

"That sucks, especially with what you do," I offer.

"And the pills they give you, make you half-dead," Dennis says. "I can't chainsaw after taking those drugs. I'd cut my frickin' head off. No, beer is the answer."

So after I help him and he pays me $20, we drink beer. We sit on his porch and his wife doesn't even care that he's drinking. She joins us for a while. Makes a pizza.

Dennis tells his wife, "Buck, here, he's a good worker."

"You should stick around, Buck," she says. "Dennis needs help. He's got more work than he can do."

I tell them I'm in the military. Air Force. Home on leave, just taking it easy for a couple of weeks. They ask me some questions and it gets complicated really fast, so I tell them I have to leave.

"You just going to walk away?" Dennis says. "You want a ride or something? A beer for the road?"

"Sure," I say to the beer. "And don't worry about it—my car is not far up the road. Was just taking a walk."

Turns out it's a long way from Dennis' house to Three Ladies, even if you know where you're going. Somehow I get turned around and find myself coming off my alcohol buzz and standing on the outskirts of Wisconsin Dells, Waterpark Capital of the World, population 2,418.

"Jesus," I say, and start hitchhiking.

I've walked most of the way to Three Ladies when I get there just before 10. I'm tired, hungry, ornery.

"You think I'm kidding? I'll flat out fire you," Chess says.

"Sorry," I say.

Bob, Miles, Rusty, they all frown at me.

"Hey, man, you're either in it or you're out of it," Rusty says.

"Yeah, we sounded like shit without drums," Bob says.

"Sorry," I say. I shake my head and mutter "fuck" under my breath.

"What was that?" Chess says. "Don't you be dropping the F bomb. You just do what you're paid to do."

"Paid?" I say.

Miles pulls my arm, gently. Leads me away.

"Where'd you go?" he asks.

"Wisconsin Dells," I say.

Bob says, "Lot of water parks there. Pricey, though."

"You were hanging with some chick, weren't you?" Rusty says.

"Yup, that's it," I say.

"Liar," Rusty says.

"He got lost," Lark says. "He was out walking around. Bet he got lost and doesn't want to admit it."

"Hey Lark," Bob says. "Want to come over to our room for a while. We got some beers."

"A few minutes maybe," Lark says.

Rusty's phone rings. He stubs his cigarette and leaves the room. No doubt it's his parents. He talks to them almost every day. He's 26 and this is like he's in tenth grade. I stopped talking to my father when I was about 14 and my mother basically never talked to me. Maybe it's different with adopted parents. Maybe they feel they should stay in touch, to make up for the whole adoption thing, the whole identity issue.

"What's your real name?" I ask Rusty when he comes back in the room. Though it's after 2 AM, the guys are watching TV. So is Lark. When you play until 12:30, you need some time to unwind. The little room is stuffy with all these people.

"Russell Weinstein," Rusty says.

"No, I mean your Asian name," I say.

"Who the hell knows. A South Korean name, if I knew it," Rusty says.

"So you are from South Korea?"

Rusty nods, lights a cigarette. "Yeah. Base bastard. Some soldier and some poor South Korean."

"So you've been in the States since you were what, a baby?"

Rusty nods again. "Weinsteins are my second family, though. First one didn't work out. I got re-adopted when I was 7."

"Bummer," I say.

"Yeah," Rusty says. "There's a lot of confusion about where I actually came from. Weinsteins saw a story about me in the paper. They looked into it. Ike is a lawyer. When they got to meet me, I was irresistible. That's what Wanda says. The Weinstein kids were grown up, out of the house. Kids thought their parents were nuts to adopt a 7 year old Korean kid with issues. They've always been nice to me, though."

"You want to be a lawyer?"

"I want to be something," Rusty says. "Something more than this."

"You been to South Korea?" I ask.

"Yeah, couple of times. Weinsteins were into the whole South Korea thing. Wanda knows a hell of a lot more about the place than I do. She even learned some of the language and tried to teach me. I didn't really give a shit then. Might be interested now."

"Yeah," I say. "Things change when you hit the quarter century mark."

Rusty says, "I suppose. I was a royal son of a bitch in high school. Always in trouble. Nothing but grief for poor Ike and Wanda, who probably wondered what on earth they were thinking."

Rusty and I compare high school bad behavior stories. Mine mostly have to do with disappearing. Rusty's are hard core.

"So what's the point of burglary if you've got rich parents?" I ask.

Rusty shrugs, smokes. "Good question," he says.

Miles has been listening. "You should have gone into the Army," he says. "That would have straightened you out."

"I was just a kid then," Rusty says. "Fortunately. Or I'd probably be wearing an orange suit."

A quarter century. I had my birthday last spring. Anna Bella got me drunk on French wine. A splurge. My mother's brothers, Karl, Ken, Kris, Kyle—they all sent me money. Uncle Ken is the weird one, but he sent me $50. I've done a lot of thinking since then. Reflecting. Looking over my life. I hope there is some part of it ahead of me, but that is hard to think about.

I had a friend who avoided reflection. Her name was Phaedra. She denied the importance of the past. Thought it was a trap. No reason for it to determine the present—that kind of thing. I found it attractive, for a while. Davey Miller, my best friend, found it really attractive. And he found Phaedra attractive, too. They are off, somewhere, discovering the present. All I have of them is the past.

So I like the past. It really happened, for one thing. Who knows if anything recorded, remembered, repeated, recalled ever did. So in that sense, Phaedra has a point. The past is slippery. Time passed, but its reality ticked away with the clock. Yet I can't help but think about it, what has happened. To me. The Audleys. The world. Even if it isn't strictly true, the past, it still makes you think. Helps you choose what to do next. Maybe compels you. That's why I look to the Middle Ages. Pre-Renaissance. Pre-Enlightenment. Pre-Industrial Revolution. Pre-Raphaelite, my favorite painters.

And this old music, this fossilized music, it's in the past. So why do I loathe it? I think because it doesn't say anything. Just because something is old doesn't mean it has wisdom. True for people. True for music. True for everything, if I may be so bold as to offer a universality. I do that with caution. I'm a relativist. I specialize in gray areas. Not because I'm insightful, critical, smart. It's because, generally, I'm confused.

I'm really confused by Saturday night at The Three Ladies Bar. It's jammed. Where did the people come from? Not from Three Ladies itself. From the Dells? From Madison? From little hidden hamlets, farms, communes? They are all white and all ages. Kids to old, old people. They love Chess. They laugh at his deeply lame humor.

"Hey, I thought this was Three Ladies. I'd say it's more like Forty Babes," Chess says, and "No one knows more about fishing than Miles here does. That's why he's the 'bass' player." I note that women like this whole thing more than men. The women outnumber men on the dance floor 4 to 1. At one point, I watch one guy dancing with at least twenty women around him.

Miles leans over and says, "You know who's going to get lucky tonight."

The women hoot and holler. The men sit and drink. After a song, women guzzle, flounce onto laps, head for the restroom. Always in motion. The men drink.

At the end of the third set, Melody Schmutz finds me. She has a friend with her, a brawny, dark-haired woman, who looks tough but uncertain. A good Wisconsin girl.

"Hey," Melody says. "What's up?"

"Going to take a break," I say.

"This is Lynne." She nods toward her friend.

"Hi," I say.

I decide Melody is ten years older than me. Lynne could be anything.

"When you boys are done, why don't you come on over to my place? We're having a little party. Night's still young," Melody says. Then she leans close to me. "I talked to Chess. I know you aren't faggots."

"Party sounds great," Rusty says over my shoulder.

"Yeah," Melody says, "I was going to tell you to bring a friend."

"Well, we don't really have a car..." I say.

"No prob," Melody says. "You can ride with me."

"Sounds great," Rusty says.

"Did you hear that, 'ride with me'?" Rusty says.

"Jesus, Rusty," I say.

I'm in the backseat with Lynne. Rusty and Melody are flirting in the front seat. Melody drives erratically. I tighten my seatbelt.

Lynne looks at me, then digs around in her jeans. "Here," she says, offering a silver flask. "Damn drinks are so expensive there. I bring my own."

I take a sip, feel my sinuses light up.

"Everclear," Lynne says. "Gets the job done."

I take another sip.

"She drives like shit when she's drunk," Lynne says. "Well, she drives like shit anyway. Amazing she's still alive."

I want Rusty to shut up, to quit distracting her. Melody turns her head to look at Rusty when he talks.

"Road curves ahead," I say, peering through the windshield around Rusty.

"I'm a fucking communicator," Melody tells Rusty. "Know what I mean?"

"That's exactly what I'm saying," Rusty responds.

She beams at him.

"Right lane," I say. "Your other right."

Lynne pulls me back so I'm sitting against the seat. She's strong.

"Christ, knock it off. You're making me nervous. Sometimes you just have to go with it," she says.

"I don't feel that way about death," I say.

Lynne shrugs. "Here," she says, passing the flask again.

Melody's house is a big split level, sitting in a dark sea of mowed grass. It's quiet outside the car. No crickets. Too early in the season. Lots of stars overhead. Trees make a black border around the yard. The air is cool, almost cold, and smells fresh.

"New moon," Lynne says. She's standing next to me. She's maybe three inches shorter than me. I'm just over six feet and shaped like Tom "Hairy Bear" Audley. From a distance, Lynne and I probably look like a couple of trolls.

Indoors it seems too bright, too warm. It smells faintly of smoke, part cigarette, part woodstove. We walk up a few stairs to a living room. It's neat, furnished nicely. Well, it looks that way to me, but what do I know. I spent my formative years in my Dad's derelict trailer. That was after the divorce, and before I moved in fulltime with Anna Bella.

I sit on a couch. Lynne sits next to me.

Melody says, "I'll get us some drinks."

"I'll help," Rusty says.

They don't come back.

I listen to a clock tick. After a while, Lynne says, "Want a beer?"

"Sure," I say.

Should I say, "I'll help"? Is that the protocol? Do you say that and disappear into a bedroom? But I sit and wait and Lynne comes out of the kitchen with a Pabst in each hand. Lynne has a lot of hair. It's more like a head pelt. It sticks out bushily, thick, dark, almost coarse. Her bangs come right to the tops of her eyes, hair curls around her cheeks. You really can't see that much of her. She's in a black tee shirt, loose, and jeans. She's barefoot.

"You always go barefoot?" I ask.

"No," she says.

We both make a long show of opening our beers and taking a few sips.

I clear my throat. "So what's new?" I say.

"Not much," she says.

I keep looking at her hair. It's like there's an animal on her head, curled up, sleeping.

"Would be a good night for camping," she offers.

"Want to take a walk?" I say.

"Sure," she says.

We grab two more beers for the road. Lynne sticks her head down a hallway but says nothing. At the front door, Lynne slips on flip flops.

We walk down the driveway into the deep night.

"Have you known Melody a long time?" I ask.

"My sister and her, they grew up together," she says.

"Your sister still around?"

"No. She got married and moved to Sheboygan. Years ago. I got 2 nephews."

"Oh," I say.

"You from around here?" she asks me.

"Nope," I say. "Argentina."

"Yeah, right," she says. "Where really?"

"Illinois."

"Thought so," she says. "The accent."

"I don't have an accent," I say.

"Yes, you do. Central Illinois I bet. Kind of a southerner poser accent. We get a lot of Illinois people come up here."

We walk for a while. Lynne turns down a gravel side road.

"Watch for bears," she says. "There's a garbage dump near here."

"Maybe we should go a different way," I say.

"You are such a wuss," she says. "Big guy like you. Oh, no, watch the road! Lions and tigers and bears!" She laughs. It's the most animated she's been. She must enjoy tossing insults.

"Not a wuss," I say. "Just careful. Balancing risks and consequences."

"Wuss," she says, laughs again. She has a low laugh that ends with a snort.

"I've been shot," I say. "Does that sound like a wuss?"

"Shot in the back probably. Running away."

"I was not. I was trying to save someone and got shot."

"Where?"

"In the shoulder," I say, touching it.

"Let me see," she says.

"It's too dark," I say.

"Liar," she says.

So I unbutton my shirt and show her the scar.

"Holy Jesus," she says, running a finger over it. "You really did."

I tell her what happened. Most of it. Mostly correctly. She listens in silence.

"Well," she says.

"Yeah," I say. "Is that a bear?"

We stop. She puts her hand on my arm, leans forward.

"Yup," she says. "Got cubs. We've got to turn around. Don't hurry. Just walk."

I can feel the bear's eyes on me, just about feel its huge paws pulling my head off. I can see the bear standing over my body, cubs nosing at me. Food? Not food? They want to know. While they decide, Lynne is watching from a tree. How she got up there so high, so fast, I'll never know, because my unseeing eyes are in the ditch with my severed head. She calls to me from the top of the tree. In her voice, a hint of sadness.

"Trevor, right?" she says, startles me back to the real world where I am alive. "Your name is Trevor?"

"I'm known by many names," I say.

"Well, aren't you cool."

I notice we are holding hands. I don't remember taking her hand, if she took mine. Her hand is rough and strong. I find it comforting, having so recently been beheaded.

"So, where would you like to go? Where's your dream destination?" I ask.

"Finland," she says without hesitation.

"Finland?"

"I'm three quarters Finnish," she says. "One fourth German."

"What's your last name?"

"Hakkonen," she says.

"My mother is a Sorensen," I say.

"EN or ON?" she asks.

"EN."

"Danish," she says. "Well, that's not far from Finland."

I don't tell her that my mom was adopted, like Rusty, but not from so far away. I know about the Audleys, the Welsh side. I have no idea what else I am.

"Do you ride?" Lynne asks me.

"Ride what?" I say.

"Horses."

"I haven't had a lot of opportunity."

"Well, have you ridden at all?"

"Yes," I lie. "I'm pretty good."

"We could do some riding tomorrow if you want," she says. "I work with horses."

"It would have to be morning," I say. "Chess probably will want us to hit the road."

"It is morning," she says.

"It would be great to get back on a horse," I say, knowing this will never happen.

We walk back to Melody's house. No sign of Rusty and Melody. We sit on the couch again, cuddle a little, and fall asleep. I'm such a stud.

When the sun lights the living room, Lynne and I stir, look for food in the kitchen. We eat toast.

"I'm divorced," Lynne says. "It was a starter marriage."

I nod. "Got kids?" I ask.

"No."

"That's what they all say," I say, and instantly regret it. But Lynne doesn't react.

"I don't lie," she says. "But you do."

"I just try to make the world a more interesting place," I say.

"Interesting to you," Lynne says. "Call your boss. Tell him you'll be there in a while. Let's go ride."

"My real name is Jason Audley," I say. "See? It's not a lie if it can be fixed."

"It's still a lie," she says.

We leave a note and take Melody's car to Lucky Bucky Stables, near Wisconsin Dells.

"Kind of a tourist thing?" I ask.

"Yeah," she says. "A lot of nose to tail trail rides. Kind of fun, though. Some people are terrified even of that. Others really like it."

"Is anyone mean to the horses?"

"Not for long," she says.

Lynne says a few words to the people working in the stables. Then she leads a big, big horse into the corral.

"This is Diablo," she says. "A mare."

"Her name is devil?" I say.

"Yeah, but that's not very accurate. It should be Bitch. But since you are such an experienced rider, I think you can handle her."

"I didn't say I was experienced, not exactly."

Lynne ignores me, puts me to work on Diablo with a stiff brush. She goes into the stable and returns with a sleek gray horse.

"My horse," Lynne says. "Her name is Betty."

We tack up the horses. Lynne watches me mount and chuckles. I know what she's going to do. I've seen it before, like in movies. She'll gun her horse and race out of the corral and I'll be bouncing behind, clinging to save my life. I'll be uncovered as a fraud, a city boy, a buffoon, a wuss. I know my part. Be humiliated, then look at Lynne with new respect. It kind of pisses me off.

But instead, Lynne takes Betty out at a walk. And we stay walking, following thickly wooded trails.

"We can see the Wisconsin River just up ahead," Lynne says, turning in her saddle, driving like Melody without looking. I'm doing all right on Diablo. She wants to eat things along the trail and I struggle to keep her head up. Lynne turns around again, watches me for a while.

"Good," she says.

I'm curiously proud of myself.

"It's nice to be around a guy," Lynne says. "And you are quite the gentleman."

"Thanks," I say.

"I haven't dated or done much of anything since I threw Terry out," she says. "That was four years ago. I just kind of keep busy with the business."

"Lucky Bucky is yours?" I ask.

"Yeah," she says. "Me and my Mom started it. She passed on."

"My mother is dead also," I say.

"Do you camp?" she asks.

"Not the yuppie camping, you know, with fancy backpacks and all, but, yeah, I've spent a lot of time outdoors, when I was younger," I say. I don't tell her that a lot of that time was in boxcars.

"You heard of the Boundary Waters?" she asks.

"Nope," I say.

"It's over in Minnesota. Bunch of lakes with paths between them. You canoe across a lake, then carry your stuff to the next lake. I go up there every year. Hard to find people to go along. It can be a lot of work."

"I'd go," I say.

She turns and smiles. It's the first real big smile I've seen from her. It changes her face.

"How old are you?" she asks. Many numbers dance through my head, but I tell her "25."

"I'm 28," she says.

"How long were you married?" I ask.

"Ten long months," she says.

Going back is not so easy. Diablo wants to go home. When I try to control her, she turns and nips at me. She tries to scrape me off on tree trunks. She jerks on the reins, makes ominous noises, and flips her ears. Then, abruptly, she rolls. I scramble off.

Lynne watches patiently. "You shouldn't let her do that," she says.

I shrug. "She's stronger than me," I say.

"You have to outsmart her. Think about what she might do and stop her," Lynne says.

Lynne makes sandwiches in a small kitchen in the employee's only area.

"If you are serious about going to the Boundary Waters, let me know," she says, and writes out a phone number.

"I don't have a phone," I tell her, "or I'd give you my number."

We drive back to Three Ladies in Melody's car. We don't say much. Lynne drops me off at the Pocket.

"I'll call," I say.

"We'll see," Lynne says.

Chapter 6

"Practice, practice, practice," Chess says. "That's the secret to success."

We have our gear set up in a pole barn. It belongs to someone Chess knows. We're outside of Munich, a farm town in the dead middle of Wisconsin. We have two nights off, then we play at the Munich Gausthaus.

"We're the Heidelberg Boys?" I ask Chess.

"Nope," he says. "Chess Chalmers and the Country Bumpkins."

"Oh," I say.

"It's funny," Chess says. "Part of the marketing. Keep things light. Good times."

So we are in a pole barn, practicing. I'm all for this. We set up while Chess is outside, talking to his buddy. Lark even helped carry things. The guys tune, and Rusty starts playing some Stevie Ray Vaughn. I didn't know he had it in him. Miles and Bob join in. So do I. We're rockin' out and it's so much fun, I get this big grin.

Chess comes in, waves his hands for us to stop.

"Yeah, Stevie Ray," Chess says. "Love him. We'll get a chance to play this stuff over in western Wisconsin."

"Hey, you're good," I tell Rusty.

"I just copy people," Rusty says.

"We got to work on the country song list," Chess says. "We got a bunch of country gigs coming up."

At least there's some variety, I discover. More, anyway, than polka and ancient rock n' roll.

I've been doing this for two weeks. Only have two months left. Seriously, if we hadn't started this practicing and hadn't done some different music, I think I'd quit, and go canoeing.

Lark has been hanging out with us quite a bit. Not saying much, but not avoiding us. Encouraged, I decide to risk conversation.

"Why do you want to seek revenge on your step-uncle?" I ask.

We are sitting on the concrete floor of the pole barn. No chairs. We're taking a break. Lark picks up a piece of something from the floor and fiddles with it, doesn't look at me. Rusty is outside smoking. Bob and Miles are doing brother talk. Chess is somewhere.

"You would if you were me," Lark says.

"Okay, something bad. So you half serious about it?" I ask.

She shrugs. "Who the hell knows," she says. "It's all pretty complicated."

"I bet," I say. "It's a big decision."

"Yes, it is," she agrees.

"Well, how would you do it?" I ask.

Lark throws away her scrap and looks at me. "You know, that's the funny part. That's why it's so complicated. He's already dead."

"Already dead? That does make it—harder," I say.

"You see, he was this terrible man," Lark says. "And now, well, he's found some way to haunt me."

"Like, psychologically?"

"That's part of it," she says.

"So, what, you are saving for therapy?" I ask.

"Been there," Lark says, gets up.

"Wow," I say as Lark walks away. "That's a pretty unusual situation."

Lark picks up her trumpet, blows a few notes. She looks at me. "Yeah, well, I probably shouldn't have said anything."

"Don't worry. I just think it's interesting."

"Interesting," she says flatly. "Well, good for you."

I tell Rusty about the conversation. He frowns. "Some of this happened last summer," he says.

"What?" I say.

"Just drop it, okay?" Rusty says.

This is very mysterious. But I can guess.

The Gasthaus is great. It's a restaurant and cabins right on a big lake. We get to stay in a cabin. It's an old one, and it smells like stale fried fish. But it has two little bedrooms, a kitchen, and big deck overlooking the lake. To us it's a palace.

"Look," Miles says. "This lamp is made out of a deer leg."

"I'm taking it," Rusty says.

We're here for three days. We go swimming, though the water is deadly cold. I don't believe in getting used to cold water slowly. It's all or nothing. So I go out to the end of a dock and jump in. My breath stops. My heart stops. My legs and arms curl in like a dead spider.

"It's great," I yell, swallowing a scream. "C'mon in."

And they feed us, the same as the kitchen staff. We get leftovers from the night before. Sausages, sauerkraut, red cabbage, pale rye bread. I love it all. The cook is a real German, a tiny, bossy woman who doesn't look at all German, but cusses in German and talks with a wonderful German accent.

"You vant beer vit da food?" she asks.

"Ja," I say.

"Vell, git it youselv," she says.

She makes us her special sandwiches the second day we're there. She calls it a Hawaiian. It's Spam, a fried egg, and a ring of pineapple, all on squishy white bread.

"Goot?" she asks.

"Ja," I say. "Danke."

I don't really know German, but I have found it useful to know some polite words in a variety of languages. When you've been around for 25 years, you learn a few things.

The employees in the restaurant wear lederhosen, white shirts, and little hats. It brings me back. I began my working career in a restaurant. That's where I met Cherry, who is now married to my Dad. Cherry, who stole Tom from my life. Part of it is Cat, Cherry's girl, who is a pre-teen and in dance lessons every day of the week. Cherry insists that Tom dote on her. It doesn't really bother me. Tom is a flawed Dad at best. He's a guy with lots of schemes to make money and all they've led him to is being a janitor at the high school. Lynwood High, my alma mater, if I had stayed there. Until he disappeared, Davey Miller, my best friend, was the god of Lynwood High.

What irks me is that I seem to be following Tom's course. I didn't go into the Army, it's true. But we have these eerie parallels. Tom Audley didn't finish college. Tom Audley is a great shot at basketball, though his shooting style is unorthodox. Tom Audley is a loser.

For the guys, the waitresses of the Gausthaus are a topic of endless conversation. Their outfits accentuate boobs. Are they really that busty, or is it a trick of costuming? If they are all that busty, where did they find them, these busty girls with braided blond hair, beguiling blue eyes, these Aryan goddesses, this troop of Freyja's? The latter is my description, actually. They sling giant mugs of dark beer like paper cups, smile, make little jokes. They're angels of man heaven, and we watch them in awe, and even Rusty knows they are far, far above him.

And, like a dream, before we know it, our time in Munich is over.

We go from the sublime to the absurd. It's a wedding, in some hall in a dreary town whose name I don't know. A Sunday wedding.

The wedded couple are in their 30's. From the start, we feel the hostility in the air, like the smell of paint thinner. The groom is on crutches. He has a broken leg, and as soon as the reception starts, he changes out of his suit into shorts and a tee shirt. The bride wails about the pictures. Her new hubby can't wear shorts in their wedding photos, she says. What will their kids think?

Her sister and the groom's sister try to negotiate peace, but they end up in a loud argument, mostly between the sister and sister-in-law. The two of them start yelling, even do some pushing. A minute later they are out in the parking lot, fighting to the death in their heels and dresses, in front of a cheering crowd of guys, until the police show up. Back inside, the bride, in tears, kicks chairs and balloons, yells "Fuck!", and collapses on the floor. She is too distraught to take part in the cake-cutting ceremony, so the groom and his sister cut the cake, he in his shorts, she in a crimson bridesmaid's dress.

The groom's people sit on one side of the hall, the bride's on the other. Both drink heavily. No one dances. We're the Flamin' Rocketmen again, and our silly music echoes dismally.

We take a break. Insults begin to fly across the room. I sense that there's a history here. It's the Hatfield's and McCoy's, the Montague's and Capulet's.

Sensing impending tragedy, Chess goes back up to the mike.

"Folks, let's take it easy here," he says.

A balloon, impelled with force, drifts across the room and taps a man on the head.

He stands. "Who the fuck did that?" he demands. His friends pull him back into his seat.

A man on the other side of the room rises. "I did it. I Brett Favre'd that sucker. Bet you couldn't."

Then shouts on both sides.

"Folks, folks!" Chess says. "We're gonna take the stage again. Here, I tell you what. I'll sing you a Chess Chalmers original. You know it. More of a country song, but you can all join in."

He glances at us, waves us back. While we get behind our instruments, Chess strums and begins singing.

Puddin' Wrasslin' Woman
By Chess Chalmers

I've been from Detroit to Cudahy
From Beloit to St. Paul
I've been all over this big world
And I thought I saw it all.

But one day, way down south
In Springfield, Illinois
I seen something I won't forget
While out once with the boys.

This little bar, it had a ring
Knee deep in brown goo
Into it there walked a gal
In her birthday suit.

She challenged all who'd heed the call
To meet her on the mat
And wrassle in the pudding
Inside that sticky vat.

She's a puddin' wrasslin' woman
So strong that it's unreal
She's quicker than a cobra
And slicker than an eel.

I could not let this challenge go
To my boxers I did strip
And entered that ring of pudding
And right away did slip.

Then the woman, she was on me
Though I tried to get away
She buried my head in pudding thick
And I began to pray.

That this wouldn't be my end
Don't want to die like this
But she pulled my head above the waves
And gave me a sticky kiss.

And though I lived to tell the tale
And drown it in many a beer

That puddin' that we wrassled in
Is still stuck in my ears.

She's a puddin' wrasslin' woman
So strong that it's unreal
She's quicker than a cobra
And slicker than an eel.

But it's no use. As soon as the song ends, the insults fly, and now the women join in. People are standing on either side of the dance floor, yelling, waving arms. A chair slides across. A kid, with a howl of rage, slides it back hard to the other side, where it loses momentum and ends up against an old woman's leg.

"Boys," Chess says. "You'd better get behind your amplifiers." Lark and Chess join me behind the drums. "You don't see this real often," Chess says.

When it's over, and the police have come and gone again, and the lone staff person cleans up the mess, we tear down our equipment. Chess tells us, "You know, some marriages just get off on the wrong foot."

Chapter 7

I think most people my age follow a map and they do it in different ways. For example, they might be tourists to their own lives, following a map designed by others. They travel in a small herd, making their way through crowds as a group, wearing matching tee shirts or matching hats, glancing to this side or that side, but staying behind the tour guide.

Some make their own map. These are the expeditionists. They've chosen their route, planned their attack, gathered their resources. They are prepared, focused. They'll complete the route or die along the way, their arms sticking out of snow drifts, figuratively or literally.

For some the map looks more like the weather forecast—a series of social low pressure systems, high pressure systems, floods, droughts, and beautiful days. It's a macro map that drives vast crowds along the whims of cultural isobars.

And a few have none of these things. They've managed to drift off the map. Strangely, their terra incognita coexists with the mapped geography of others. They inhabit the same places, breathe the same air, drink the same beer, touch the same doorknobs. But you can spot them. They're the ones who never ask for directions and they have bad luck.

"Where to next?" I ask Chess.

"Backwards," Chess says. "Back to Lake Michigan." Chess watches me load drum cases. "How's your jaw?"

"Fine," I say. It hurts like hell. I worry it's busted.

"Okey doke," Chess says.

There was this table. They looked really young. They got carded and could drink, so over 21, but not by much. Five girls, two guys. They sat off to the side, were there all night, closed the place down. The girls were pretty, animated, alluring. They talked on cell phones between songs. They ignored the band, except to laugh at Chess once in a while. And at Lark. One of the guys imitated Lark's puffed trumpet cheeks on a beer bottle. I watched him do it. Such easy targets.

I go to the bar during a break. I'm in the mood to drink and play. I order two beers to bring up to the stage. At Swig's, this busy, crummy bar, we have to buy our own drinks. No comping the band. One of the girls comes up next to me, orders a captain and coke.

"Having fun?" I ask her.

She does a little rabbit jump because I talked to her. Eyes look startled.

She doesn't respond.

"Having fun?" I say again, louder.

She glances at her friends. She's afraid of me. It pisses me off.

"Hey," I say even louder. "How's it going?"

She ignores me, which I expected, gets her drink and walks quickly back to the table.

I know who they are, what they're doing. College kids, slumming. What college, who knows. But it's small, private, and probably religious. They've wandered in here for the thrill of mixing with the animals, of drinking cheap drinks and watching the locals be pitiful. It reminds them of the life they don't want, and of the lives that will disappear beneath their feet. Their map leads to the suburbs, to the golf course, to the loan officer, to the divorce courts.

This is what I've learned from being cold-cocked, from being slugged at Swig's. That I don't have a map, or I would understand these things better. See myself in a mirror, see myself in the eyes of the girl I frightened.

At the end of the night, I go outside to cool off, for just a moment, before tearing down the drums. The 5 girls and 2 guys stand around a car with the hood up. All 5 girls have their arms crossed. One guy is on a cell phone, the other looks under the hood. I watch for a minute or two, then go over.

"Car dead?" I ask.

The guy on the phone says "I'll call you back," and turns to me.

"All under control," he says. He sounds drunk.

"Mind if I take a look? Got a flashlight?" I say. My dad's car was a wreck and I learned a few things when it died as I drove around our trailer court. That was when I was fourteen. And working for Millers, they had all these old trucks they let the demo guys use. We tore things down. People with skills built things up. The old trucks had their problems and you learned how to get home.

"Back off," the guy says to me. The other guy straightens up from under the hood. "Let him look," he says.

"Forget it," I say.

"Let him help," one girl says. "I want to get out of here."

I'm not the only one who's noticed them. Various small groups of guys lean against their cars and trucks, keep half an eye on the girls. This is the hard core, the stuff that staggers out the door when a bar closes.

"Hey," the friendlier guys says. "Go ahead and check it out."

So I do. It smells funny under the hood. A bad, metallic smell. I don't recognize it, but I have a suspicion.

"Flashlight?" I say.

A girl moves forward, does something with her cell phone to cast a little light. "Does this help?"

I pull the dipstick and try to read it in the feeble light. It's easy to read. There's no oil.

"There's no oil," I say.

The girl leans forward almost imperceptibly to look. One of the guys looks over my shoulder.

"Christ," he says. "You fucking idiot."

"Probably burned the last of it getting here. Engine's all seized up now," I say.

"Shit," a girl says.

"Can you fix it?" a girl asks.

"Nope," I say. "Requiescat in pace."

"Rest in peace," the under-the-hood guy says.

"Shit," someone says.

Some guys come over. "You girls need a ride somewhere?" one asks.

"No," the cell phone guy says. "Back off."

"Back off?" the guy says. "Just trying to be civil, asshole."

And I'm just standing there, off to the side, when the two guys start to get stupid and yell at each other and push each other.

I say, "Hey..." and cell phone turns and punches me in the mouth. He's smaller than me but I don't see it coming and he punches hard and I fall onto my butt, still holding the dipstick that says empty.

Other guys intervene, including Bob, and then Miles, and it all calms down, to the disappointment of onlookers. Bob calls a tow truck. We stand around, waiting. My jaw hurts and I can feel the heat rising. I'm no fighter. I used to wrestle, though. If cell phone gets close to me, I'm going to take him down.

"What's the name of your band?" a girl asks me.

She's too pretty to look at. Button nose, blond-red hair tied back in a long ponytail. Halter top. She looks athletic.

So I don't look at her, mutter, "Chess Chalmers and the Shit-heads."

"You guys were good," she says. "Can I see your face? I do sports medicine."

"It's fine," I say.

"Here," she says, and gives me a business card. I can't help but try to read it, strain in the parking lot light. The only print I can read says, "Macey Beckman, MD. Sports Medicine."

"Jesus," I say. "You're a doctor. Are you all doctors? You look so young."

"Not all. It's the fitness lifestyle," the doctor says. Then she puts her hand on the side of my face. "Move your jaw, slowly. Stop if it hurts." It hurts, but I move it anyway.

"You guys slumming?" I ask.

"Birthday party," Macey says. "You need to put ice on that. Ten minutes on, ten minutes off."

"You should have kept the fucking dipstick," Rusty says. "Keep it, a souvenir."

"That was a Volvo she killed. Not a new one, but still a nice car," Bob says.

We're in the van now. All packed up, heading east in the middle of the night.

We're at Stony Beach Resort. It's on a stony beach, right on Lake Michigan. The water is flat and dull. An overcast sky, but not rain clouds. Too high.

My face is swollen and I have two purple spots. Could be worse, everyone tells me. Yes, I could have been fed to alligators or gotten cholera. That's so comforting, the fact that no matter what happens to you, it could be worse. Or maybe at some point you say, wow, this is it, this is the worst that can happen to anyone, at any time, ever. That's an achievement.

Stony Beach Resort has a few lumpy campsites and that's where we have pitched our cheap tents. Chess did not buy sleeping bags, but the old caretaker took pity and brought us some heavily pilled sheets. We'll be warm and toasty tonight, as we slip into the sheets on the rocks in the 40 degree damp. It's freezing here, with the breeze off the lake, and I think the fog will roll in, dense, dark, like your eyes have gone bad.

I sit on the beach watching the flip of pathetic little waves. I'm thinking about things, about being a doctor, if I can draw the map. I know I can't. It's a mental exercise to try, like anticipating six moves ahead in chess, like the pro's do. If this happens, and this happens, etc. etc., then I will be in medical school. I've got the Latin. I say that, but I don't use it much anymore. I used to read compulsively. My map was self-education. But that phase ended, apparently. And I'm on to a new phase where I basically rot. I sense this could be a long phase. I sense that what I do at 25 will be it for life. I sense I should start eating better, start exercising, start using my brain, start making a plan. I sense these things, but instead I sit on rocks and look for chips of agate. I find two, red-brown and smooth.

"Hey," Rusty says, walking up.

"Fuck you," I say.

"I talked to Melody. Guess what, Lynne likes you," he says.

I start to laugh. "It could be worse," I say.

Our day off is over, a day in which I do absolutely nothing. Andy, the care-taker, drops off some firewood for us.

"You can have a fire on the beach," he says. He's an old guy, wearing a flannel shirt with frayed cuffs, old jeans. He smells a little.

"You boys got some food?" he asks.

We are not welcome in the lodge itself. This isn't The Gasthaus. No one offers food to the band.

"Nope," Miles says. "Thanks for the wood."

"Tell you what, I got some stuff in the freezer. I'll bring it down. You can cook on the fire. You need a potty , just use the one in the shop. I leave it unlocked."

It gets dark and the fog rolls in. We start a fire, find a flat rock to sit on. We're pretty quiet, because this pretty much sucks.

The caretaker appears by the campfire, carrying a plastic bag.

"Here you go, just like I said." He opens the bag, takes out some long metal forks, like you'd use to roast marshmallows. He takes out a ziplock bag.

"Mourning doves," he says. "Shot 'em last fall. Been froze ever since. They're all cleaned. Just poke 'em on the stick and roast 'em over the coals. They're great to eat."

Our fire has died down and we're nearly out of wood, mostly because Rusty kept dumping it on. We all criticized him, but didn't do anything to stop him.

"Looks like you could use some more wood," Andy says and leaves us with the forks and doves.

We're hungry. We ate some fast food earlier when we made a beer run.

"Well, hell," Miles says. "I'm going to try one."

So we all get a fork and skewer a slippery, cold, skinned dove. No heads or feet, thank god, but they still look primeval.

"Chess is missing out," Rusty says. Chess and Lark went to check things out in town, and as usual, never came back.

We roast the birds. There's a good smell after a while and our spirits rise a little. We crack more beers. Everyone has their own roasting strategy. Bob's bird is high over the fire. "It's hottest up here," he says. Miles and I, we keep our doves close to the coals. Miles slowly rotates his, like a rotisserie. I hold a position, then after I judge enough time has passed, rotate the carcass. Rusty moves restlessly around the fire, thrusting his bird here and there.

We eat. "Hey, this is damn good," Rusty says. We gnaw in silence.

I look at Rusty. There's a little line from the corner of his mouth.

"What's on your face?" I ask him.

He wipes his hand across his face, looks at it. Moves closer to the one sputtering flame we have left. "It's dark," he says.

"Look at me," I say.

"God, it's blood," Bob says. "Did you bite yourself or something?" We all start giggling.

Rusty spits into his hand. "Christ," he says. "It's the bird. It's all bloody."

Bob pulls out a flashlight, examines his bird. "Jesus H. Christ, hardly thawed in the middle," he says. He shines it around. "Look at you guys."

We all have bloody mouths. Miles has a little channel of blood, just like Rusty. We all jump up, like that will help. Miles spits out a mouthful.

"You look like a bunch of fucking vampires," Bob says, beginning to laugh hard. We are kind of horrified and hysterical at the same time, pointing at each other, spitting our dove.

"God damn, that has got to be the grossest thing I've ever done," Bob says. We all stop and think for a moment. Miles says, "Maybe not the absolute grossest. It's hard to say."

So we talk about what we've done that was grosser. Miles says he tasted cat poop when he was a little kid. Just once. No one can top that.

Andy appears, drops a load of firewood and holds up a plastic bag.

"Squirrels," he says.

So, I need a plan. A map. The challenge is choosing a destination. The entire destination concept runs aground on my suspicion that I won't be around long enough to get anywhere. I'm not an expeditionist. I can't pursue a goal, no matter what cost. It's a problem really, not being that goal oriented. Without it, you lack a major source of motivation. I feel the lumps under my chin and under my arms. Are they bigger? Are they smaller? I don't know. I should go back to the oncologist. That could be a destination, to try again and beat this. I could abandon myself to the doctor's plan. Why don't I just do that?

Maybe I'm going about this wrong. Maybe the question isn't where do I want to go, but instead, who do I want to be? Maybe I should look for possible role models. Do I want my life to be like my father, Tom? No. Chess? No. Rusty, Miles, Bob? No.

Uncles Karl, Kyle, Kris, and Ken? Maybe, but it's awfully Wisconsin-centric.

Anna Bella? Maybe. I could see being a professor. Davey's Dad, Marlin Miller? Yes to be a good man. No to rebuilding shopping malls. This is harder than I thought.

Do I have other possible models? Lynne Hakkonen? No. Too horse-oriented.

Macey Beckman, MD? Maybe. I could see being a doctor.

Davey? Phaedra? No, no. Lost in Neverland. Or maybe just lost.

Jason Audley? Be myself? Most likely, but there is no self. Well, yes, there is a self. There is no substance to it. When I was 14, I often felt like a ghost, wandering among the living. In many ways, that hasn't changed, except I might be a real ghost in a short time if these lumps are really bigger. At least that's a destination.

Chapter 8

"Hey, Macey," I write in an email. I'm sitting in the Stony Beach Resort lounge and reception area, where, for the convenience of their customers, there's a computer. The band is not supposed to be in here. I've got my nicest clothes on. I'm sitting straight, looking confident, entitled. I'm in disguise. "Hi, Macey. It was great meeting you at Swig's. I'm the guy who got hit by your friend while trying to fix the car. I just wanted to let you know that I'm doing fine. The old jaw feels better.

How could I get into medical school?

Regards,

Jason Audley"

I don't write a lot of email. I know that puts me in a minority. I don't own a TV or a cell phone or anything digital. I don't own much of anything, except a ton of books mildewing in Anna Bella's basement and a bicycle named Aretha that is rusting in Tom's carport. I'm not materialistic, you might say. But I'd like to give materialism a chance, just to understand it.

Dr. Jason Audley. But what kind of doctor? I'm thinking surgeon. I have steady hands, patience, and experience in demolition. That title, that's what I really want. Just a few small steps to get there. 1) finish college, taking many science classes and achieving all A's; 2) take the whatever test you take and kill it; 3) apply to medical schools and be accepted; 4) complete medical school, with honors, and go onto to a successful and satisfying career; 5) live long enough to complete 1-4.

"Hi, Jason," Macey writes back, within 10 minutes. "You should get an x-ray. Macey Beckman, MD."

I think we've bonded.

What I think about besides my clicking jaw is how young they looked, Dr. Macey and her friends. I leave the computer and stare at myself in the workshop bathroom, in the small, cloudy mirror that hangs over the sink. I do this dispassionately, objectively. I look like a thug, the first guy the hero shoots in a movie. The guy that never gets any lines, never gets to say, "wait, don't shoot! You don't really know me! I'm more than this!" Nope, the thug takes a bullet and topples backward through the window, off the bridge, or over the balcony, falling silently off camera.

I borrow the van, go to the address on Macey's card. I introduce myself at the front desk as a friend of Macey's, oops, Dr. Beckman. The receptionist tells me just a minute and makes a call. A man comes out and tells me I'm getting an x-ray so follow him.

Then I wait in a little room and read Medical Aviator.

Macey comes in, wearing glasses and a white lab coat. She looks a lot different than in the parking lot. She mutters hello and slaps a film on the light box.

"No fracture," she says. "None that I see anyway. I'll have a colleague take a look. How does it feel?"

She puts her hands on the sides of my face and turns my head. "Soft tissue damage. Any teeth loose?"

"Don't think so," I say.

"You're swollen, right into your neck. Did you put ice on it?"

"No."

"You still can. Let me see your neck again."

I shy away from her touch." So where did you go to medical school?" I ask.

"Madison," she says, dropping her hands. "Are you really called Chess Chalmers and the Shit Heads?"

"Yes," I say. "I'm not proud of the name."

"I would think not," she says. "Okay. You're good to go."

"You busy tonight?" I ask.

"What?" she says, turning back to me and turning red.

"Never mind," I say.

"What did you say?" she says.

"Well, nothing," I say.

Dr. Macey sits down in the guest chair. I'm sitting on the exam table.

"Tell me," she says. "Is this what you do? You're a Shit Head?"

"That's a complicated question," I say.

"You are interested in medical school? Where did you go to undergrad? What was your major?"

So she read my email all the way through.

"I'm still in the planning stages," I say.

"No college?"

"Yes, some. No point in blowing too much money on it until I know what I want to do," I say.

"Take a lot of science classes. Get great grades," she says, standing up.

I nod. "Will do," I say.

"Ice," she says, and leaves.

I find out Rusty steals things. We get really drunk after playing, the four of us, on the chilly beach. Rusty starts bragging about it. Then he pulls something out his pocket. It's a necklace.

"Is that a real diamond?" Miles asks.

"Hell, yes," Rusty says.

"Where did you get it?" I ask.

"Melody, after she went to sleep."

"That's like a felony," I say.

He shrugs. "She'll never see me again. She probably doesn't even know it's gone, and then she'll be too embarrassed to do anything about it, if she ever does notice," Rusty says.

"Jesus, Rusty. Are you insane? I say. "Think about what happens if you get caught."

"I won't," he says.

"Of course not," I say. "You could be throwing your stupid life away with one dumb stunt."

"Cool it, Jason," Rusty says.

"You're a fucking idiot, Rusty."

"Jesus, what's it to you?" Rusty says, getting mad. He puts the necklace away.

"Give it back to her or I will," I say.

I can't stand to see a life wasted.

I found out there was asbestos in the trailer where Tom and I lived. Asbestos has been linked to lymphoma. Not only did I suffer through living there, in that smelly little wreck, but it poisoned me. Tom found out about the asbestos when he tried to sell the trailer for scrap. They told him then, that it was hazardous waste.

"God, why does everything happen to me?" Tom says.

A guy was on the same chemo schedule as me. We'd sit, sharing this small room, sitting in recliners, hooked up to drips. He was 47. This was his second bout with colon cancer. His wife sat next to him, knitting mittens. When he died, she gave me a pair.

"You've really got to get out of here and do something," Anna Bella says, coming downstairs to talk to me. She noticed me poking at lumps. She told me to go to the doctor.
'No," I say. "Not yet."
"Well, don't hold me responsible if you keel over," she says. "Thank god I didn't promise Astrid anything. About you, that is."
She says things like this a lot, using Astrid like a chemical weapon that's supposed to drive me out of my hole. She wears me down, and I agree to visit Uncle Karl. He sells ag implements and he does pretty well. Lives in Wisconsin, like all of Astrid's family. I used to visit up there when I was a kid.
"Don't mope," he says.
"I don't mean to," I say. "I need a job."
"Damn right," Uncle Karl says, and then strokes his red beard. "I can find you something," he says.

Chess gives us each $400, in twenties. I'm glad to see the money. I suspected we'd never get paid. We're leaving Stony Beach. We have a day off, then an afternoon gig at some festival, followed by a bar gig that same night. Two jobs in one day. He tells us this and we don't look happy.
"This festival," Bob says. "It's not on the schedule you gave me."
Chess shrugs. "New gig. More money for everyone. It will be a long day, that Friday, but we can do it. The bar is just a one-nighter. Then we have a real cushy gig at the Red Wolf Casino."

We're the Heidelberg Boys again. It's been a while and I nearly fall asleep tapping that polka beat. We're at the aptly named Hokotaw Days in Hokotaw. There are like twenty people in attendance and they look embarrassed for us.

The gig that night is more interesting. It's my first gig in a strip bar.

"I thought all of these were in western Wisconsin," Miles says. "Man, this is the real thing."

We don't know what town it's in. It kind of sits out in the middle of nowhere, a dark building up against a pretty grove of birches. No windows, one small sign.

BB Club

Girls

"It's even darker inside. "That's to hide any female imperfections," Rusty says.

It's empty when we get there. They don't really serve much in the way of drinks, just canned beer. Everything is cash only.

"Why are we playing here?" I ask Rusty.

"We'll be background noise for some of the dancers. Maybe play a few songs between acts."

Lark says, "Count me out. I'm not playing in here."

"I know, I know," Chess says. "You can take the truck when we unload. Go on down the road to Wilson. I'll catch a ride with the boys."

Where we set up, we can't see the dancers. It's both a disappointment and a relief. Mike, the manager, tells us to help ourselves to beer, and when we're not playing, head on back to the lounge.

"The lounge?" I ask.

"Green room," Bob says. "You'll see."

Some dancers want the live music, some don't. We are up and down, on and off a lot. But we get to play music that's more fun, even some blues. The place goes from totally empty to totally full in about ten minutes time. These guys know when the acts start. The whole place closes at 11 PM. The men carry flashlights.

We play a little and then get sent to the lounge. It's a stuffy room with a few sloping couches and a card table. There's a water cooler in the corner. A couple of girls walk through, one in street clothes, another in running shorts and no top. There is a certain contrast to Hokotaw Days and the BB Club, especially to experience them in the same day. I would like to see them blended, Bare Bear Hokotaw Days. There'd be hot dogs, and brats, and popcorn, and school bands, and strippers. It would be best to locate them next to the beer tent. It would put Hokotaw on the map.

"You're doing it again," Rusty says. "Poking at yourself."

"Habit."

"It's not polite," he says.

"We're in the back room of a strip bar," I say.

"Civility is always a good thing," Miles says. He always seems to hear our conversations.

"I'll remember that," I say.

Chess is restless, doesn't like sitting around. He sticks his head out the door to look into the bar.

"Oh my god," he says and shuts it. "Don't look."

We spring to our feet.

At the BB Club, at Swig's, all over I have seen these biker dudes. I don't know where they come from, or who they are, or how they pay the bills, if they have any. But they look like the real deal, like Hell's Angels. Are these guys who didn't make Hell's Angels? Like Wisconsin is the farm league for the biker majors? Are these guys accountants with double lives? They look scary, walk scary, smell scary, some of them. Would I like being one? The farther we go west in Wisconsin, the more we see. I need to research.

It occurs to me as we load the truck after a weary night at the BB Club, a night in which one becomes inured to boobs and tired of leering males, that I am in a kind of spiral. I picture a bird floating on thermals, a noteworthy, soaring bird, like a vulture. It banks into the uplifted air, curves gracefully away, and then rises again. But to my eyes at least, a bird can't stay that way forever, and slowly and surely it descends. Maybe not the albatross, who soars above oceans its whole life. But I bet it flaps a lot. Really has to fly, not only soar, glide, bank, and rise.

You have this brief launch experience. You are born. You live in some kind of social unit. You may go to school. At some point, though, you level off, plateau. Then you slowly spiral down. At 25, I am a quarter century, I have some perspective, and my fear is that I've already begun to descend. We circle around Wisconsin, on a more or less geometrically flat plane. Yet I feel the descent in me, like this endless circling with Chess Chalmers absorbs my thermal. As did the last seven years or so. It may be that I peaked in high school. Reached my full potential as a human being, fulfilled my destiny, rendered my greatest service. This occurs to me as we load the truck with everything in exactly the same place, to be secured with the same tie-downs, to be then unpacked in the same order, set up, and then packed again. It's a circle, but somehow it loses ground.

Here's the other bad thing about spiraling. You never get anywhere. And another thing, the lymphoma, that's like a kite string, tugging at my spiral, robbing me of any chance to find a way to fly.

Maybe it's not a spiral at all. Maybe you're floating on the surface, and growing up is only the process of becoming self-aware, self-aware that you're floating over the abyss. And there you drift, until you are drawn into the maelstrom, the whirlpool, where you gain speed as you descend.

In either case, you can watch other vultures, other victims of the vortex. You see the little motes drawn inward, downward. They might be people, or ideas, ghosts. Down they go.

Into the wormhole.

These thoughts do not make me social. I crave beer, but not company. We go back to our tents—no motel tonight—and get drunk.

"You look glum," I tell Lark the next morning.

"So do you," she says. She's riding with the boys today. I don't know why she isn't in the truck with Chess. She's in the back seat, with me, but not really with me.

"You look depressed," I say.

"Thanks," she says. "You look homeless."

"Your smile could touch my heart with laughter," I say.

"Your drumming is getting worse," she says.

"I know," I say. "I've lost my muse."

"Didn't the BB Club inspire you?" she asks.

"No," I say. "It bruised my soul."

"Well, I liked it, "Rusty says, turning around. "Though some of girls were definitely not that hot."

I like that Lark wouldn't play the BB Club. I've found that when she's in a certain mood, I can talk to her like Anna Bella. I wonder if Lark is a poet. She's got the aura.

Chapter 9

We eat fast food at a park. Kids are playing here. One girl screams a lot. If you shut your eyes, you'd think it was the Inquisition at work, but she's on a swing. I find it difficult to swallow my cheeseburger.

"I wish that little brat would stop screaming," Rusty says.

"Maybe she's caught on something," Bob says.

Lark puts down her fish sandwich and goes over to the girl. She talks to her for a while. The screaming stops. The girl gets off the swing and runs off.

"She got stung by a bee," Lark says when she gets back.

"Why did she keep swinging?" Miles asks.

"She was afraid more would get her if she didn't keep moving," Lark says.

"Where did she get stung?" Bob asks.

"On the leg," Lark says.

Then we eat in silence. Bob, Rusty, and Miles wolf their food, get up. Rusty leaves his wrappers.

"Thanks for going over to the kid," I say to Lark. "It was driving me crazy."

Lark says nothing, chews.

"I mean, we just sat here and you got up and did something. Bob could have been right. She could have been pinched on the swing or something."

Lark looks at me. "I didn't do it for you."

"I know," I say. "Just wanted to..."

Lark interrupts. "Got it."

I find this annoying. I try to swallow it but I say "Jesus, I was trying to be nice. How about a little civility?"

Lark glares, tosses her sandwich down, gets up, starts to walk away.

"Well, Jesus, eat your sandwich," I say. Then for some reason I walk after her.

"Hey," I say when I catch up to her. Just tell me this. What's so tough about being civil?"

She keeps walking. I follow, still stewing. Part of me is tempted to grab her, turn her around to face me, but I don't. I just keep talking.

"Everyone treats you like, like you're a house of cards. Collapse with a puff of wind. But you just bitch back. Do they know something I don't? Am I missing something?" I know I am and I'm hoping she'll tell me. "Because that isn't the way I think people should act."

"You should talk," Lark says, stopping. "Mr. Big Words, sneering at us."

"I am not sneering…"

"Oh, no. Little smirks. But, no, you're so nice and kind to everyone and you help people and get punched and you're just the victim."

"What?"

"Mr. Sneering Big Words Perfect," she says.

For a moment we just stand there.

"What's your deal? Why are you bothering me?" Lark says.

"I don't know," I say. I do know. I liked that she helped the girl. Whenever she seems kind of human, she does something ugly and pisses me off. Now why it pisses me off, I don't know.

I see an odd look on her face. It's pained and playful at the same time.

"You don't know me," Lark says.

"You don't know me either," I say.

"I have secrets."

"So do I. So does everybody."

"Mine are worse," Lark says.

"Bullshit," I say. "My secrets are like Superman vs. a baby."

"That's lame," Lark says. "For Mr. Big Words Sneering Perfect Smart Ass."

"My name is getting kind of long."

Lark starts walking. I walk beside her. It's a little park in a little town, and we're soon walking down a shady street of middle class homes, all painted white.

"Tell me a secret," Lark says.

"My best friend ran off with a crazy woman when he was sixteen, and it ended up with me getting shot," I say.

"Is this truth or dare?"

"No," I say. "That's the truth."

We walk. Lark stops. "My step-uncle, he raped me last summer," she says.

I nod. "I thought it might be something like that," I say. "Sorry."

"And the police got involved and before he could be charged with anything, he drove through a railroad crossing and got hit by a train."

"Trains are good for that."

"He was drunk," Lark says. "I think he did it on purpose, though. Killed himself, just so he didn't have to face the consequences. He never even got in trouble, at least in public."

"At least he's gone."

"Too quick," Lark says.

"Not necessarily," I say. "Depends on what happened. He could have been slowly crushed or ground up."

"It was quick," Lark says. "They said he was somewhat dismembered."

"That still had to hurt," I say.

"Yeah, I suppose," Lark says.

"So Chess kind of watches out for you?"

She sighs, starts walking again. "My family blamed me," she says. "Everyone but Chess. I'm not doing very well."

"I suppose not," I say. "Did you get counseling or something?"

"It didn't work out," Lark says.

I am curious about a lot of things then, but I stay quiet.

"Well," I say. "Thanks for telling me. It must be hard to talk about."

"It is."

The little town has a flea market and one guy sells used books. Really used books. And they smell like cigarettes. But I have a sudden urge to read, so I browse his table.

"What are you looking for?" the man asks.

"Oh, just something to read," I say.

"Most of these books are crap," he says. "People buy them just to sell them again. Try to get them from me for next to nothing and then sell them, make maybe ten cents a book."

"Hardly seems worth it," I say.

"It isn't. It's the game of it," he says. "I do the same thing."

"I'm used to crappy books," I say, thinking of what Tom Audley used to buy for me.

I pick up a worn guide to the Boundary Waters Canoe Area.

"That's pretty old," the man says. "Probably out of date."

I thumb through it. A dried mosquito corpse drops out.

"I'll take it," I say.

"Okay boys, next stop is the Happy Badger Casino. Be there a week or more," Chess says, when I ask him about our schedule. "You need money?"

"No," I say. "Any time off for us, like a vacation?"

"This is a vacation," Chess says.

"You know, like a block of time off, like a week."

"Nothing like that, but things change. But Jack, if we got a week off, that would be bad, don't you see. No gigs, no money. We want to play."

"I know. And I totally agree. Just that, well, my mother's sick."

"I thought she died," Chess says.

"Yes, my real mother died," I say. "Sorry. I should be more clear. The woman who has been a mother to me, that's who I mean."

"Who's that?" Chess asks.

"Her name is Cherry. She lives with my dad." Cherry was a server where I worked. She really was nice to me for a while. I wanted my dad and her to be a pair. I thought they'd get along. They did, though Cherry is a lot younger. It's all kind of creepy now. And Cherry has no use for me, only her kid. I'm just competition for Tom Audley.

Still, I hope she's not sick.

"She's real sick, Chess. Real sick," I say.

Chess rubs his face with his hand. "She gonna die?"

"I hope not, but the docs, they are kind of stumped by her condition."

Chess thinks. "Maybe, just maybe we can work out a little time off for you. You be sure to call her."

But I want to call someone else. I dig through the scraps of paper in my wallet. I find Lynne's number, borrow Miles' cell phone.

"Hey, Lynne," I say. "It's..." and then I freeze. What did I call myself to her? But I can't be silent this long. As the name Trevor pops into my head, I'm already saying Jason. What comes out is "It's Jabar."

"Jabar?" she says. "Hold for a second. I have to put a kid on a horse."

I hear vague chatter, a kid's voice, Lynne's voice saying, "No, you can't bring your pop."

"Hello?" she says, back on. "Jabar?"

I hang up. I have to think this through a little.

The Happy Badger Casino is large, garish, and busy. And that's just the outside. I think of casinos as hell's pimples. Every once in a while, some of the corruption of hell bubbles to the surface, creating a boil. Wherein one may find most of the seven deadly sins. Casinos aren't purgatory. That's the bus station. No, they are little outposts of Satan.

This is what I tell the guys as the van pulls into the parking lot. We find Chess already there.

"I got two rooms for you boys over in the casino hotel. Nice place. Miles and Bob, you got one. Rusty and Jake, you got the other."

We boys all smile. This will be our most deluxe accommodation, at least in terms of density.

"We're kind of the house band for a week. We do the warm ups for acts they got coming through. Plus we play some private parties here. We'll be playing quite a bit." He gives us each $100. "Get some food and rest. We're gonna be busy."

I call my sister Lydia, collect, from the room.

"Hey, sis," I say.

"Who is this?" she says.

"Jason Audley," I say.

"Oh, hey, Jason. I'm just heading out the door. What's up? Anything wrong?"

"No, just called to say hi."

"I'm good," she says distractedly.

"Me, too," I say.

"Hang on a minute," she says and muffles the phone.

"Jason, I have to run. Can I call you back?"

"Not really. How do you like medical school?"

"That's not a short one. It's good, I suppose. Lot of work. Hey, call me back sometime," she says.

"Sure. Bye."

"Bye," she says, then, "wait. How are you doing? Any swelling of the lymph nodes?"

"Nope," I say.

It's like this. That's what my Uncle Karl says a lot. "It's like this, Jason..." and then he tells me something I don't want to know or don't want to hear.

It's like this. I'm $50,000 in debt. If there hadn't been a charity fund at the hospital and folks hadn't chipped in, god only knows what I would owe for being foolish enough to get cancer.

It's like this. I don't see any way I'm going to pay that. Realistically. I don't have prospects. Lark said my drumming seems to be getting worse. What does that say about my ability to apply myself, my potential for growth and self-improvement? I'm basically doing nothing nowhere.

So it's like this. I've had a long life, an unusual life. And the world is a fucked up place. Take Lark. Assaulted by her step-uncle. When she told me that, images flitted through my head, images of terror and violence and god knows what. I've been thinking about this ever since. How did this happen? Why does her family blame her? Is that even true? I know it happens all the time, blaming the woman. But inside the family?

And then the step-uncle gets trained.

And Rusty steals things. Not just Melody's necklace. He showed me a crucifix he grabbed from the house that put him up when we were the Bible Boys. A Bible Boy stealing a cross. "It's pure silver," he said, like he knows.

And Uncle Ken's become a drunk since he shot that guy on the tracks. Anna Bella looks ten years older than she did a year ago. Entropy. You enter an entropic world. As soon as you're born, you are surrounded by decay. You hurt your mother in the process and she is never the same. Your parents never get along as well once you're there. Every birth is a further decline. I see Phaedra's point, that thinking about the past is pointless, and thinking about the future is doubly pointless. Ask any of the glassy-eyed old people sitting right below me, right now, pressing a button on the slot machine, feeding it hope.

So it's like this. I'm ignoring these lumps. If it's cancer, fuck it.

Chapter 10

I might be James Bond wandering the casino. Things haven't gone well for James. Age, illness, bad habits. But he's still working, undercover, casino security. Drawing on the old instincts, the old training, his eyes are everywhere. The old lady with thick glasses who slumps in front of the quarter machine. Is she really what she seems? A depressed old lady squandering her social security? And the glassy-eyed waitress, slinging drinks to the slot drones. Is she really a woman? And the noise, the hum of hundreds of machines, chiming, chirping, blended with a choir of sighs. Why does it seem to have meaning? Does he really hear voices in it? James absorbs it all as he makes his way to the poker table, to play his game. Texas Hold 'Em, the game of choice for spies.

James scans the table for the high-rollers, for Mr. Big, enveloped in women, dressed for the evening. But no. Who are these middle-aged drunks? These angry retirees? The dealer, he attracts James' interest. No one could be that empty. What's his real story?

"You a poker man?" Rusty says beside me. "I'm frickin' awesome. No one can read me. No one knows what I'm thinking. I don't know what I'm thinking." Then he whispers, "I count the cards. I can do that. My memory is awesome."

"I know," I say. "James Bond knows everything."

"James Bond," Rusty says.

"I'm looking for Mr. Big," I say. "Take me to him."

"Well, I don't know about Mr. Big, but you won't have no trouble finding Mrs. Big," Rusty says, looking around. "Some real plus size ladies here."

"You guys want a drink?" a surprisingly pretty girl asks us.

"Rum and coke," Rusty says. "Shaken, not stirred."

I say. "I'll have your finest tap beer. The reserved stuff."

"Bud or Miller or Pabst," she says.

"Pabst."

Near us, a man wins something. A light whirls on the top of his machine and he gives a hoarse cheer.

"You guys with the band?" the waitress asks when she returns with the drinks.

"Yes," Rusty says. "We're on tour."

The casino smells of breath and musty carpet and cigarettes. The waitress' muscular perfume makes me sneeze.

"Bless you," she says. She's in no hurry. She's older than I first thought, and there's something clever hidden in her eyes.

"Thanks," I say. "I'm an anthropologist."

"Bullshit," Rusty says. "He's a drummer. I'm the lead player."

"Working on my dissertation," I say. "I'm studying the music subculture. Field work."

"Right," she says.

"What are the hidden rules for members of the performing arts culture? You know, power issues, gender issues."

"Right," she says. "7 bucks, please."

"When do you get off work?" Rusty asks, but she turns away.

James Bond continues his rounds. His back is acting up. Old bullet holes ache. He's getting a headache.

"Hey." It's the waitress. She motions to me to follow. I do.

We stand by the wall, next to an employee door.

"So you're an anthropologist," she says. "Where do you go to school?"

I weigh the risks of locating myself. "University of Minnesota," I say. Not in Wisconsin, but close enough to be possible.

"Wait," she says and goes through the door. She comes back with her purse, digs in it, pulls out a quilted wallet.

"Here," she says. It's a University of Minnesota student ID. "I'm an anthropology grad student," she says. "I'm studying gambling culture."

"What a coincidence," I say.

"Who do you work with?" she asks.

I rub my chin.

"You're full of shit, aren't you?" she says.

Yes. "No," I say. "Truth is it's a complicated situation. I'm doing this through a kind of correspondence curriculum. Online, of course."

"Huh," she says. "That must be new."

"Actually, it goes back to the 1920's, when correspondence courses first originated. This was one of the earliest."

"A doctorate in anthropology?" she says.

"It seems unlikely, I know."

"Yes, it does."

"So, you are like a spy?" I say. "You work here but, you know, observe the lab rats around you?"

"I'm here with permission. I'm sharing my results with the casino."

"To make it more effective at parting people from their money?" I ask.

"No, to improve the programs for people who are gambling addicts."

"Well, be sure to catch the band," I say.

"I already did. You look bored to death up there."

"It's my stage persona," I say.

"And it's very appealing," she says with stone face sarcasm that, just for second, makes me miss my sister, Lydia. "Okay, just wanted to check with you on the anthro thing, just in case we had something real to talk about." She turns.

"Wait," I say. She turns back, just a little.

"I'm really very complex," I say. "I would make a fascinating study." She turns back.

"I'm dying," I say.

"That's not funny," she says.

"It's true."

"And this is your way of living large before you go?"

Truth is, I just want to keep talking to her. She has cat's eyes, a bit slanted. And her forehead wrinkles when she talks, like everything she says is very serious. And when I talk, she tilts her head, which makes a small protruding ear appear through her straight brownish, blondish, rather thin hair. She wears no makeup.

"That's strong perfume," I say.

"It's hand lotion," she says. "This air conditioning dries me out."

She angles her head and it seems to ask a question.

"What time do you get off work?" I ask.

"Anytime," she says. "I'm an intern. I don't get paid."

"What about tips," I ask.

She smiles, for the first time. "I keep them," she says.

"Want to go for a walk or something,"

"I don't think so," she says.

"I'm James Bond," I say. "Don't laugh." I offer my hand.

"Nora," she says. We shake. Her skin is warm and soft.

I'm at a highway wayside. It's hot and flies buzz me as I sit on a blistered picnic table. The casino gig is over, and we are taking this two lane somewhere else. Chess is not clear on this. It's an old-fashioned wayside, with two pit toilets and four picnic tables on an overgrown patch of grass. We spent the night here, camped behind a screen of trees. Rusty and Lark took the van back into town to get some food. Chess sits in the truck with the door open, his legs half out, looking at a map. Miles and Bob sit on a different table, talking quietly.

Chess slaps the map down. "Where are those two?" he says. "We need to hit the road."

"I'm hungry," Miles says.

"Why don't you boys break down the tents and pile things up out here? We can at least be ready when they get back," Chess says.

I think we all feel reluctant to move, but we slowly get up, wave off flies, and start heaping up the gear. We almost never fold up the tents because they just get smelly.

"I found something," Bob says, holding a sheet of paper. "From Lark."

"Let's see it," Chess says, but Bob starts to read.

"Dear Losers. Rusty and me are gone and we aren't coming back. The van is a piece of shit and it's our pay. You will never see us again. So long. Rusty says bye. P. S. Sorry Uncle Chess but I'm a woman not a little kid. Lark."

"Jesus Christ!" Chess says. "Throw this junk in the truck. We got to go find them. If that little son of a bitch Rusty lays a hand on that girl, I'll cut his balls off." Chess is really mad. We open the creaky back doors of the truck and try to cram stuff in.

"In the cab!" Chess commands. Bob and Miles crowd in with Chess. I try to squeeze in.

"No," Chess says. "They might come back. You stay here."

"I don't want..."

"Jack, this is a military operation now. No place for you," Chess says. He digs out his wallet and hands me some bills. "Here," he says. He guns the engine.

I just stare. "Wait," I say and Bob and I get in a tug of war over the door. Bob wins. Chess floors it and the truck chatters away.

"They went the other way!" I yell, trotting after the truck.

"Shit!" I say, watching the truck disappear.

I'm sitting on the picnic table at this wayside rest, the blistered table, ignoring the flies, the smell of the outhouse, and the occasional car. It's been hours. I'm hungry, thirsty, pissed.

A sheriff's car rolls slowly into the wayside. It stops and a uniformed guy gets slowly out of the car. He walks toward me, slowly, stops five feet way and just looks at me.

"So what's the story?" he finally says.

"Hmph," I say and look the other way.

"It's kind of odd for a young man to be out here by hisself, out here at the rest area. I don't see no car," the officer says. He pauses, then goes on. "This might be the sticks to you, but we know a thing or two at the sheriff's office. A deputy sheriff like me, I've seen a few things. Only one reason a young man hangs around a wayside rest and I think you know what I'm talking about, and I'm going to tell you right now we don't want that in this county."

I look at him. "What?" I say.

"You know, you should be ashamed of yourself. All the things a young man could be doing, and you're out here."

"Doing what?" I say.

"You know. I'd like to see some ID."

I dig in my pocket, show him my driver's license. Chess' money falls out of my pocket. Three $100 bills.

"I think you better get in the back of the car," says the deputy, handing me my wallet and looking at the cash.

It's not so bad. I get a ride back to town. Get to sit in an office while the deputy makes a few calls. A guy comes in and the deputy points to me. He takes me to a little room and carefully talks to me about the dangers of male prostitution. I listen, agreeing wholeheartedly with all he says. Then a cop woman asks me a lot of questions and I fill out a form.

Then they let me go.

The good thing is that I have $347, almost $348. On the negative side, I've lost the band, my duffel, and I guess my job. I don't know anyone in Clayton, Wisconsin. I could call my uncles or Anna Bella, or even Tom Audley, my feckless father. That's how it should go. My wild adventure goes down in flames. Hey, no one got hurt. Jason goes home, finishes school, becomes an actuary, marries a nice Lutheran girl, and throws himself under a train. Or, a lot quicker, the illness spreads and I croak. Isn't cancer more virulent in young people? My only defense is to depress my life force, to undercut the vital energy of youth. It's holistic chemotherapy, in a sense.

I head for a bar.

I choose the ugliest bar. The front is a blank wall of cheap siding, featureless except for a steel door set in an unpleasantly asymmetrical spot. No windows. It's called Bobs Bar, with no apostrophe.

The door handle is sticky. Inside it's close and dark and I trip over a chair with someone sitting on it.

"Asshole," he says.

My eyes adjust. Linoleum floor. Cheesy paneling, festooned license plates from different eras. Sconce lights with red bulbs. Three old men lined up before me, elbows on the bar. There's a farty smell. I go to the other end of the bar, which is only about 3 feet past the last old drunk.

"Whiskey," I tell the bartender.

"Neat?" he asks.

"Neat. Double."

"Bad day," he asks.

'No," I say. "Great day. Celebrating."

I'm surprisingly not drunk when I leave. And once I find the door and relieve myself on a car parked out in front and fall off the curb two times and clunk my head on a streetlight pole, I decide this would be a good time to visit my old friend at the casino. My old friend Nora, with the wrinkly forehead and cat's eyes. She will be glad to see me, I know.

"Oh, James," she will say. "Where have you been? I've been going crazy."

Chapter 11

But the next day Nora is not so happy to see me. It's been a long walk to the casino and I know I look like hell, because I feel like hell. I will stick to beer next time.

"I'm working," Nora says. "You'll have to leave."

"Truth is," I say. "I'm kind of abandoned. The guys took off without me—long story—and they still have my stuff."

"Truth is," Nora repeats.

"Yes, truth is, I just need a place to crash for a couple of days, 'til the band comes back."

"You get in a fight with them?" she asks. "You have a scab on your head."

"Chicken wire. Or a curb. Tripped last night. No. Not a fight. Just some confusion."

"Well you aren't staying with me," Nora says. I take the fact that she is still talking to me as some encouragement.

"You got a car I can sleep in?" I ask. It's actually already evening again. The days just fly by when you get older.

"You are not sleeping in my car. Look, I know of a place. Empty camper. Kind of rough. No electricity."

"Where?" I ask.

She's quiet for a moment, probably considering whether she's offered too much. "Wait here," she says finally.

It's a dump. I can't believe I'm back in a trailer, one that's even worse than what Tom Audley found for us after the divorce. It's an older camper trailer, up on blocks. It sways as I step in. The mouse pee odor is overwhelming. First impressions are important. We make so many judgments from first impressions. I have to admit the mouse pee puts me off, as does the hole in the floor and the broken windows.

"It's worse than I thought," Nora says. "It doesn't look so bad from the outside."

Yes, it does, to a practiced trailer trash eye.

"I see what you mean," I say. "Kind of deceptive."

"Someone has stolen the toilet," I say, poking around the inside.

"James, come back out of there," she says. "Is James Bond your real name?"

"No," I say from the doorway. My mind races. "It's Fergus McDoodle."

"No it's not," Nora says. "Let me see your driver's license."

It's a pretty little spot we're in. Summer cabins, for those who can't afford lakefront. Nice trees, wildflowers, a woodsy, evening smell. Nora lives on the same gravel road, a few properties down. It's a pre-fab cabin, a simple unattractive box with two bedrooms and a room that serves for cooking, dining, and living. She wouldn't let me inside, but I know the type. They are around Uncle Kyle's cabin near Holdfast. She got it cheap, because the parents are dead and the kids who inherited it don't know what to do with it, and cabins become wrecks in one year if no one lives in them.

"I'm not ready to reveal my identity just yet," I say.

"Fine," she says. "I'm Nora Bjorklund, of Chanhassen, Minnesota. Maybe that will help."

"Ah, the Chanhassen Bjorklunds," I say.

"Why didn't you buy some stuff, stay in the casino hotel. Some clothes, you know," she asks.

"All the stores were closed. Sunday," I say.

"Oh," she says. "Right."

"And I don't' want to blow my money on a motel room. I have $347 and who knows how long that will need to last."

The mosquitoes are coming out and a humming cloud envelopes us.

Nora stares at me for moment. Her forehead wrinkles. "One night on my couch, if you take a shower," she says.

"Thank you," I say.

Nora goes back to the casino, returns later with an old tee shirt and sweatpants for me, borrowed from a security guard. She tells me she is staying with a friend for the night.

"Don't..." she starts to say, but pauses. "Okay. See you tomorrow."

I sit on a chair in my NASCAR tee shirt and faded pants. It's stuffy in the cabin. No TV, no radio, and almost no food. I drum my fingers on the kitchen table. I miss drumming, even the tappity-tap of drumming Chess Chalmers style. I wonder about Rusty and Lark. Rusty has stealing tendencies, but I didn't see him stealing Lark. Lark does not think much of herself, but I didn't see her choosing Rusty. I, for now, am an alien, in strange clothes, in a strange town, in a strange life. As it grows dark, I get depressingly reflective. What does it mean to be here when reality is a random organization of subatomic particles? Solid, liquid, gas—it's all about space, how much space between atoms and molecules and the like. A wind blows through it all, through all that empty space. Why don't we all blow away, diffuse, blend, drift like the smoky clouds that birth stars? Why don't I sink and morph into the chair, or into the stale cabin air? What if there's a planet like that, where if you stand still long enough, you sink into the ground, become part of it. You've got to keep moving. So I go out onto the gravel road and stare up at the stars. No moon, no clouds. Just the Milky Way, born of Hera's milk, spilled by the overenthusiastic suckling of Hercules.

"I have this curiosity about things," Nora tells me the next day. Nora Bjorklund, junior anthropologist. She is dressed much like me, appeared that way, knocking at her own door early in the morning. She's brought coffee and two donuts. Two. That is what a woman would do, one donut for each. I would eat three, at least, and wish I had input.
"So that's why you've helped me," I say.
"I suppose. Curious about people mostly. Culture."
"Have you learned much at the casino? I ask.
She shrugs, cocks her head. Her forehead wrinkles and then smoothes. "Not really," she says. "But it won't look that way when I write it up. I can apply a model for analysis and make something of my data, but me, personally, any insight? Not much."
"Are you planning to teach at a college?" I ask.
She nods. "That's the plan." She looks out the window, then at me. "You could get some work at the casino. Security or something. You have that bouncer look."
"Thanks.""
She gets up. "I'll take you to town," she says.

We ride in her Subaru, small, old, but spunky. Clayton has a second-hand store and I buy a few musty, tired shirts and a pair of blue jeans that look like brand new. I go to the casino and apply as security. I mention Nora Bjorklund. The man talking to me flashes a quick smile, white teeth under his big black moustache. "She's a pretty girl," he says. "College kid."

They hire me, pending a background check.

"Might be short term," the man tells me. "We got some big events here in the next couple of weeks. Don't know if we'll need you after that."

"That's fine, Mr. Nelson," I say. "I appreciate the opportunity."

My background check comes out okay. "Nothing serious," Mr. Nelson says, holding a computer printout. "You should see some of these."

"I got the job," I tell Nora, "on the basis of my clean background check."

"So, you're no worse than what we see," Nora says.

"Right. Can I stay at the cabin?"

Nora pauses. She is a person that speaks carefully. Thinks first. I fight the urge to fill in the blank space, to talk about something else.

"Fifty bucks a week. Or you could do some maintenance stuff. Are you one of those handy guys?"

Pretty much," I say, and it's true. My experience runs more to demolition, but there is something in my genetics that makes me good with tools, good at figuring things out. One of those things I actually like about myself.

Chapter 12

None of the spare uniforms fit, so I am a floor walker. I really am James Bond, wandering a beat in the casino, looking for stuff. I sat through a two-hour training video and then shadowed Mike Nelson for an afternoon. I am now an expert in casino security.

I replumbed the toilet in Nora's cabin. Bad flapper. I cut back brush. Nora said it needed a fire break. I've earned one month of rent, she says.

I have never lived with a woman before. It's easy. Nora is never there. She goes home a lot, to visit her boyfriend. This came as something of a blow. It might have gone like this:

"James," Nora would say, "you must marry me or I will die."

"Well, then, yes, or course, old girl," I will say.

We have three beautiful children. Two girls, one boy, whom we name Tennyson. The two girls are twins, one evil, one even more evil. No, they are both good girls, but very, very young. They are two years old, talkative, lively. Tennyson is 14. We have been married some time now.

We live in a lakeside ultramodern home. The walls and floors are actually computers, thanks to Tennyson, who is a genius. Nora is very famous. We are rich, thanks to my many money-making schemes, all of which work and are legal. Nora and I share a passion for strong black tea from England. That's just one of the many things we share. Others include values, principles, and childrearing philosophies.

But no. Nora has a boyfriend. I tell Nora I am spoken for as well, by several women.

"Good for you," she says. "My boyfriend doesn't want you living here."

"I'm not surprised, with our three kids and all," I say.

She has already learned to ignore me. "I told him tough luck, buddy. If there is anything I have learned about relationships, it's never compromise."

"I bet that works really well," I say.

Nora has made one of her rare evening appearances. She is a little drunk from something at work. We are sitting at the table, drinking beers, while it grows dark. I can hear mosquitoes whining against the screens, and a few tweets of sleepy birds.

"It does," she says. "When you compromise, you lose yourself. If you lose yourself, what have you got?"

"I don't know," I say.

"That's the point," she says. "You don't know what you've got. Probably nothing."

"I don't think it works that way," I say.

"Hey," Nora says, looking at me with a cocked head. "I talked to Mike Nelson. You are Jason something or other."

"I could be," I say.

"And guess what, Mike said that Chess Chalmers called the casino, asking if they had any idea where you were."

"What did they tell Chess?" I ask.

"That you were working security now."

"Oh." It sounds so banal. I suddenly know I can't do this much longer. Maybe four days is not long enough to really sample a career. In this case, maybe I should at least wait until I catch someone doing something wrong, to get the thrill of the hunt.

"What are you going to do with your life?" I ask Nora. It's dark in the room now.

"Hell, I don't know," she says. "I want to get this doctorate and then teach. But what are the odds? Know what I mean? Hardly any jobs and most of those in awful places like deserts and cities. Anyway, I should have published by now. I haven't even given a conference paper. I'm a nobody in the field."

"Want to do shots?" I ask. I found whiskey in the cupboard. I might be ready to face it again.

"Sure," she says.

We get drunk and make love.

I'm in love. She's not. She didn't sleep with me that night, but went to her bed, leaving me on the couch. It was cramped for two. Impossible, really. But I think she left too as a way to tell me something.

This is the one thing I learned from my mother. Astrid Audley didn't say much. She communicated through quick looks, faint gestures, imperceptible nods. She had a complex inner world that had little to do with words and conventional communication. It was the job of other people, particularly the males, to interpret scant signals into concrete plans and deep-felt opinion. So much could go wrong. Tom tried to understand his wife, but he'd shift his gaze at the crucial moment and miss volumes of communication. Tom lived in a world of guesses and surprise. Astrid found him dense. They had to divorce, I see that now.

So I know a great deal about women. I know that what they say may or may not be what they mean. I know that the nonverbal cues are legion but elusive. I know that I am usually wrong, and I am often sorry.

"So, we're sleeping in separate beds now," I say. I'm making coffee for Nora. She wears a big, loose tee shirt and won't look at me.

She stirs and I realize she has been motionless. She looks at me.

"I have to pee," she says and heads for the bathroom.

I see the writing on the wall now. That look, the shuffling walk, the little groan as she stood up. She wants me to go. My heart sinks and I smile ruefully at the cup of coffee in my hand, the coffee for Nora. I grab my little bundle of things from where I stuff them, under the end table with its little vase of plastic flowers. I walk out the door.

"Where are you going?" Nora says. She's leaning out the screen door. I'm about to step on the gravel road. I pause.

"Are you just walking away?" Nora asks.

I turn. "Your coffee is on the counter."

"I know," she says. "Did you want a ride to work?"

"Yes," I say. I walk back into the house and grin.

"Jesus," she says. "Don't you have a hangover?"

"No," I say. "Let me get you an aspirin."

"I need some food first," she says. "I feel like shit."

"You look great, I say.

"No I don't."

She's right. She looks like a wreck. Her eyes are puffy. She has a certain pallor. Her hair is dirty and hangs like seaweed.

"Oh, yes, you look great," I say.

She gives me a little smile and heads for the bathroom.

Wow, I think, that was easy. Just a little compliment and I got a smile from Nora with a hangover. Thing is that she does look great even though she is a wreck. Love is complicated.

"Good news," Mike Nelson tells me. "Got you a uniform. Doesn't match ours. Got it from a nursing home where my wife works, but you will look more official."

"Won't I scare the old people?"

"Only the ones from Little Bit of Paradise Lutheran Home," Mike says.

So I wear a tight uniform of dusty green and tan. I look like an overstuffed boy scout. It's hard to walk, as the crotch is tight and no matter how I shift around, I have to walk with a clenched butt. I patrol the parking lot, standing still as much as possible. An old lady gives me a quarter to especially watch her minivan. After a while I can't take it. I feel like I'm wearing an anaconda, slowly tightening its grip. I'd like to go to the Amazon, home of the anaconda and countless other malignant creatures. I'd like to walk through the claustrophobic jungle, slashing my way through the impenetrable tangle. So easy to get lost. You can't really see the sun and you can't keep a straight line as you hack your way. And then insects lay their eggs in you, or you step on a poisonous snake, or sink in a bog. I think about this all day and fail to notice the car fire in the parking lot. Well, fail to notice the early stages. But I fully notice the blazing car, sputtering, pinging, under a column of black smoke. I call it in, glad it's not the old lady's minivan. I keep people back until the fire department arrives.

Then I have no real function there, so my mind wanders. I think, what if this is a diversion, and someone is robbing the casino or plundering other cars. I scan the lot. Other than the crowd around the burning Ford, it seems calm. I picture ski-masked bandits holding cashiers at gunpoint in one of the back rooms where they do the counting. I edge away and then jog stiffly to the doors where they meet the Brinks truck. No Brinks truck, but as I watch, two figures in ski masks slip out of the door.

This is what should have happened.

I charge toward the robbers, my uniform suddenly flexible. They spot me. One pulls a gun, levels it at me. I dodge to the side, a split second before the gun fires. And then I'm on the gunman before another shot can be fired, a wrestle take-down, just like I learned in my brief high school wrestling career. The other figure hesitates. Run or fight? He can't decide. While he pauses, I work to pry the gun loose while wild shots spray the air, falling harmlessly somewhere. The second robber now joins the fight. For a while, it's dicey, robbers are tough. But through lightning quick wrestling moves and the conviction that I'm right, I subdue them both, just as the police arrive and say, "Wow, how did you do that? It's only then that I notice I've taken a bullet.

This is what really happens.

"Stop!" I yell, holding out my hand like a traffic cop or one of the Supremes. One of them pulls a pistol and shoots.

Chapter 13

My mouth tastes like metal. When I open my eyes, my head implodes, so I close them. Then I open them. I smell hospital. I instantly feel nauseous. I hate hospitals. I hate the smell, the lights, the sounds, the rough sheets, the unhealthy food, and the all of the other inmates. I have a tube in my nose. My fingers and toes are cold, but they move. I stare into the round face of a woman with over plucked eyebrows.

"Well," she says, "good morning, sunshine."

I close my eyes.

"No you don't," she says. "Wakey, wakey." I hear her turn. "Tell the doc he's awake," she says to someone else.

Soon I have a small collection of smiling medical personnel. An older man in a doctor coat sits next to me, chats while he shines a light in my eyes, which hurts like hell, and checks my pulse.

"Uneven pupil dilation," he says to those behind him. To me, he says "Welcome back," he says reasonably. I decide I will look at him.

"What happened," I mumble.

"Get him some water," the doctor says. Someone sticks a straw by my mouth. God, that tastes good.

"You have been unconscious for almost two days," the doctor says. "You got shot in the head."

"Shot?" I say.

"Just a ricochet," the doctor says, done poking at me. He sits back in his chair. "Don't know the details. You got hit just above your right ear. Didn't penetrate the brain or anything. Gave you quite a neat little fracture. Small caliber, lucky for you. Not sure why you've been out so long."

"Okay," I say. I'm having a little trouble following him, but I gather that I have a hole in my head, which is alarming. "Am I a vegetable?" I ask warily.

The doctor smiles. "No more than you were before," he says.

The doctor gets to his feet. "I'll keep the police out of here for a while yet, but they do want to talk to you." He turns and speaks quietly to the others in the room—nurses, I think.

Actually, I don't feel that bad. I'm hungry and thirsty. My head hurts, but I've felt worse. Half of my head is shaved. I'm very tired and get woozy if I try to sit up. But soon they are coaxing me out of bed and I take slow journeys to the bathroom. In a day, I feel pretty much fine, except for the headache. This is a lot better than the first time I was shot.

A cop visits me. "Hi there, young man," he says. "How are you feeling?"

"Good," I say.

I'm sitting up in bed, reading a sports magazine. He inspects my head.

"What do they think," he asks. "You gonna live?"

"For a while anyway," I say.

"Hey, that was pretty brave and dumb, trying to stop those guys. You remember anything?"

I think for a moment. "I remember a burning car and then yelling at someone."

The cop nods. "I'm Len," he says, giving me a delicate handshake. "Couple of amateurs. Didn't get a thing. Had no idea how casinos lock up their money. Between you and me, don't think they meant to shoot you. Bullet bounced off a light pole, and then a curb, and then hit your head, far as we can tell."

I hear some commotion outside my room. Chess Chalmers strides in, followed by a nurse.

"Jake-o!" he says. "Wow, look at you! You look like shit. Not really. But you don't look great..." Chess notices the cop and frowns.

"Officer," he says, "let's get one thing clear. Jake here had nothing to with this business. Just because he knew Lark and Rusty and traveled with them and was real good buds with them, don't mean he had anything to do with this. They shot him for Christ's sake."

Len the cop looks at me with more interest.

"Rusty shot me?" I ask.

"Nope, Lark did," Chess says. "You aren't gonna press charges now, are you? She's just a kid."

Nurses hustle Chess out of the room. The cop hesitates then stands. "We'll talk more," he says. "Didn't know you knew them."

A while later, the doc comes back. I'm in for observation. I was out for too long. They want to see what my brain is doing, so I get a CT scan. I have a small hematoma, they say, small brain injury. Should be fine. May have some symptoms in the meantime, like bad balance, fatigue, memory problems, instability. I check these off as they tell me, feeling all of them. But I've had all these before getting shot.

"I have lymphoma," I tell the doctor. He orders more tests and tells me a day later, "No, you don't."

"Do, too," I say. "I had it. Real bad. Now I have swollen glands again."

"No, you don't. It's still in remission. You probably had Lymphadenitis--that's an infection--and the lymph nodes still have some swelling. Can take ages for that to go away. I'll check with Dr. Ong, the oncologist. I can have him stop by."

"Well," I say. "I still think I have it."

"You don't need it," the doctor says. "You have a brain injury. That's all you need."

So I spend the whole day pretty much alone, except for a nurse or two who come in and ask me where I am and what my name is. I am sorely tempted to say something like "Tunisia and my name is Amy," but I don't. I call Anna Bella, collect.

"Again?" Anna Bella says when I tell her. "What is your problem? Why did you let her shoot you?"

"I'll be fine," I say. "Really just grazed my brain," I say, as we carry on our usual parallel and unconnected conversation.

To bridge the gap, I ask "How's your poetry going?"

"Working on your epitaph," Anna Bella says. But she continues, "I'm writing a Spoken Word piece. Has potential. Are you okay? Maybe you should head back here."

"Can't," I say. "I'm in love."

"Oh," she says. "Well."

"Yup," I say.

'Okay, talk to you later,"

On my third day in the joint, Nora visits.

"They wouldn't let me in," she says. "I'm not family. How are you doing? Your head is shaved, part of it." She touches the bandage on my head. "How do you feel?" she asks.

"Good."

"Really," she says.

"A bit dizzy still. Vision is a little blurry. Strange dreams. Really strange." It's true. Whether it's my swollen brain or the constant waking by the nurses, I have had unusually vivid dreams. Even when I nap, which I've been doing out of boredom. I don't like to think about them.

Nora nods. "The nurse told me they are going to release you tomorrow. What's this about knowing the suspects? It was on the news. That guy you worked for, he was interviewed."

"They were in the band but ran off. Guess I didn't really know them very well."

Nora leans toward me. "You aren't mixed up in this, are you?"

"No."

She looks at me, her forehead crinkles a lot. "I don't know if I should believe you," she says.

I look at her hard. I don't do that much, look at anyone like that, ever. "I had nothing to do with it," I tell her. She stares at me. There's a silence.

"Okay," she says finally.

We sit for a moment or two. "I need to tell you something," she says.

Doom, I think, a yawning pit of doom. I don't know what she is going to say but I know it's bad.

"John, in Chanhassen," she says.

"The boyfriend," I say.

"He's not my boyfriend," she says. "He's my husband."

"Oh," I say. Falling into the yawning pit of doom makes you dizzy.

"We separated," she continues. "But, well, we are going to try to work things out. I'm moving back to Chanhassen."

"Oh."

"We've been married three years. Been separated for almost a year now. I need to give it a chance."

"I can't think of anything to say," I say.

"Well, I just had to let you know. You rest now. I'll be gone when you get out."

"I think I get out tomorrow," I say.

"I know," she says. "I checked."

An hour later, Len the cop comes back with a friend. The man with him is tall, suited, crew cutted. He has lines that run from his mouth like a ventriloquist's dummy, making him look dour.

"Jason," Len the cop says, "this is Frank Plynth. He's the county prosecutor."

"Jason," Plynth says, nodding.

"Hello," I say.

Len pulls up a chair right next to me.

"We have a problem, Jason, "Len says. He looks at his hands for a moment. "The two suspects in the attempted robbery of the casino, they say, well, they say you were the mastermind of the operation. The inside guy, the one who planned the whole thing."

Plynth adds quietly, "Those are serious allegations, Jason. Very serious."

"How's your head?" Len says, leaning to peer at the side of my skull. "We hear you will be released tomorrow."

"Here's the problem," Plynth says. "We need to arrest you."

"Oh," I say.

"Just because there are allegations doesn't mean that we think you are guilty," Len says.

Plynth frowns. "Not so fast, Len. These are serious allegations."

"But Frank, it doesn't all add up," Len says.

They both look at me, not at each other.

'I'm not sure I agree, Len," Frank says.

Out in the hall, a woman is crying and for a while we go quiet.

I clear my throat. "So what exactly did those guys say?"

"That you were the mastermind," Plynth says.

"I mean, what exactly did they say that I did?"

"Inside job. You knew the security rotation. Started the car fire. They didn't really try to shoot you. You knew them. Played in a band. You're all broke. Motive. One of the suspects has a record. Burglary, shoplifting. It all adds up," Frank says.

"Did they get anything?" I ask, knowing they didn't.

"No," Len says.

"That might only mean you are not a very good mastermind," Plynth says, "not that you are innocent."

"They say it was kind of like a cult. That you are a Charles Manson type guy. That they were, well, sort of in your spell. Didn't know what they were doing."

"You gave them drugs," Plynth says. "They were your sex slaves."

"Frank," Len says, still looking at me, "I just don't buy all of that."

"It's a free country, Len," Frank says.

"I didn't do any of that," I say. I try to look aggrieved, shocked, and innocent, but I detect a note of falseness in my own performance. The story is strangely plausible, compelling, even though I know it's bullshit.

Len nods. "Here's the problem, Jason. I'm going to read you your Miranda rights now. You need to get a lawyer. We can't take you out of the hospital against the advice of your doctor, and we don't have the manpower to put a guard on your door until tomorrow."

"We'd like you to voluntarily come with us now," Plynth says. "Doc says you are stable."

"I want to confront my accusers," I say.

"Can't do that just yet. We'd like to take you with us, ask you some questions," Len says, "straighten this whole thing out." He reads me my rights.

"Let's go," Plynth says.

"No," I say. "I'll stay until tomorrow."

"Stalling won't do you any good," Plynth says. He and Len try to persuade me to join them. Len promises everything will be fine.

"When did the 'suspects' say I was the mastermind?" I ask.

"After their apprehension," Plynth says.

"Like immediately, or later?"

Len and Plynth exchange a quick look.

"That's not important, Jason," Plynth says.

"Oh yes it is," I say. "They didn't know it was me in the security uniform. They only told you this after they found out."

Len and Plynth are silent. "Come with us, Jason," Plynth says.

"No," I say. "I'll stay here until tomorrow."

Plynth motions Len to the corridor. Len rises slowly and follows Plynth out of the room.

"Jason," Len says when they return," I want your solemn promise that you will not leave this room."

"Until tomorrow," I add.

"Until tomorrow," Len agrees.

"I promise," I say.

At 12:30am, I slip out of the room. I feel bad about it. I kind of liked Len in spite of myself.

Chapter 14

I am a fugitive.

Someone took my clothes from my room. Probably to keep me there. I walk in the chilly night air, with stars overhead, no moon, a lazy chirp of crickets, an occasional car in the distance, thick summer night smells, down a sidewalk in a residential street near the hospital.

I wear my hospital gown. It flaps in back. I'm barefoot. Have half a shaved head, a small head dressing. Just another neighbor taking a walk. But this isn't easy. It's one thing to walk to the bathroom or stroll down the hospital corridor, and another thing to run off into the night. My head pounds with every careful step. My vision blurs. I'm dizzy. My heart thumps in my chest. I have my arms crossed, cold hands in my armpits, head down, trying not to step on anything pointed.

This is incredibly stupid. I know that. I say out loud to myself, "This is incredibly stupid." I can't help but agree. I just couldn't stay there. Something deep in my animal brain made me go. Maybe it's brain damage. Maybe it's a control issue. Maybe it's just another in a long line of poor decisions. But it's my life and I can fuck it up any way I want to. I tell myself with some defiance and then I say out loud, "This is incredibly stupid," and I can't help but agree, and I go through it all over again.

I am heading for railroad tracks, at least where I think they are. My plan, the plan of a mastermind, is to find a train, hop it, and disappear from Wisconsin forever. To start a new life, under a new name. I already have many of these. It will be an easy transition. I've never hopped train barefoot before. I know what the rocks are like in the gravel beds that line the tracks. They are sharp. Nothing to do with trains welcomes bare feet and bare butts. I am scanning the dark neighborhood for a clothes line, hung with clothes that fit me. Surely someone would leave clothes hanging in the damp night air, just my size? It would be nice if they left some shoes with them. And some cash.

Will they send dogs after me? Should I be jumping from tree to tree, or wading up a creek, or doubling back on my trail. Instead, I stop to pee. Can't help it. Not a good way to disguise my trail. I tie my gown tighter in back. What a ridiculous garment. Who ever dreamed this up, and why? Is it like a practical joke that amuses all the hospital staff, every day? Is it designed to reinforce submissive behavior? I think about this, and a car turns down my street. I freeze. I am next to a house with absolutely no landscaping. It's a rambler perched on a dark lawn. Not a bush or tree. I consider diving onto the wet grass. But the car is on top of me. I turn and face it, wave at an old man behind the wheel. He waves back and passes by.

Maybe I should go back to the hospital. I doubt anyone even knows I'm gone. I'm still a potential fugitive. I'm just out for some air. I can fix this before it gets worse. But I am feeling slightly nauseous and the idea of creeping back into my hospital room is almost more daunting than going on. It's easy to just walk forward. So much harder to turn around. I just can't do it. "This is incredibly stupid," I say and keep walking.

I find the tracks. I'm an old pro at this, I tell myself, and there is something familiar and comforting about the smell of train tracks in the night. That does not say anything good about me, I realize. I walk carefully up the tracks, stepping from tie to tie, slowly, until I am between streets. I find a patch of bushes just off the gravel bed and huddle down, yanking at my stupid gown, waiting for a train.

I always notice the sound of trains. Wherever I am, awake, asleep, somewhere in between, I hear their subsonic rumble, their calls. I am seldom so far away from trains that I can't hear them, somewhere off in the background, like distant drumming. Towards dawn, I feel rather than hear the rumble in the earth, the pulse of an approaching train.

So, it's like this, I hear my uncles say in a chorus in my head. Anna Bella adds, Astrid, your mother, she would be disappointed. My dead mother adds, I am disappointed, Jason. My father stands in silence, because he is not watching me. He is smiling at his waitress wife, Cherry, the woman who was my friend and then stole my dad. And Davey and Phaedra, they beckon me and welcome me to a life with no hope, no expectations, no past, and no fears. This is what I dream, balled up on the small platform on the rear of a container car. I doze on and off, cramped but out of the worst of the wind, pierced like Saint Sebastian with arrows of sunlight as we rattle among trees and fields, heading north. Poor Saint Sebastian, who survived being feathered with arrows, only to be beaten to death and thrown into a privy.

As I ride, I really miss Nora. We'd been together almost a week, got drunk together, made love. Okay, it's not much, but I don't have much to compare it to, and it was good, in its short, one-sided, married woman way.

I get off the train behind a shopping center. It's night. I'm hungry, thirsty, cold, in pain. I'm everything bad and very little good. I've been on several different trains, still in my hospital gown. Now I'm rummaging through a dumpster. I'm hoping for tossed-out hamburger buns and tossed out clothes. I'm not finding either, just a lot of cardboard, plastic, and a lifetime supply of straight pins. A door opens and a janitor comes out, pushing and pulling a couple of rolling garbage cans. He gives a cartoonish double-take, as I rise from the dumpster.

"Good evening," I say.

"Are you from a mental hospital?" he says in clear but accented English.

"Yes," I say. "I'm a lunatic. But not dangerous except to myself."

"What are you looking for?" he asks.

"Clothes. Food."

He is totally bald, short, and stout. He rubs his jaw.

"Wait here," he says and goes back inside.

I assume he is going to call the cops. That would be the rational thing to do. But I just stay there, hip deep in cardboard, plastic strapping, foam peanuts, pins. The door opens and the man reappears. He has a very, very small woman with him.

"So," she says. "You the crazy one? You look crazy."

"I have had some bad luck," I say. "I'm not really crazy in the way you mean. Crazy maybe in terms of some of my choices," I say.

"Out of dumpster," she says. She's Asian, but I don't know from where. I get out of the dumpster. She and the man share a sniggering laugh.

"You from a hospital," she says, gesturing towards my gown.

"Yes," I say. "Couldn't pay the bill, so I ran. Got this bump on the head. Pushed a stroller out of the way of a bus. Got grazed by the mirror."

"Right," the woman says. The man grins at me. "I believe maybe the bill part."

I shrug. "This is not a world for heroes," I say.

"You got that right," the man says.

"Wait here," the woman says. Now they will call the cops, I think. The diversion in their routine is over. They'll go back to work and the cops will slap me around a little and haul me away. Maybe they will shoot me, a real shot this time. None of this ricochet stuff. A just get it over with shot. That's what should have happened.

What happens though is that they come back out with a tee shirt that says Sale-a-thon with little firework designs around it. A pair of khakis with a long grease smudge. A baseball hat. Flip flops.

"I could use a belt," I say, pulling up the massive pair of pants.

"No belt," the woman says. I finish dressing and throw the gown in the dumpster.

"You still look crazy," the woman says.

"Put on the cap," says the man. "Your head is..."

"Crazy," the woman finishes.

I try, but it hurts. Hits my head hole exactly.

"Wait here," the woman says. I wait.

She comes back with a stocking cap. Still hurts, but not so badly. It's green, with a Green Bay Packers logo. They look at me and both start laughing.

"Sorry," the man says. "The best we can do."

The woman hands me a plastic bag. "Hope you like Vietnamese," she says. "My lunch."

"I can't take this," I say. "You need to eat."

"Okay," she says, and takes it back. The man and woman look at each other. It's clearly a conversation. They know each other well. Finally, she nods and says to me, "Wait here. Three hours."

He goes by Roger, though he is from Iran and has some other name. He says he has a degree in architecture. She is his wife, Mai. They are Roger and Mai Tehrani. They have their own business, cleaning the offices at the mall, and a few of the stores. They have three kids. They look small and intelligent in the pictures, with sharp dark eyes and round faces.

"I am Muslim," Roger says. "A Muslim must help those in need. It is a basic tenet of my faith. I believe you are here to receive our help."

"I completely agree with that," I say. I have eaten an Iranian Vietnamese meal, with lots of rice with bits of meat and vegetables in a spicy fish sauce. They got off work at 1 AM, collected me, and brought me to their home, a smallish split level with strange décor and many exotic smells. They have a dog named Okar, or Oscar, or Ochre, or something.

I hate dog," Mai says, feeding it table scraps.

They give me tea.

"Tell us your story," Roger says.

I tell them about my life as the son of a wealthy businessman. An old family business, I say, going back over one hundred years of selling plumbing supplies. Van Helsing and Sons Plumbing Supplies, Incorporated. I tell them how my sister cheated me out of my inheritance, how I devoted my life after this to helping the homeless, never dreaming I would end up as a homeless wanderer myself. How my sister, Katarine, had a change of heart, reconciled with me, and then suddenly died of mysterious causes, without ever legally granting me my share of the family business. How our half-brother, Nestor, the offspring of our father's secret polygamist marriage to his bookkeeper's sister, wrested the plumbing supply enterprise from all members of the Van Helsing side of the family. How I knew it would only cause pain to pursue this through the legal system, but did so for the benefit of my sister's special needs children. How it all failed, leaving me in debt, and working as a roofer, where I actually received the head injury, saving a fellow worker, Juan, who came all the way from southern Mexico to earn whatever he could to feed his family, who had run afoul of the drug lords in the area and barely survived, growing their own food at an impossibly high altitude, on the flanks of a live volcano.

"Your mother, she not know of second wife?" Mai asks.

'No," I say.

"Baloney," Mai says. "Woman know."

"I can't say," I reply. "My mother ran off with her tennis coach. I didn't see her much after that."

Mai nods. "She knew."

So I go on to tell them how Nestor, filled with spite for all Van Helsings, kept messing with my tubes as I lay helpless in the hospital, and I feared the worst.

"Why he so mad?" Mai says. "He got the business."

"I don't know," I say. "I think Nestor is just not a happy man. His wife ran off with the plumber who was updating their bathroom. Ironic."

"The men in your family are weak," says Roger. "Let the women behave in such ways."

"Maybe these men have small penis. Women not happy," Mai offers.

"I don't know," I say. "But anyway, as soon as I was able to stand, I slipped out of the hospital and found my way, well, where you saw me. I can't thank you enough."

Roger and Mai both nod.

"He is crazy," Mai says to Roger. Roger smiles and nods.

"You sleep on couch. I don't think you a problem. I can smell crazy when it is bad crazy. You a different kind," Mai says to me.

"Like the village idiot," Roger says. "Or Mai's Uncle Liu Vang."

"Liu Vang!" Mai says, bursting into a laugh. "Oh, my!" She and Roger laugh until they have tears in their eyes. Mai wipes her eyes.

"So in the morning you meet the kids and we take you to thrift shop."

I settle on the couch and wonder why Roger and Mai have not thrown me out the door, or even helped me in the first place. Maybe I will wake up in their basement dungeon, surrounded the skeletons of other dumpster vagabonds.

I wake up with a toy truck on my forehead, moving toward my nose. A small boy stops and stares when I move. He squeals and runs away. I eat Fruit Loops with the kids and Mai takes me in her minivan to the thrift shop, where she buys me some clothes that fit. I wear my Green Bay Packers hat in the August heat, to cover my semi-hairless head and the dressing over my head hole.

At home, Mai changes the dressing.

"I see much worse," she says. "Nail gun?"

"No," I say, not knowing what to add.

It's a Saturday. The kids have lessons and Mai leaves. "Go help Roger in garage," she commands.

I help Roger change the oil on the work van, then we replace three brake pads. He gets lots of calls on his cell phone. "Family in Los Angeles," he says to me. While he talks I check out the two motorcycles in the garage. Honda Gold Wings, big cruisers.

"Not new," Roger says, joining me. "But we got a very good deal on them."

"Can Mai handle a bike this big?" I can't help but ask.

"No," Roger says. "She rides with me. Had to buy the pair. One is for sale."

His phone rings again and this time he goes back into the house. I toy with the idea of stealing a bike. No, not me. Instead, I find a pile of magazines on the workbench and thumb through them. Motorcycle magazines, not for hard core bikers or bad biker posers, but for the weekend cruiser types. Articles on BMW cruisers, rallies in Alaska, and Florida, fancy ads. I am paging through my third one when I pause on an article. "Winter Lake Rally. Touring the Wisconsin Back Roads." I turn the page and look at a nearly full page photo of a woman on big bike and man in the sidecar attached to the bike. I look more carefully at the two smiling people. First I recognize Phaedra, sitting astride the bike, arms crossed, big smile. I look more closely. And the man next to her, wearing sunglasses, sitting low in the sidecar. It's Davey. His blond wavy hair is swept back, like he's in a wind tunnel. He's smiling, too. "Birdie and Wilhelm Rommel show their 2001 Harley-Davidson

Sportster 1200 with sidecar." That's the caption. I scan the article. Nothing about them. The article is mostly photos, but I gather that the Winter Lake Rally is an annual event, on Labor Day. I see this magazine is four years old.

I don't notice Roger come back into the garage. He's standing next to me. "Nice bike," he says. "We thought about a sidecar. Mai says it is too low. Too close to the road."

"Where's Winter Lake?" I ask.

Roger shrugs. "Let's get a map," he says. He takes a Wisconsin map out of the glove compartment of the van.

"I need my reading glasses," he says.

"Let me look," I say. I find it. It's a small black dot of a town, on a lake that is shaped like a turkey baster. It's a big lake, with lots of islands and bays. Winter Lake, the town, sits at the long skinny end of Winter Lake, the lake. It's in the northwest corner of the state, not far from Superior, which not surprisingly, is on Lake Superior.

Roger is staring at me. "You look very interested in this," he says.

"I know these people," I say, pointing at the photo. "I haven't seen them in a long time. I'm surprised, I guess."

Roger nods. "Want to help me change a belt?" he asks.

"Sure," I say.

I feel weirder and weirder in this happy home. I go with them that night to clean. I pick up trash, all they will let me do unless I have training. That night I colonize a little part of the basement, against their protests, and sleep on top of a musty sleeping bag. My head hurts. I only notice it when I'm not doing anything. But this will be a long night on this hard, cold floor, and I know it was foolish. I sit against the wall. Davey and Phaedra.

Where did they come from? Where do they live? That bike couldn't have been cheap. What are they doing to live? Wow, I think, they were still together, as of four years ago. So 3 years after I last saw them, after Davey told me he was running away from his life, his family, high school, to be with Phaedra. Davey the good kid, from the Miller household, kind and patient people. Have they ever heard a word from Davey? Should I contact them? He looks older in the photo. Phaedra, who we met while hopping trains, she looks the same. Her smile has a feral quality, like her eyes. Can't see Davey's eyes behind the sunglasses, but I think they would tell me a lot. He looks so open in the photo and she looks so closed. Yet they both smile at the camera. Birdie and Wilhelm Rommel. Any doubt of who they are goes away with that name. Rommel. The Freight Train Riders of America poser, or maybe he was real. He was smart, demented, and nearly killed me. Shot me in the shoulder with Davey's gun. Then my uncle shot him dead. All of this seven years ago.

I feel a conflict in me. A desperate longing to see Davey and Phaedra. I don't know why. And a strong reluctance to find them, to talk to them. Do I want to hear about their happy life? They bought a Harley. How did they do that? That's not Phaedra, at least as she was seven years ago. She was an outsider, an off-the-grid wanderer, running from something, but I never knew what. Older than Davey and me, and a woman, and aware of her effect on us. We traveled by freight train to see Mark Twain's home in Hannibal, Missouri. It was hot, then stormy, then Rommel took her away. And we found her. Then it got complicated, and the two of them, they left me. I didn't have the courage to follow, or maybe I had the good sense to stay behind. But what good was that? I was there to see my mother die, to see my father and Cherry forget all about me, to fall in and out of college.

Now look at my achievements. I am a fugitive from the law. Wanted for a casino robbery, betrayed by my bandmates. Isn't that supposed to be some kind of brotherhood? We went through a lot together. I hear Lark's voice in my head, saying to me, "Loser."

When I fall sleep, I dream, more of those dreams of a damaged brain. A man in a gray robe points a bony hand at me. "Pillbug," he says and I am struck with terror, as water rises around me and I just can't seem to run fast enough to escape the hail of bullets. I'm hit and man in gray closes in on me until a fiery bat hovers like a luna moth, tells me to go north. Which, the next day I do.

Chapter 15

I go north, but not to Winter Lake.

"Roger," I say. "I'd like to rent one of these bikes." We are in the garage and I am seated on one of the Gold Wings, one with saddle bags that match.

Roger holds a wall socket. The outlet in the downstairs bathroom doesn't work and Mai wants him to fix it.

"One of the bikes?" Roger says without looking at me. "I will have to talk to Mai."

Another night at the shopping mall, hauling and breaking down boxes mostly. I have some stubble around my head hole, and Mai has buzzed the rest. I almost match, and wear a small dressing that comes off a lot. No more Packers cap. My energy still seems down, but what's new. I still get headaches and get dizzy if I move too fast. I still have strange dreams. But I feel like I've turned a corner on this.

"So, you want to rent bike," Mai says after work. "Why? Where you going?"

"North," I say. Roger and Mai nod.

"Time to move on," Mai says. "You doing a lot better. We don't want jail. We got kids."

"I'm grateful," I say, more than they can know.

Mai nods. "Good," she says.

Roger says, "We've talked. You can borrow my ten speed. Not rent."

"Ten speed?" I say.

"It's an old Trek, but it works fine," Roger says. "We'll go over it, tune it up."

"Okay," I say. "How about renting one of the Hondas?"

Roger and Mai laugh. "You a funny man," Mai says.

On a sunny morning in the second week of August, I set off.

"Bye," Mai says. "Go away now. But bring back bike."

"I hope you have better luck," Roger says.

After an hour, my ass is killing me. I'm not used to riding a bike. I also discover that Wisconsin is full of hills, long, long, long uphills and brief downhills. I pedal doggedly along a paved section of road, a lumpy blacktop that passes among dull-eyed bovines, monstrously tall corn fields, and little settlements of houses and outbuildings. I suppose it's a beautiful day with postcard scenery. I am suffering too much to notice.

But I do have a destination in mind. Uncle Karl. I need help. I have fifty bucks, thanks to Roger and Mai, and a little backpack with a few things I picked up. But I am missing my wallet. It is in my jeans, either in some hospital storage room or in some investigative lab being analyzed for forensic evidence. The fugitive thing is not going to work, at least the way I'm doing it. I'm open to suggestions. This is a new experience, running from the law. But as a criminal mastermind, I should be able to devise a clever way to evade detection by detectives, those who detect things like runaway masterminds. I guess being detected wouldn't be so bad. It's the arresting and jailing that follow, and the frankly hilarious innocence I proclaim.

It would go like this.

"I'm innocent," I say.

"You've been detected," they tell me. "As a criminal mastermind. You masterminded a moronic attempt to rob a casino. Now you must pay the piper."

"I know that it looks bad," I admit. "But besides knowing my alleged accomplices, my shady and alternative life style, and my problems with holding jobs, going to school, and alcohol abuse, and my fucked up family, and the damning defenses offered by Chess, my personal Charon, the boatman of Hades, who has ferried me into a personal hell. Besides all those things, look at my eyes. Look at this face, which looks like an expendable henchman in a terrible American kung fu movie. Besides that, you can see I'm innocent."

"Are not," they say.

"Am," I say.

"Not," they say.

"Am too, and that's final. No backs," I say.

I need a drink of water. Or a Dairy Queen. I find neither. From Roger and Mai's house to Uncle Karl's implement dealership is 62 miles. It's not far. In all these wanderings, I've almost gone back to where I started. I finally hit a town, Mesitgot. I buy a map at the gas station. I have covered 16 miles. I'm exhausted. I buy a coke and sit on the curb next to my bike, hoping a passing milk truck will run me over. I would be a flat John Doe. At least partially flat. Much would depend on my orientation vis a vis the truck tires.

Two kids walk by. "Do you know where I can recycle this?" I say. It's what Nora would have asked. The kids look at me and one says "Faggot," and they run. I go back in the gas station, buy a nasty looking sandwich out of a refrigerator case, a bottle of water, and sunglasses. Only 46 miles to go. I have the route fixed in my head. I calculate that at the speed I am riding, I will get there about 2 AM. Maybe a little earlier.

Three hours later I get a flat tire. I was coasting down a hill, daydreaming, hit a hole in the road that almost sends me flying. Within seconds my tire is completely deflated. I get off and start pushing. Not much else I can do. Deer flies find me and circle my head. I ignore them for a while until one actually bites me. Then I realize they mean business and I try to wave them away, even knocking some out of the air. When it starts to rain, they leave me alone. It happened suddenly. One minute I'm sweating in the afternoon sun and the next minute, dark clouds rush in, with almost no wind. The wind comes after it starts raining, just to make sure I get thoroughly soaked.

My bandage on my head falls off and won't go back on. My pack feels like a tortoise shell. My shoes squish and I start to shiver. I stop at the crest of a hill, wipe the rain of my face, and look around.

The glaciers really did a number on this landscape. I don't know what it looked like before, but know it looks like corduroy, long, lumpy hills everywhere, most covered with dense woods. Pastures and fields of corn claim the valleys. It's a beautiful combination of lines and curves, rocks and trees, in all shades of greens and browns. And from where I am, lots of sky, dark, misty hanging clouds, intensifying the colors. I hear nothing but the rain and the rustle of wind. No cars, no planes, no people. I feel a strange peace.

Thunder grumbles in the distance and I decide to move off the hilltop. I am still feeling this odd glow when a pickup slows down beside me. An old man looks at me while the truck glides by. He drives a hundred yards or so and then stops. The backup lights come on and the truck slowly reverses towards me.

"Looks like you need a ride," says the man, leaning toward the passenger window. "Throw the bike in back."

"Got a flat," I say and as I get in, "I'll get your seat wet."

He shrugs. He's a small man, thin white hair, bristly white beard, flannel shirt.

"I can take you to town or we could stop at the farm and I can fix that tire."

"Let's fix the tire," I say.

The man doesn't say anything, but puts the truck in gear. We cross a bridge over a creek and glide up a hill. After the bike, this seems miraculous.

The man glances at me a few times.

"Hey, thanks for picking me up," I say. "I got this crazy idea to go visit my uncle. You know, spur of the moment, ride my bike over, and got a flat and then this rain."

He glances at me again. "What happened to your head?" he says.

"Industrial accident," I say. "Looks worse than it feels. It's pretty much healed. Nice truck," I offer.

He nods, then says "That stand of pines was planted by the WPA. Norway pines." Under the dark sky, the pines are shadow black, impenetrable.

"WPA did a lot of good," he says.

"I agree," I say. We ride in silence for a long time after that.

He turns on his signal and about three minutes later we turn onto a gravel driveway, drive half a mile, and pull up in front of a weathered barn. Near it are a couple of long Quonset huts and a simple two-story house. No porch, old wood storm windows, storm cellar doors on the side. We get out. Just drizzling now. The man slides the heavy looking barn door and we go in. It's dark and chilly in the barn, smells like dry straw, dirt, and old wood. He walks over to a steel utility door, opens it, reaches inside and flicks a light switch.

"I'm just going to step in and see what I got for your bike. You can stay out here," the man says.

I can feel warm air coming from the door and I wouldn't mind stepping into the room. But I wait. The man goes in, shuts the door behind him. I stand for a while and start to shiver, pace around in the barn, flap my arms, stick my head outside. It's almost as dark as inside. Finally I go over to the door. It's not locked. I open it a few inches and say "Hey, can I come in? Getting a little chilly out here."

No response. I look around the barn a little more then go stand by the warm door breeze. This time I open the door. "Hey," I say, a little more loudly. Then I walk in.

It's a small room but brightly lit, white walls, clean concrete floor. Fluorescent lights give a buggy hum. It's entirely empty, except at one end, stairs lead downward, with a blue metal railing. I hear some noise from down the stairs, walk over and look down. Concrete stairs, with even yellow stripes marking each tread. I can see six stairs and then a landing.

"Hey," I yell. I hear some rustling but no one answers. I have no reason to go down the stairs. It is indeed much warmer than in the barn, warmer, and drier, and oddly new. I tell myself this is a bit strange and I should stay where I am, but that would violate my code of stupid decisions, and anyway, I'm curious.

I go down the stairs, take a turn on the landing and go three more steps into another room. It's a spacious room, bigger than the one above. One end of the room contains a sort of fenced cage and inside are guns. All kinds of guns. I take a few steps closer, walking softly. I see handguns, rifles, automatic weapons. Maybe two dozen firearms. The rest of the room is a kind of workshop, and a couple of doors going who knows where.

"Asked you to wait outside," the man says. He's holding a bike inner tube.

"Got cold," I say. He looks at me closely, then nods.

"Here," he says, offering the tube. "Got a patch kit, too. How are the spokes? Did you damage them?

"I don't know," I say.

"Better bring it in," he says.

I go get my bike out of the truck. After pausing for a moment, I carry the bike down the stairs. He has a bike stand and flips the bike upside down, spins the wheel. "Spokes aren't true" he says.

"Oh," I say. "Will it still work?"

"Depends on what you mean by that. Could you ride it? For a while maybe, but the wheel is warped and it will get worse."

"Can it be fixed?" I ask.

He looks at me. "You don't know anything about bikes, do you?"

"Not really," I say.

"It's good to know about bikes. There'll come a time when people are going to use bikes a lot. Chaos everywhere. No fossil fuels. You want to hang on to this bike. Nice old Trek. "

"Okay," I say. I'm stuck on the chaos part and can't help but glance at the guns.

The man walks over to the cage and deftly unlocks it, takes what looks like an Uzi off a shelf. "You know firearms?" he asks.

"Not really," I say.

He eyes the gun closely. "Getting dusty," he says. "Should be in a cabinet."

"You a collector?" I ask.

"Kind of." He flips the gun around, aims at the wall, and then puts it back on the shelf.

"Not so much into the weapons themselves," he says. "Just want to be ready for when it falls apart."

"The end times," I say.

"Could be," he says.

"Like the rapture?" I ask.

The man snorts. "Hell no. None of that nonsense. I'm talking about the end of government. Anarchy. Chaos. Every man for himself. Survival, son, that's what interests me."

"Do you have, I don't know, water and food and other stuff all stored away?"

He looks at me intently. "Why do you ask?"

"No reason," I say.

He picks up a pistol. "Desert Eagle," he says. "Kind of a hand-held cannon. Got a kick."

"Well, maybe I could just fix this old tire and get out of your way," I say.

"No hurry, unless you got to be somewhere, which I don't think you do." He continues to play with the Desert Eagle, turning it this way and that. "Son, why don't you tell me what you're really up to."

"Nothing, "I say. "Just out riding."

"Just out riding, with an injured head, in a thunderstorm. Well, I guess that can make sense, if your brains have been scrambled." He chuckles. "One of my favorite dishes that my mother used to make, scrambled eggs and calf brains. Ever had it?"

"Scrambled eggs and hot dogs," I say. "No brains."

He sights down the pistol, then puts it down. "Do you read history?"

I nod.

"What did you learn?"

"Well, I read mostly about Romans." Just getting into the Middle Ages now.

"I asked what you learned from it."

"I don't know," I say. "Maybe that it doesn't matter when or where you live, people wreck everything they build. They wreck their lives, their families, the natural world, everything. The grass is always browner on the other side of the fence."

"Browner, huh? Maybe only when you get there. Not everyone tears things down. Some just wait for the collapse and then get on with things"

"The survivors," I say. "Like those who had a natural immunity to the plague."

"Plague, huh? You're a strange one to talk to," He rubs his hands. "You hungry? The boys are coming over tonight. I got to feed myself before they get here, get a few things ready. C'mon over to the house."

"I might just fix my tire and..."

"No turning back now, son. You come get something to eat.

"I think I should probably get on my way."

"Won't hear of it," he says. "Let's head up. We'll finish the bike later."

It thunders again, a big crash, even down these stairs.

I could run, I think. As soon as he turns his back and starts to walk toward the house, I'll take off into the woods. I'm not sure about this guy. That's a lot of guns. But I'm tired of that, the running. I think I still have some of that peace from watching the hills in the storm. I can still smell the cool, living air, with almost a hint of fall in it. Makes me passive, cow-like.

"What's your name?" I ask.

"Bill."

"Me, too," I say.

When we are in the house, Bill fries up a couple of hamburger patties and opens a can of baked beans. We eat like cowboys, off of metal plates, with quaint wood handled forks. He makes strong black coffee. He never looks at me, never says a word, even when I say "Thank you," and "This is delicious."

We are still sipping coffee when they start to arrive, the boys. It's like they lined up outside. Within two minutes, four new faces crowd the little kitchen.

"Living room," Bill says.

"Who's this?" one of the men asks. They are all graying or white-haired, except the one who spoke, who might be 35 or so. They are all dressed like Bill, in flannel shirts, jeans, boots. Three wear baseball caps. Two are blank, one says Brewers. They are good sized men, thick, strong looking. A bit of belly, but solid. The living room is small, with a couple of worn chairs and a couch. We're crowded. I can smell cigarette smoke on someone.

Bill nods toward me. "This is Bill, or so he says."

They all look at me.

"Hey," I say. "Good to meet you."

"Found him on the highway. Flat tire. His story doesn't make a lot of sense," Bill says.

"You think they sent him?" one asks.

"No, not this guy," Bill says.

"Where's his car?" someone asks.

"He was on a bike. A bicycle," Bill says.

"Out in the rain?" another says.

"Yes, out in the rain," Bill says.

They eye me darkly. "On a bike," one mutters.

"I've given him some food. He's seen the armory," Bill says.

"I think it's time for this little bird to sing," says the younger one.

Bill turns toward me. "Bill, or whatever your real name is, we don't mean you any harm. But you got to be careful, especially around folks like us. We got to know the truth from you, son."

"Maybe we should ask him some questions," one man suggests.

"Who sent you?" asks the young one.

"No one," I say.

"What happened to your head?" another one asks.

"Already told Bill," I say.

"He said an industrial accident," Bill says. Bill looks around at the other four men. "So what do you think?" Bill says to them. "Is this worth a shot?"

The men glance at each other.

"Oh, hell. He might be the one we need," says one. "So hell, just put our cards on the table. Agreed?" No one responds, so he keeps talking. "This group is the Wisconsin Coalition for Post Apocalypse Survival."

"WICPAS," adds Bill.

"Why were you snooping around?" says the young one.

"I wasn't," I say. "Bill brought me to the barn, to help fix my bike."

"Bill? That true?" says another.

"Well, yeah," says Bill. "I was testing him."

"Let me keep talking," says the one explaining. "We started as just a few guys who cared about the future back, hell, back in the 70's. I think we were the first group in Wisconsin."

"But it's hard to tell," says Bill.

"We can agree to disagree on that one, Bill. Anyway, we go back a ways. Some other groups formed but we were kind of the leader and started this Coalition thing about 10, 15 years ago."

"We had a lot to share," says one who hasn't spoken yet. He has a surprisingly low voice, like James Earl Jones. He half rises from his seat, offers his hand and says, "Hi. I'm Daniel."

"But these are dark times," says the young one.

"Short of it is that we all got different reasons for thinking we are seeing tough times for civilization. Daniel here thinks it's a religious thing."

Daniel says, "Not the rapture, but the numerical code in the Bible tells us that we are nearly done on this earth."

The young one says, "It's them politicians. Our government's gone to shit. Money going to all the wrong people. Corruption, double and triple dealing. Prostitution."

"It always comes down to prostitution with Tony here," Bill says.

Tony shrugs. "Or television," he says.

"Or satellites," Bill adds.

"So we've pooled our resources, learned a few things to keep us alive, like emergency medicine, wilderness survival, barter economies, all that. We've been studying this for decades now."

"We got families to watch out for. Or had families. Or wish we had families, at least a wife," says Daniel. There is huge flash of lightning, followed by a thudding boom.

"Jesus," Bill says. "This thunderstorm is really hanging around."

"Odd for this time of year," Daniel says. And then continues, "Mesoconvective complex. These storms are trailing, one following the other. Could get some strong winds, even a tornado." Then he smiles. "Weather's my subject," he says.

"So you guys don't pay taxes, that sort of thing?" I ask.

They all wince, simultaneously.

"We aren't Posse Comitatus," Bill says. "Not that kind of thing at all." There's a hint of exasperation.

"So," I say. "Anyone want to take me to Sorenson Implements?"

"Why would we take you there?" Bill asks.

"My Uncle Karl runs it. I was riding over to visit him," I say.

"It's past five o'clock. They'll be closed, and it's over 30 miles away," Bill says.

We lapse into silence for a minute or two, listening to the rain and a wind that begins to howl.

"Did BOWS send you?" Tony asks.

"BOWS? I say.

"Brothers of Wisconsin Survival," Bill says. "Kind of our archenemies."

"Bunch of a-holes," says Daniel.

This is what I should have said: "No."

This is what I say:

"Well, guys. It's like this. I don't mean no harm. Really, I'm not in any group of any kind. Well, I was in a band, but it fell apart, even before I got shot."

"You got shot?" Daniel asks.

"Caliber?" Tony asks.

"9 mil," I say. "Ricochet, actually."

"Oh," Tony says. "That's why you are still here."

"So I was kind of set up. A couple of guys in the band, well, actually one is a girl. Woman. Looks like a girl. They tried to knock off this casino..."

"Saw that in the news," Bill says. "Story checks out so far," he adds, with a sarcastic smirk.

"I was working security, undercover. Kind of a side line of mine. Private contractor. Was doing some undercover work, well, I can't go into that. Let's just say I was traveling with this band, and leave it at that."

They nod. "I'm curious, though," says Daniel.

I really want to launch into my extensive undercover experience, but manage to swallow it. With difficulty. "So these two in the band, they were associated with some group. I don't know who. I was looking into that, but kind of on the side. Wasn't my main assignment."

"Are you a hit man?" Tony asks.

"No, but I have special skills," I say. "Anyway," I continue. "They try to pull this casino job. Of course, I knew all along, but it wasn't my job to stop them. Or to help them. Kind of morally neutral on that one, as I don't really support casinos and I don't support robbery."

They nod.

"So they botch this job, and then tell the cops I'm behind it all."

"Were you?" Bill asks pointedly.

"No," I say. "I already went over that."

"Next thing I know, I'm on the run," I conclude.

"From who?" deep voice says.

"Excellent question. Truth is, I'm not sure. Oh, there's the small town cops. Not worried about them. But who were these two working for? That's what I wonder."

"Why do think they were working for anyone?" asks Bill.

I lean forward. "They talked about the need to fund a group. Some organization they were part of. It felt to me almost like they were in a cult. Here we are a traveling band. Neither smoked, drank. No partying at all. And they kept talking about the government this, the constitution that, eco-nazi this, voter fraud that, it went on and on."

"So?" Daniel asks.

"I'm just saying, it's all they thought about. No 'how about those Brewers or the like."

They still don't look convinced.

"There was one other thing," I say.

Tony leans back, crossing his arms. I'm losing him.

"Brother of Wisconsin Survival," I say.

"You head that from us," Bill says.

"I've heard that from a lot of people," I say.

"Ned?" Bill asks, turning to the only man who hasn't spoken. He's the oldest, with rheumy eyes, magnified by trifocals. He's listened without expression.

Ned stirs himself, clears his throat with a damp sound.

"Total bullshit," Ned says. "It's all total bullshit."

Tony snorts. "Thought so," he says.

"It's not total bullshit. There are some areas of – adjustment. There is a lot I can't reveal," I say.

"Self-aggrandizing son of a bitch," Ned says.

They all nod.

I sense I am losing ground fast.

"Definitely not BOWS," Bill says.

"Could be Pioneers for Patriotic Wisconsin," Daniel suggests.

"Or the Wisconsin Trumpets of Freedom," Tony says.

"Or the Soldiers of the New Order," Bill adds.

"You got tattoos?" Tony asks me.

"No," I say.

"Not one of the White Supremacists," Tony says.

"They don't all have tats," Bill says.

Ned interrupts. "I think this young man needs a conversion. He knows too much now. Can't let him walk without a conversion. Orwin, that's your department." He speaks to the largest man among them, barrel-chested, ruddy faced. He's been mostly silent.

"You sure about that, Ned?" Bill asks.

Orwin stand, slowly. "Okay, I'll get the tools of conversion." He walks to the door, opens it. "Look at that rain," he says, and goes out.

"Lots of people, they don't understand this part," Bill says.

"It's how I lost my wife," Daniel says.

"What are you going to do?" I ask.

"Get the truth out of you," Tony says. "See what a man can take."

"It's been nice meeting you all," I say. I stand up. They stay seated.

"You might as well sit down. Can't be converted standing up, leastways not for long," Bill says.

I stay on my feet, cross my arms, edge toward the door. They just watch. The door opens and Orwin comes in carrying a box. With a grunt, he puts it on the floor, looks at me. "Have a seat," he says. Orwin opens the box. "Whisky or bourbon," he says.

"Orwin makes his own," Bill says.

"Only difference is that bourbon has corn in the mash," Orwin says. "Right from my field. Smoother than the plain whiskey."

The men nod. Bill gets up, comes back with small glasses. Mine has a screw top, like a mustard jar. I sit.

Orwin knows what each man prefers, pours a hefty amount in each glass. "Want to try the bourbon?" he asks me, with a bit of a smile.

"Sure," I say.

We all settle back with our glasses, sipping.

"Okay," Ned says to me. "You got some ID?"

They all laugh. I laugh, too.

"I'm serious," Ned says. "I want to know who the hell you are."

"I don't have my wallet," I say. Tony snorts.

"This was a spontaneous thing." I force a laugh. "Didn't even check the weather before I hopped on the bike..."

"Cut the crap," Ned says. "Talk, and tell the goddam truth."

"He needs another dollop," Daniel says. "Try the whiskey." I do. It's like paint stripper. "Not my best batch," Orwin says. "It's harder than hell to make good whiskey."

I sip, feeling the warmth spread from my torso to my head.

"I'm on the run," I say finally.

They nod.

"From the law," I add. The rain and wind rattle the windows. Bill rises and turns on two lamps.

"Go on," Bill says.

I'm struck by how stupid this will all sound, seek somewhere to start a narrative, some point in time, struggle with making it a real point or, so much easier, just making something up. I gulp the whisky, and then just start talking.

I tell them everything, random, out of order, full of backtracking. I'm not good at telling my own story, not nearly as good as inventing one. I'm not used to fact, if that is what it is, because so many things I say sound foolish or false to me, no matter how hard I try to say them right, to tell the truth.

Ned interrupts with questions now and then. So does Bill. Tony rolls his eyes and shifts in this seat, but remains silent. Daniel and Orwin watch me with owl eyes, tuned in, not missing a thing.

I go back, back to high school. I tell them about my friend Davey, and the Phaedra, and hopping trains, and my father, and my dead mother, and my sister, and her disinterest and sarcasm. I tell them about Chess, and my uncles, and how I got shot, twice. I tell them about college, about drums, about the types of train cars, about Nora, about casinos, about the Romans, that I once saw a tornado, and bears. I tell them about cancers come and gone, about lymph nodes, and Christian girls, and girls with horses, and a lady doctor who I think likes me.

Bill brings out some stale pretzels and smelly cheese. They taste fantastic with the whiskey, I think, and ask for more of both, though I hardly have to, as Orwin has been most attentive in keeping my glass filled. At some point, I notice that they are drinking coffee and ask for some, and pour my whisky into it and burn my mouth and ask for ice cream and Bill says he doesn't have any. And then the night goes quiet and so do I, and tears come to my eyes.

"I miss my mom," I say. "I miss them all."

Chapter 16

Bill is a retired engineer—worked at a metal fabricator. He is good with tools, though you would never know it from looking at his house and outbuildings. He's got ten acres of woods and farmland gone to weeds. He is a member of the Coalition's Executive Committee. The other members are the four guys to whom I sort of embarrassingly told my life story. Well, they got me drunk. I'm not sure about the conversion part. I don't think I'm a survivor. If an asteroid was about to collide with earth, I'd run toward it to be instantly vaporized rather than experience a lingering death in a world I didn't recognize. Not Bill. He and the Coalition not so secretly hope for a Cataclysm, something that will end Life As We Know It. They say things with gravity and scarcely contained excitement. They all have their own theories for the root of the Cataclysm, but they're united by preparing to survive it.

Tony, the youngest one, sells auto insurance. Orwin owns a mega-farm. Daniel, with the sonorous voice, teaches high school math. Ned, the old guy, is a retired county judge.

In the time it took me to recover from the whiskey, the executive committee of the Wisconsin Coalition for Post Apocalypse Survival did a little checking around, called in a few favors, and offered me a deal.

"Jason," Ned says. They know my name now, though I held onto my alias as long as I could. "Here's the deal. Let's begin by reviewing your situation. Basically, you have nothing and you are nothing."

"That's a little hard, Ned," says Daniel. It's the evening of my second day at Bill's. For the past day, I've been weed whacking and racing around on the garden tractor mower—my contribution for my room and board.

Ned glances at Daniel, irritated. "Don't interrupt," he says. "I'm not used to that. I'm used to owning the floor when I want it. Anyway, young man, turns out you have not been charged with any serious crime. Oh, you have piled up some misdemeanors, running off like you did. Lucky for you, the casino picked up your hospital tab. Lucky for you that the two robbery suspects are now telling different stories about your role. One now says you had nothing to do with it."

"Who is that?" I ask.

"Doesn't matter," Ned says. "Just thank your lucky stars. Still, the sheriff's office and the prosecutor, they want you. They've been thwarted and they don't like it. I know these boys well. They thought they really had something here and it's not going to grab headlines like they thought. So they are pissed, mostly at you, which makes no real sense, but you are probably the most powerless person in the whole thing, with no attorney, so maybe it does."

"Jeez, Ned, get to the point," Bill says. "I'm hungry." They are planning on going to Perkins after the meeting.

"This is important stuff," Ned says. "You got to understand the context, the motives. Anyway, here's the deal, like I said. We can clean this up for you. Get your wallet back, your gear. We can get the sheriff's office to lose interest in you. Still, you will need to talk to them sooner than later. Give your statement, but maybe, just maybe, we can work out a different way for you to do that. If we are lucky, we can make this like it never happened, and maybe even get you a little something besides, a little contribution to your welfare from the casino.

"To avoid any kind of lawsuit from you—lack of training, inadequate equipment, that kind of thing," Daniel says.

"That would be great," I say.

"I said we 'could' do these things," Ned says, "not that we would. You need to do something for us."

"Not much of a thing," says Bill.

"What?" I say.

Ned continues. "Frankly, we need to know what's going on with BOWS."

"Brotherhood of Wisconsin Survival," Bill says.

I nod.

"We want you to go to a couple of BOWS meetings. Talk with them. See what's up. And then talk to us."

"Spy on BOWS," I offer.

"Yes, that is essentially it," Ned says. "You are perfect. An unknown. A kind of rough around the edges kid. No local connections. Don't seem all that bright."

"Thanks," I say. "I do have relatives around here."

Ned nods. "We know. Two of them belong to the Coalition, though they aren't all that active."

"Which two?" I ask.

"Can't reveal that," Tony says. He's been quiet, mostly fiddling with his cell phone. "I don't like this idea. I don't trust you. But I did get the others to agree to this." Tony hands me a folded paper from his pocket. I scan it. "It's what Ned has been saying," Tony says, "only we ask you to sign it. And it makes clear we aren't getting you off the hook for anything until we get some real reports from you."

I fold the sheet back up. "I have some questions," I say. "Does BOWS have guns?"

"Of course they have guns," Ned says crossly. "Doesn't mean they'll shoot anyone."

"Truth is, we are losing members," Bill says. "Dues are down. The bunker still needs work, among other projects. A lot of people are moving over to BOWS. We want to know why."

"My next question. Why don't you guys just go talk to them?" I ask.

"Doesn't work that way. We are secretive organizations," Daniel says. "We aren't really supposed to know who belongs to what and all that kind of thing."

"BOWS meets a ways from here, so this will require some travel. We are prepared to lend you a vehicle. You do have a driver's license?" Ned asks.

"I do," I say. "Where is BOWS? Where do they meet?"

"Up in Winawan County, near Winter Lake," Bill says.

"I'll do it," I say.

"What do you mean, you'll do it?" Ned says. "Don't be hasty."

"I'll do it," I say, unfolding the contract. "Got a pen?"

"The boy is interested," Bill says. "Let's take him at his word." Tony produces a pen and they watch me sign. Tony takes the paper, folds it, and puts it back in his pocket. "You better not be screwing us," he says.

We go to Perkins, riding in a caravan of pickup trucks. I ride with Bill. We sit in the back corner. It's a Tuesday night, and it's not busy.

"How do I get in touch with BOWS?" I ask.

The five men glance at each other and finally Bill shrugs. "Don't know," he says.

"Okay," I say. "What's my cover? My identity?"

"Hell, you're a bigger liar than all of us put together," Ned says. "You figure it out."

"One thing you should know." Daniel says. "You got to seem like a true believer. They will smell out a phony. And, well, from what we know, BOWS is a little more ..." Daniel trails off.

"Intense," Bill says.

"Committed," Tony says.

"Paramilitary wackos." Ned says.

"...so you have to come across real serious," Daniel finishes.

"I understand," I say. "No problem."

"We want to know who's running this group, what they plan to do, what they're promising people —anything you can dig up," Ned says.

"I'm in," I say, "But I'd like to do a couple of things first. All anyone knows is that I wandered off. I mean, my family, my uncles, they might be wondering what I'm up to."

"I doubt it," Ned says.

"See, that's the thing, you are invisible now," Daniel says. "You can go anywhere, do anything." He adds wistfully, "You're free."

"You need to keep a low profile in this area. Up around Winter Lake, no one knows you from Abraham Lincoln. Round here though, best you stay close to the farm and then just head north," Bill says.

I nod, telling myself that once they turn me loose I can do what I want.

"I'm spying on a paramilitary group," I tell Anna Bella's voice mail. I'm standing at a small town gas station. They have a pay phone on an outside wall, right next to the air hose. "You can let the family know that I am fine. My head is fine. I've got this job, kind of a secret thing, and I'll be in touch."

Then I stare admiringly at my truck, my temporary truck. It's a Ford F250, at least 20 years old, but it's hard to tell, as it is a crazy quilt of mismatched pieces. Orwin has a whole pole barn full of 250's. He loves them. This was a parts vehicle, but it still runs great, even if the doors don't match the quarter panels, which don't match the hood or the bed, and all of it is seriously rusted. One wheel looks bigger than the others, and it definitely pulls to the left, but this could be an illusion created by the sagging frame. I think I am getting about 8 miles per gallon and have already added oil. But it purrs when you fire it up, and I love driving it, even with the three-on-the-tree manual and no power brakes or power steering. I have the bike in back, locked with a cable through rust holes in the side of the bed. I also have some of my gear, my wallet, and a handful of cash.

I've had some time to think and have been in no hurry as I've worked my way to the northwest corner of Wisconsin. I'm not doing deep thinking. That could be too revealing. Rather, I'm just below the level of surface logistics. I have stopped musing on how I got here, stopped wondering where I am going, in the existential sense. I think about how I will find BOWS, how I will look for Davey and Phaedra at the motorcycle rally, which, if it's like in the magazine, is only two weeks away on Labor Day. I think about Lark and Rusty, and which one of them started telling the truth, and what will happen to them. I can't help but think about Nora, and whether she is back at the casino, wondering where I am, her attempt at reconciliation a failure. I think about these things and get back in the truck.

At the next small town, I see a barbershop.

"You catch a rock from the harvester?" the barber asks me, examining my head through his bifocals.

"Yep," I say. "Went to the doc. I want my hair real short"

"Sure," he says. He looks like the ideal grandpa. "I'll give you buzz cut."

Fifteen minutes later, I look like a Marine recruit, or a paramilitary wannabe. I've lost weight with all this drama. I'm back in my own clothes and they sag in unfamiliar places. The lethargy that followed the stay in the hospital is gone now, gone since the second day at Bill's.

I spend the night in a state forest campground. It's mostly empty, with a few families that have grabbed sites next to a small lake, and in the woods, a group of people maybe my age who seem to have been partying all day. I pull in at dusk. I get out of the truck to stretch my legs and quickly hop back in. Mosquitoes. There is hardly air enough for all of them to fly. I sit in the stuffy cab, eat the food I've picked up. Two beef sticks, a bag of licorice, and orange juice in a plastic bottle. I watch it get dark, watch the raccoons wander thought the campsite, hear some kids and dogs, and fall asleep.

I wake up in the middle of the night, get out of the truck. It's cool, mosquito free. I walk out from under the trees and look up at a spectacular display of stars. I walk down to the lake, to the boat access. The water, thick and drowsy, reflects the starlight, so that even with no moon, I can see clearly around me. A splash out in the lake, dim sparks of starlight in the ripple, and I look up again, deep into the Milky Way, the galactic core. I feel like I'm floating, suspended in a spider's web of cold, alien light. I take a deep breath, then sit on the cold sand and listen to the crickets tell their long, dull stories.

After a short drive the next morning, I arrive in the town of Winter Lake. I buy some coffee. No one even looks twice at me. I am feeling human again.

"Thanks," I say to the young woman who hands me the cup.

"You're welcome," she says, and I grin.

"Is there anything else?" she says.

"How are the muffins?" I ask.

"Good. Maybe a little soggy," she says. "The banana chocolate chip is from yesterday and is half price."

"I'll take it," I say.

I find a city park, much like that one in BERF, with a bandshell, playground, and lots of picnic tables. I find a place to sit in the sun, as it's cool, and just watch, smelling the pine needles from the tall trees next to me and slowly eat my muffin. It's good, and so is the coffee. I could stay here the rest of the day, but I am a spy and I need to get to work.

I walk over to Main Street. It's a highway at either end, but slows to a crawl in town. Diagonal parking places line the street on three or four blocks of old storefronts, some haphazardly modernized. I see a used clothing store, a beauty salon, a couple of diners, a real estate office, a bank, a dollar store, a hardware store, a pizza place, and nine bars. I suppose it was too much to hope that there would be a BOWS office.

I go into the used clothing store, thinking I might buy a jean jacket or sweatshirt or something, as these have disappeared from my duffel bag.

"Can I help you?" a woman asks.

"Sure," I say. "Darn government has stolen all my money and my initiative with their high taxes and interference in my personal life. I'd like to buy a used jacket."

"We only sell women's and children's clothing," she says. "Sorry."

I do no better at the dollar store, where I tell the two employees that it would sure be nice to find like-minded people who understand the plight of the common man, reduced to dollar store shopping by government oppression.

"You might try Alcoholics Anonymous," one of the employees sniggers.

I go back to the park to reconsider my approach. Then it's time for lunch. Then I get in the truck and take a nap. Then I think I should find a motel. Orwin has scrawled a motel name on a Perkins napkin, saying it's a good deal.

I pull up to the Motel 5.

"Used to be part of a chain," the clerk tells me, a pale young man wearing a sweater vest over a white tee shirt. "But it like closed and my boss bought it and renamed it."

"Is that blood on the carpet?" I ask.

"Yes," says the young man. "We had an incident last night."

"Like what?"

"Fight," the clerk says. "We have lots of vacancies. Cheaper if you pay with cash."

I take my key and head down a dingy hallway, past two boarded up rooms that smell of fire, and then to my room,

135. This is the kind of place Chess would put Rusty, me, and the Tierney brothers. The plastic lined curtains block all light. I pull them back and slide a squeaky window open, hoping to dilute the dungeon air. I turn on the TV and it immediately turns itself off. No dial tone on the phone. The worn bedspread has three very visible crusty spots. Not a great place to hang out, so I go spying again.

It's 4 PM. Bar time.

"Damn government," I tell the bartender in bar number one. "You look just like the barber in Dunston," I add.

"My brother," he says.

"No shit," I say.

"No shit," he says. "What can I get you?"

"A beer," I say. "And some information."

He draws a Miller for me and then smiles. "What would you like to know?" he asks.

"Well, I'm thinking of buying some land around here. Do a little hunting on it. Put a trailer on it."

"You want to talk to the real-a-tor," he says. "Bergen's, down the street."

"Thanks," I say. "Anything I should know about this area?"

"Nope," he says.

"Like, does it have lots of forest fires, or do you have a bear problem, or are there like any paramilitary camps?

He stares at me. "Nope," he says.

I drink some beer. "Yeah," I say. "If I get some land, it would be great to just have a place to fire off my automatic weapons, like my Desert Eagle."

"Right," the bartender says. "Why don't I turn on the TV for you."

I am really striking out and think maybe I should call Bill and tell him. But I finish my beer and walk up Main Street, past the realty office. The window is plastered with ads for individual properties. Many have a red "Sold" stamped on them.

The next bar I come to, Ed's 19th Hole, is forlorn and abandoned, as I can see from the dirty window in the door. A faded sign says "Open."

I never make it past bar number three, Winter Lake Pub. I have a couple of beers, eat some bar food, hang around, playing pool, chatting with a few people, not talking much about the government because I am tired of it. A band came in and started setting up, a bunch of old guys in their 50's and 60's. They look tired and slow, so I help them haul things in and set up. They do a sound check, run through a few songs. They play country, maybe more rockabilly than country. They sound pretty good.

"Nice drum kit," I told the drummer.

"Old as Jesus," he said. "I had these drums in high school, believe it or not."

"You guys sound good,"

The drummer shrugs. "I am so sick of these songs I could cry," he says.

"Well, I'd be happy to sit in a little," I offer.

Between the second and third set, he walks over and hands me the sticks. "Play as long as you want," he says.

It's more tap-tap stuff, kind of like playing with Chess, but I enjoy it. Makes my head throb a little, but a couple more beers takes the edge off. I'm having a great time.

"What are you called?" I ask at the end of the night.

"Black Mambas," the guitar player says.

"Cool," I say.

"He's shitting you," the drummer says. "We haven't really settled on a name."

"How long have you been playing together?" I ask.

"Forty-one years," the drummer says.

On my way into the motel, it's the same thin, young man. I notice he has a name tag that says "Robert."

"Hey there, Robert," I say, in a beer jolly voice.

"I'm not really Robert," he says. "I just have to wear a name pin thing."

"So what's your name?"

"Dylan Duncan," he says.

"Say, Dylan, I may be here for a while. I'd like to talk about a rate discount, you know, a multiple night rate."

"You want to stay more than one night?" Dylan asks, incredulous.

"Yeah," I say. "What can you do for me?"

"I'd have to talk to the boss. You know, it's only a week and a half until the rally. We're all booked up that weekend. I don't know if you can stay."

"Well, talk to your boss. I'm offering $25 a night, and back to full price during the rally," I say.

It's 2 AM when I get back to room 135. It's filled with mosquitoes. I left the window open. After swatting mosquitoes for half an hour, I try the TV about twenty times. It just keeps turning off, but it stays on differing amounts of time. I begin counting the seconds and this actually entertains me for far too long. I should have asked the Executive Committee for a cell phone. I feel like calling someone. I want to talk. I'm not sleepy. I want to do something, not lie in the crusty bed. But I know I have a long day of spying ahead of me, so I peel off the bedspread, throw it in the hallway, and finally go to sleep.

Chapter 17

Winter Lake Hog Rally
August 29-31
Bergen's Tree Farm and Tubing
3 miles east of junction CR D and 167th Street
Scenic rides in northwest Wisconsin
Visit the vendor Fair—Over 25 Harley Dealers
Food, Bands, Contests, Ladies, and Hogs!

So says a colorful flyer in the window of the hardware store. I'm cruising Main Street again, seeking inspiration. I'm thinking too much about the rally, and the possibility of seeing Phaedra and Davey, and not enough about BOWS. I stop in a diner and get breakfast, the Dairy Farmer Special. Lots of eggs and lots of cheese.

I get back in the truck, figure I will wander around the countryside, look for a paramilitary compound. It's a ridiculous plan, but it's a cool, overcast day and the greens and browns of the countryside are deep and compelling, the air full of scent — hay, cows, dirt, clover. I drive for two hours, become thoroughly lost in the fields, small towns, lakes, cottages, and cheese shops. I slowly find my way back to Winter Lake, tired and dispirited.

"Dylan," I say. "Do you ever go home?"

Dylan shrugs. He's wearing a polo shirt that is much too big for him. It says Motel 5, Winter Lake, Wisconsin. He sees me looking.

"You can buy these," He says, picking at his shirt.

"What should I know about Winter Lake?" I ask.

"What do you want to know?"

"Tell me the inside dope, like this was a TV show, an exposé on Winter Lake."

He looks to the side for a moment. "Not much to say," he says. "You going to the rally? That's the big thing. Iron Butterfly is going to play on Saturday night."

"Okay, that's a good start," I say. "Sure, I'll go to the rally."

"You might want to register," he says.

"Even if you don't have a bike? Not open to the public?"

"Some is. Some isn't," Dylan says.

"Okay," I say. "What's weird about Winter Lake?"

Dylan thinks. "There's a castle out on an island," he says.

"Really? Where?"

"On an island," he says. "Built by some crazy lumber guy like in the 1800's. It's been used for a lot of things since back in the day, then it became a wreck. We used to go there and hang out. Supposed to be haunted. You could always get girls to go, because of the haunted thing. But this lady bought it. Maybe she is fixing it up."

"Cool," I say, and I mean it.

"This lady's a re-la-tor," Dylan says. "She sold the Harbor Resort to the Scientologists. Made a bunch of money. She's an urban type, like the ones who build those big lake mansions and come to them like once a year. You know. Fancy hair. Make up. Real chatty, but in a 'aren't you a cute little country moron' kind of way."

"So you've met her?" I ask.

"My mom told me about her," Dylan says. "She used to work at Bergen's, selling lake lots, like my mom. Only my mom got laid off. And then my Dad got shot turkey hunting. So I work here like a thousand hours a week."

"Sorry," I say. "Is your Dad alright?"

177

"Dead. Oh, the boss says $30 a night and you got a deal."

"Sounds good," I say.

The town of Winter Lake is not actually on Winter Lake. Maybe the lake moved. If you want to see the lake, you drive a mile or so to a marshy area, where there's a boardwalk, and that brings you out to open water. You can see a small marina past the marsh, but I don't know how to get there.

I like the boardwalk. It's pretty well rotted, so no one goes out on it. Standing out here on this cloudy, and now windy, day, I'm all alone, just me, the white caps foaming into the marsh, and a few lake gulls, checking me out for food. It starts to rain, then stops. I head back for the truck, which I have named Carmen and plan to buy it from Orwin, one way or another.

I didn't see the castle on the island. I was hoping it was close to shore. I could see some other islands. Could be it's behind trees or behind taller islands, but I want to see it.

It's back to Main Street. Here's how it should go. I see a man in camo walking down the street.

"Damn government," I say.

"I heard that," he says, shaking his head. "Have you thought about surviving the next cataclysm and sticking it in the eye of the government, all at the same time?"

"Why, yes," I say. "Could such a thing be possible?"

"BOWS," he says. "You look trustworthy. Follow me."

But it doesn't go like that. Instead, I go to bar number four, Logger Inn. It's aimed at tourists and cabin owners and has veggie burgers and lots of salads, along with real food. I hear some middle-aged guys talking about the Hog Rally. One of them has long hair in a neat ponytail.

"Excuse me," I say. "Are you the rally organizers?"

They look at each other. One laughs and points to the man with long hair. "He is the rally."

"Need any security?" I ask. "I'm looking for some short term work."

"Got any experience?" the man replies.

"Worked casino security," I say.

"Minimum wage, you know. Just three days. But I do need some more people. We'll have to run a background check." He looks meaningfully at me.

"That's fine," I say. "I'm interested."

He pulls out a card, tells me to stop by and ask for Lucy tomorrow morning.

Security got me in the thick of things once before. I figure it can do that again. And I'll be in a good position to see who's there, like Davey and Phaedra. And I won't have to pay registration. And as I find out the next day, I get a black tee shirt that says "Rally Security" that I get to keep. And I pass the background check. It takes like fifteen minutes. I'm thinking they just pretend to check, to see if you will come clean that you are one of the ten most wanted.

I feel good about this. The Coalition gave me a good amount of cash, but it won't last forever and working will keep me guilt-free on the spying gig.

And I see overlap between the two. I find the Walmart, just outside of town. I buy some running shoes, shorts, and some tee shirts, including two camouflage models that are a size too small. I buy some hand weights, and a notebook and some pens. Then I go to the library — a great old building with lots of dark wood inside — and read up on fitness training, workout schedules, and positive attitudes. I am going to get in shape. If I naturally look like a thug, I might as well be a fit thug, and I'm thinking this will help me find the right people.

I call Bill.

"Where the hell are you?" he says.

I tell him.

"We wondered if you ran off. You should have called days ago. I've got news for you, if it isn't too late. About giving a statement for that casino crap."

"I haven't had anything much to report," I say.

Bill ignores me. "Ned has arranged so that you can give your statement over the phone. Ned — remember him? Used to be a county judge. A conference call, with the prosecutor, sheriff, and Ned. You need to call Ned right away. He put some time into this."

"Sorry," I say. "Give me his number."

Bill does. "Anything on BOWS? What exactly are you doing up there?

I fill him in, more or less accurately. "I'm thinking, just a hunch, that there's a connection between the Hog Rally and BOWS."

"Why on earth would there be any connection at all?" Bill says.

"Like I said, it's a hunch. Just, you know, from talking to people, reading between the lines."

Bill is silent.

"Well," he says finally. "I guess it's up to you. Bikers and so-called survivalists. I don't know. I don't see it."

"Tony has a Harley. He talked about it at Perkins," I say.

"Tony also has wife. I don't see you trying to get married," Bill says.

"If it doesn't work out, I'll try something else," I say.

We finish by talking about the weather and how much I like the truck. After I hang up, I go running.

My mother, Astrid, she was a runner. She took it up after she moved out of our house and in with Anna Bella. She ran a lot. Every day. She said it came natural to her, felt more normal than walking.

I feel like a marshmallow on toothpicks. I can't figure out how to breathe and run, can't find a comfortable pace, don't know what to do with my arms, and keep trying to wipe the look of pain off my face. I can run from the Motel 5 right out into the section roads between the cornfields and cow pastures. But it's hilly, or at least maybe slopey. I'm conscious of the slightest grade and it all seems to be up, just like on the bicycle. I finally just close my eyes for a moment, feel the cool breeze, listen to the crickets, and relax into a slow trot. This seems to work, and I plod along for half an hour before I give up and walk back.

In three days, I can run. Not great, but a whole lot better. I think my body just needed a reminder, a wake up call. I've never been much of a runner unless it was part of something else, like wrestling practice. But I am getting a glimmer of what entranced Astrid. It's primal, a connection to our essence. We are a terrible animal — tippy, vulnerable, hideless, clawless. We freeze, we overheat, our babies are feeble and rather repulsive. We fight too much, we acquire too much, we have no self control. We're never really happy. All we can do well is run—run down any other animal, given enough time. Run, and think, and be aware of ourselves as eternal misfits.

So a week goes by. I work out. I go to the bars at night. I sit in with the rockabilly band a couple more times. I drive around. Bikers start to filter into town. A banner goes up across Main Street, welcoming the Hogs. I go to security training.

"Hey" says the head security guy, a big guy with a big grey beard and no hair. "Good to see so many of you back from last year. You know what to expect."

The thirty or forty guys in the room pretty much all look like bikers, except for me. And they are all older than me. When we sit down, they look at me with curiosity.

"Jason here comes with real security experience, from a casino. He's a martial arts expert," the man with the grey beard says. I shift in my seat. Wish I hadn't told them that.

I fold my arms and try to look ready for anything.

"Doc," says someone, "is this the same drill as last year? We just work the gate?"

Doc is the grey beard . "Well, sort of. We are working the gate, but we're also supposed to do some crowd control."

"Screw that," a guy says. "We could get killed."

"Nothing major. It's on private property, so the cops will be pretty much out of it, unless things get too crazy. Nudity is okay, unless people get too riled up. You know, nothing too…"

"Hard core," someone says.

"Right," Doc says. "We're just here to have fun. Let's see. New this year. Got some new charity rides, and it's included in the registration fee this year—no more collecting money. And we got more cop escorts."

"Praise Jesus," someone says.

Doc continues. "We got a frozen tee shirt contest. More drag racing than last year. More workshops, like Yoga for Bikers, Eat Healthy, Ride Hard. That kind of thing. Let's see—oh, more bands."

"Iron Butterfly," one says.

"Who's that?" another says.

"Hell," says Doc. "Them guys are as good as Steppenwolf."

"Why can't we get Kid Rock?" someone says. "Or Ted Nugent?"

"Just be glad it ain't Chess Chalmers," Doc says, and everyone laughs.

I go out to Bergen's Tree Farm and Tubing. You head east out of Winter Lake, turn up this little county road, cross an old trestle bridge and you are there. Lots of pine trees in rows, and a place where you can rent big inner tubes to float down the Marinette River, a small river by anyone's standards. It flows into Winter Lake. Bergen's goes and picks you and your tube up about five miles downstream. They've got special tubes that hold beer coolers. The river looks a little suspicious to me. Kind of dark. Smells like farm run off. No one's tubing. Too cool. But there's a lot of activity at Bergen's. Stages going up. Mowing places for parking and camping. Setting up a domino line of portapotties. Checking the surface of the track and the drag race strip. Fencing it all. Running power. Vendors setting up tents and good trailers and beer gardens. There must be a hundred guys working here.

I see Doc.

"Hey, Jason," he says. "Let me show you around."

We spend an hour wandering, meeting people, looking at things. It's an amazing amount of work to put this together.

"I'm gonna put you at the gate most of the time, but I might have you wander around when we got them bands going at night. People get a little crazy, but it's not bad. You get some tension over stupid stuff, but it's all pretty self-regulating. Most of these guys watch out for each other, especially if they're in a club. And we get all kinds—the posers, the wannabes, and some real, straight-up bikers. Mostly we're just here to show we care. Anything real bad goes down, you call me on your radio." I nod.

The first day of the rally comes and goes. I don't see Davey and Phaedra, though I'm at the gate all day. I only see one side-car, but that's a woman and her dog. It's hot, and then thunderstorms roll in and the bands don't have many people hanging around to listen. Still, I look very cool. Black security shirt, new jeans, belt radio, sunglasses, and a 4-day old goatee. The running shoes add a note of discord, but, heck, I'm on my feet all day. People ask me a lot of questions. I call Doc a lot. I'm not seeing the craziness. Girls keep their shirts on. The guys seem pretty mellow. It's loud as hell, with the track racing and drag racing and just the general din of idling hogs. It smells like exhaust and dust and corn dogs. There are some kids running around. There's a Biker for Jesus tent. Are any of the bikers against Jesus? Tattoo vendors, custom shops, accessories, tee shirts, leathers, an insurance guy, all kinds of vendors. Lot of guys with big arms and big guts. Lot of women in tight tops, regardless of their heft. No one cares.

The next morning, it's still raining, and dead at the gate. No Davey, no Phaedra, no BOWS, and it's cold as hell. My feet are soaked. I've drunk too much coffee trying to stay warm. I need to pee, but there's no other security guy in sight. Where is everyone? I sit on a stool, under a borrowed umbrella, next to the ticket booth, watching the rain sweep across the mudflats where people are parked and camped.

Blue tarps everywhere, over bikes, over tents. Looks like a refugee camp.

"Need the umbrella," Doc says, coming up behind me. "My wife's coming."

I hand it to him. The woman in the ticket booth says, "Here," she hands out her poncho to me. It has flowers on it.

Doc looks at me as I pull it on. Doc is wearing tall rubber boots, red rain pants, and a yellow rain jacket over a leather vest and no shirt. "You look ridiculous," he tells me, kind of giggling.

The day drags along. About the time the bands start on the stage near the track, the clouds break up. But a chilly wind comes with the blue sky and only a few hundred people watch the local bands and Iron Butterfly. A few people are wearing warm coats. I guess this is late August in northern Wisconsin.

"So," Doc says as we watch one band exit the stage and another quickly set up. "Where are you staying?"

"Motel 5," I say.

"Just passing through?"

I shrug. "Sort of," I say.

"Looking for work?" Doc asks.

"Sort of," I say.

He nods. "Well, let me know. I have a couple of ideas for you."

"Say, do you remember a couple from last year, a woman and a man on a Sportster with a sidecar? They'd be about my age. Woman's a bit older. Names are Birdie and Wilhelm."

Doc laughs. "Yeah, but that's not their names. You saw them in the magazine? They just gave those names. Really funny, those two. Too bad what happened."

"What happened?" I say, with my pulse in my ears.

"Well, they split up," Doc says.

"How do you know?" I ask.

"'Cause they moved here the next year," Doc says. "The woman, Jasmine, she went to work for Bergen's Realty. An agent. Made a few big sales. Now works on her own. She bought that frinkin' castle out in the lake. Don't know what she's going to do with that old wreck. Used to be an insane asylum."

"You know her?" I ask.

"Yeah, she and my wife, they are in the same book club."

"And the guy?"

"He was here, too. They split up, like I said. Don't know what happened to him. Nice kid. Quiet." Doc looks up to the left, thinking. I wait. "Last I heard, he was janitoring at the Lutheran Home. Don't know if he's still there. That was, like, two years ago. Haven't seen him around, that's for sure."

We watch the band play its set, then we watch Iron Butterfly. Doc's wife shows up, a stout, friendly woman, and she bounces and sways with the music.

When I finally leave, I'm surprised to see people in lawn chairs at the bridge over the Marinette River. There are lots of cops, too. I find out later this is an annual thing. People show up to watch the cops bust drunks leaving the rally, as they come back onto country roads and leave private property. There is a party atmosphere among the onlookers, and they bring their families.

Eventually I find myself back in my room, in a kind of daze. They have been here all along, Phaedra and Davey. Now she's Jasmine. Could be a different person altogether.

A realtor? It's a stretch. Don't you have to be licensed, pass some tests? She has a castle? Now that has a Phaedra ring. She's in a book club? And Davey, here or not here?

"Dylan," I say, returning to the front desk. "Do you know anything about this Jasmine that bought the castle?"

"What I told you already," Dylan says.

"Where does she live?"

"I don't know," Dylan says. "Maybe on the island."

"Do you have a boat? Can you tell me where the island is?

"No boat, but you can rent one at the marina. Costs a lot of money, though. And yeah, I know real well where the island is. It's off of Devil's Point, where the bible camp is. Good walleye hole, though, me, I'm not much into fishing," Dylan says.

"I'll pay you to take me out there," I say.

"If I ever get off work," Dylan says.

"Call in sick," I say.

"And then get spotted out on the lake? Nope," Dylan says.

"Well, when do you get off next?"

"Don't know." Dylan says. "Maybe after all the bikers are gone."

I call Bergen's Realty from the front desk, leave a message, say that I have a question for Jasmine and I wonder if they have her number.

Our Savior's Assisted Living and Nursing Care Center, run by Lutherans, sits on flat land with spindly pines and a lot of asphalt parking lot. It's a two story building, long and plain. The front has flower beds with yellow marigolds and red geraniums. The entrance is a double glass door shaded by an awning, a door wide enough for plus-size wheelchairs, gurneys, and coffins.

"Hello," I say to the woman dressed like a nurse who sits behind the front counter. "I'm looking for someone."

"I can't reveal the names of our residents," she tells me, with a polite smile.

"No, this guy would be an employee. A janitor, David Miller."

"Sorry," she says. "Doesn't work here."

"Might go by a different name," I say.

"Not the kind of people we hire, people who go by different names," she says. She's not helping but there is nothing hostile in her responses, just facts.

"Okay," I say. "About my height, maybe an inch taller. Blond hair. Big smile. My age. Friendly guy," I say.

She hesitates. "Why do you want to know?"

"He's a friend. I was in town for the rally and I'm talking to some people and for some reason, this guy comes up. If it's David Miller, I haven't seen him for seven years and we used to be best buds. I just want to look up an old friend. I'm not sure it's him, but, boy, would that be great if he is right here."

The woman answers a phone call, turns away from me. She talks for quite a while, quietly. Finally she hangs up and turns toward me. "Here," she says, pushing a pen and slip of paper my way. "Why don't you leave a note?"

"So he does work here," I say.

"Not sure. Okay, there's someone who is kind of like what you describe, but not exactly. Works nights. But I'll leave him a note if you want to write something down."

I do.

Davey, I write. Jason here. Is it really you? Can we talk, if it's you? Jason Audley.

I write the number for Motel 5 on the bottom, thank the woman, and leave.

Chapter 18

It's the morning of my conference call to give my statement for the Great Casino Robbery. I'm a bit nervous about this. I'll use the tiny manager office at Motel 5. Dylan has set that up. It's not a long call. Introductions, swearings in, a bit of chat, then a lot of questions. No one really asks for my narrative. It's more out of order questions, non-chronological, to trip me up, I figure, to make me inconsistent. When they are done with me, Ned says, "Stay by the phone. I'll give you a call."

A few minutes later, Ned calls.

"You did well," he says. "If you were my client, I'd have told you to think that every word you say costs you a dollar. People usually get into trouble by talking too much."

"Make sense," I say.

"I think this will blow over," Ned says. "At least your part. Chess Chalmers—I guess you know him—has been working hard to get his niece some kind of break."

"I hope she does," I say. "I don't understand why they did this."

"Love," Ned says. "Love and its attendants, like lust, rage, control, possession. I always thought that if we didn't have love, we'd have a much simpler legal system."

"I guess so," I say.

"You may still have to testify, if they take this all to trial," Ned says.

"I'd rather avoid that," I say.

"I'd like to try this case," Ned says. "I miss the courtroom. God knows it's depressing, but it is interesting all the same." He pauses. "Anything on the Brotherhood of Wisconsin Survivalists?"

"Are you sure they're around here?"

"Well, in the area, yes, we're sure about that."

"I can't seem to find a trace of them. Or any group like that. They seem pretty normal around here."

Ned is silent. "Sorry," I say.

"Who knows what's normal," Ned says. "Well, if it's a dead end, then it's a dead end. I thought you were the guy for the job, but if you can't find them, you can't find them. I'm a realist. Looks like the casino will cough up a little money for you. We can settle it all out and send you on your way."

"I'm not done looking," I say. "I'm still in."

"Glad to hear that," Ned says.

I hang up the phone, walk back toward my room, stop and buy a Coke from the hallway machine. Then I walk back to the front counter.

"So," I say to Dylan, handing him the Coke, "I got a question for you."

"I don't drink Coke," Dylan says. "Can't handle the caffeine or the sugar. I have an irritable bowel."

"Geez, Dylan, yuck," I say.

"What really happened to your head?" he asks.

"I got shot," I say.

He nods. "You can hardly notice it now," he says.

"So, Dylan. Are there, like, paramilitary or survivalist groups around here?"

"Sure," Dylan says. "A couple of different groups. There's this group, right in town, sort of survivalist-minded Civil War re-enactors thing. You can watch them practice drill in the park sometimes. There's this sergeant guy who yells at them if they screw up. It's pretty funny."

"And the other group?"

"Called BOWS," Dylan says. "They are sort of the real deal. Meet out near Turpid."

"Turpid?" I say.

"On a farm near there. Turpid's a town."

"BOWS," I say. "Never heard of them. So what's their thing?"

"They see certain signs that say the world is headed for collapse. The world as we know it. They learn a lot of survival stuff, and a lot about self-defense, to secure a place of safety, liberty, and power in the new world order."

"You know a lot about this?" I ask.

"I'm a member," Dylan says.

We talk for quite a while about this. Dylan's mom's last boyfriend was in BOWS. He brought Dylan along to a few meetings. They have sort of a junior chapter, kind of like ROTC for survivalists. Dylan doesn't go there much. No car and the motel job. But in his short time with them, he's picked up a lot of Armageddon lingo and got to fire automatic weapons.

"And we were addressed by the commander," Dylan says.

"The commander?" I say.

"Yeah. My unit of new recruits, we had to go through some workshops, take some tests, a whole weekend of stuff. Then we shot off these very cool guns. Then the commander comes and asks us if we are ready for the preliminary oath, the oath that says we are serious about pursuing this, so that someday we can become full citizens in BOWS."

"Citizens?"

"Yeah, we are a militia of citizen soldiers, preparing for the continuation of an orderly, secure humanity."

"Isn't that a lot to take on?"

Dylan looks at me. "What do you mean?"

"I mean, I don't know how big this group is or anything, but isn't the continuation of humanity, etc., a big goal?"

"People will gather to us, to become citizens."

"Oh," I say. "And if you aren't a citizen, or don't want to be a citizen, then what?"

Dylan shrugs. "I don't know," he says. "I'm still pretty new."

"Does BOWS have any connection to the Harley guys, the bikers?" I ask.

"No," Dylan says. "Unless one of them wanted to join, then yes."

I'm driving Carmen, the Truck of Many Colors, around town, end up at the marshy park on Winter Lake. It's time to pause and think.

"Carmen," I tell the truck. "I've gone from no information to too much information."

I sit with the doors open. It's mid-afternoon, a warm and humid day. Not hot. Probably as pretty a September 2 as you can get, with classic cotton ball clouds, blue sky, and buzzy bugs all around me. The warm air drifts through the truck and I find myself just staring and not thinking. Well, maybe that is thinking. I should be out running, not driving around. Something about the plodding pace makes me, well, it doesn't make me think either. It puts me in the same state of staring. Thinking, I decide, is work, and you naturally want to conserve energy. We are a species adapted for subsistence living. Our history has been tenuous. Our success unlikely. Our problems come from too much thinking and not enough staring.

Another truck pulls up. A man and two dogs jump out of the cab. The dogs immediately start fighting and the man kicks and swats at them until they stop. How did they ride in the cab together, I wonder. They are German shepherds, maybe mixes. Not my favorite dogs. Too alert, too toothy. Now the dogs race around after each other, growling. Maybe it's play. The man lights a cigarette, walks over.

"Sorry about the noise," he says.

"No problem," I say. "I used to train bomb dogs."

"No shit," the man says. "Where? Always wondered how they did that."

"Cambodia," I say. "Takes a lot patience and positive reinforcement."

"I bet," the man says, stomping on his partially smoked cigarette. "See you around." He calls the dogs who bound into the cab and he drives off.

The smell of cigarette lingers in the air. The bugs ratchet up again and I hear a bullfrog in the marsh.

I stare some more, get out and pace a little, do a few push-ups. Try to do a push-up one-handed and fail. I end up sitting in the gravel, picking up small stones and trying to toss them into Carmen's rust holes. Then I think this is probably not a good idea. So I stand up and my thinking is done.

It's pretty clear what I need to do. Get Dylan to take me to BOWS. Already knew that. Wait for a response from Davey, if it's Davey. Though even if it's him, he may not want to respond. So maybe surveil the place some night. Find Phaedra/Jasmine. Find the island. Storm the castle.

Chapter 19

"Hey, Jason," Dylan says to me when I return. "My mom wants to talk to you."

Dylan's mom is Pam, maybe 40. She's pale, like Dylan, but bigger boned, with short, curly hair and a guarded look in kind eyes.

"Jason this, Jason that," Pam says. "That's all Dylan says." We sit in a neat, small kitchen, in a neat, small rambler, probably built in the 60's and little altered. I'm drinking herb tea out of a hand-thrown mug.

"Good tea," I say.

"How long are you in town? Are you working? What are you doing in Winter Lake?" Pam asks me. "What's this about hiring Dylan to haul you around the lake? He's just a kid, you know. A very special kid. My kid. In fact, my only kid. Are you with the bikers? Why are you still here, then? Don't you have a job somewhere? Can I get you more hot water? Do you want a cookie? They are whole grain, don't have any sugar. But they taste better than you might think, because of the dried cranberries. You know, Dylan is very susceptible to men, especially older men, on account of father figures abandoning him. And I think Dylan may be gay, though he doesn't want to admit it. What do you think? Do you get that vibe from him? Are you gay? But that's not the reason I wanted to talk to you. I am happy to say that I don't sense any threat from you, and I am very sensitive to that kind of thing, and your energy seems positive. Confused but positive. Is it true that you got shot in the head? But let me get back to business. I have a room for rent. If you are going to be here for a while, you could rent it cheaper than the Motel 5, and I will provide some meals for an additional cost. But not that much of a cost. Nothing like a restaurant. We are frugal here and we eat healthy. No smoking." She pauses and looks at me. "Well, what do you think?" she says.

Pam stands and turns on the electric kettle. It hisses and pops as it heats water. I look out the window so I don't look at Pam. She has a voluptuous figure. I see a small, neat backyard, bordered by a fence and, on the other side, a cornfield. I see a birdbath, two apple trees, a hanging bird feeder, and a gnome with a red hat.

"That little guy is supposed to scare the squirrels, keep them away from the feeder," Pam says, following my gaze.

"Does it work?" I ask.

"No, but I've gotten used to him," Pam says and she sits down. "Well?"

"Can I see the room?" I ask.

It's in the basement. It's always in the basement. That's where I lived with Astrid and Anna Bella. It was either that or the trailer with my dad, and that had spiders. At least this basement has windows.

"Got your own bathroom," Pam says. "$250 a month." "It's furnished."

It's a spacious room, by my standards.

"This is an unusual bed," I say. That isn't the only thing unusual. It smells of incense and it has a lot of mirrors.

"I'm a massage therapist," Pam says. "This was my studio. You know, working out of my house. Neighbors didn't like it, so I moved my business to this place that does hair and massage. Not what I wanted. So this is for rent. That's a massage table, but you will find it very comfortable. I don't know if you are interested, but there's a head cradle that plugs right in the end of it."

"Very firm," I say, pushing on the table.

"Good for your back. Look, I'll throw in one free massage a month," Pam says.

"Deal," I say. "But this has to be month by month, because I don't know how long I'll be in town."

"We need the money," Pam says. "Stay as long as you want, long as we all get along."

She looks nervous.

I try to smile. "Okay, when can I move in?"

"Today," she says. "Let's start the rent clock ticking."

She still looks nervous.

"May I please have a cookie?" I ask.

"Yes," she says.

I find Doc. He runs an auto parts store near the Walmart.

"Hey," I say.

"Jason," he nods.

"Looking for a job," I say.

"Just a minute," Doc says and helps a guy buy headlight cleaner.

"See the garage out back?" he asks me.

"Nope," I say.

"We do oil changes, wiper blades, radiator flushes. Simple shit. Can you do that?"

"Sure."

"Good timing," Doc says. "I just fired one of the morning guys. I won't even tell you why, because if I did, I would get pissed off all over again." He mutters a little.

"I could start tomorrow," I say.

"You got it. I should go through the apps, but you did good at the rally. Always on time. No fuck ups. Be here at 5:30 AM."

"5:30?" I say.

"Yeah, you get to come in later. Hammie will open the place. You don't have to get here early. He'll take care of all that stuff and then train you in. Hammie's a good dude."

So, I am planting roots in this town. Not big roots, more like exploratory runners, like crab grass. But it is all part of my plan. My plan is to think up things and do them and hope that, in the end, they all fit together. It's not a great plan, but it is flexible. Okay, the rented room was not part of the plan. It is now. Flexibility. I have three simple quests. One, send a BOWS report to the Coalition, who seem long ago and far away now. Two, find Davey and—do something. Three, find Phaedra and do something else. Those parts of the plan are a bit vague. And go to the island castle, mostly because I just want to see it.

Dylan watches me carry my things through the Motel 5 lobby. I pause.

"How come I never see your boss?" I ask.

"He lives in India," Dylan says. "My mom is going to invite you to dinner. I hope you don't mind vegan. She's kind of a hippie"

"I eat just about anything," I say.

It is a stilted, polite meal, very ricey and vegetable-y. Conversation runs hot and cold. I discover that Pam speaks in a rush, followed by long silences.

"The massage business?" she says in answer to my polite question. "It's good, but you can't make a living. A lot of farmers here with a lot of back and muscle issues. That's mostly who I see, working men. Guys in a lot of pain. And I play this new age music and talk about energy and use therapeutic oils and they could care less. They want the kinks out of their shoulders, their backs, their necks. They are all knots and lumps. Honestly, I don't know where to begin with some of them. But I don't have enough clients to do it full time. So I work at the library on weekends. Just shelving books and other grunt work. And I work at the greenhouse, when it's the right season. And I wait some tables during tourist season. And I do some proofing for the local paper. And I make earrings, which I sell in a couple of the shops."

"You can do a lot of things," I say.

"Maybe, but massage school cost some money, and I'm trying to pay that back, and keep this house going, and put away some money for Dylan to go to college."

"I'm not going to college," Dylan says.

"He'll go to the University of Wisconsin Superior," Pam says. "He did good on the college entrance exams."

"Not going," Dylan says.

"He's nineteen, so there's time, but I'd rather see him just go to school now, like right now. But he never even applied, so he's lost a year. But he'll get there." Pam smiles at Dylan.

"Nope," Dylan says.

"So, Dylan tells me you are an expert in martial arts?" Pam says.

I regret telling Dylan that. I told him a lot of things. He was the motel clerk. What did it matter? Now it's become intimate.

"Yeah," I say modestly.

"Good," Pam says. "That's good."

When I finish my quests, I can go back to school. Now that I know the lymphoma is not revisiting me, at least not right now, and things are settled here, I can go back with nothing in the way. Just burn through the rest of college and finish a degree in, well, anything. It seems simple to me, like it's already done. Just a few little things to take of first. My uncles will be pleased. Anna Bella will be amazed. Lydia, my medical school sister, will be condescendingly proud. And then I will go to work, doing something, and my life will be over.

The massage table is like sleeping on a tree limb, and my simian falling reflex is busy that long, uncomfortable night. New sounds. The upstairs bathroom is right over my head and the people upstairs have no bodily mysteries. They have a cat. This would never be a dog house. A dog would not fit this culture. The cat, named Raccoon, jumps on my precarious bed and swats my face, and then jumps down, making the table wobble. The cat's face is expressionless as he swats me. I try to look him down, stare him into submission. He stares back and swats me. It's not a tap. It's a cat punch.

"Ow," I say. "Jesus, cat. Go take a long climb up a short tree."

Dylan is a strange kid. Not that many years younger than me, but way younger than me nonetheless. Those few hours when he isn't at work, he plays computer games, where he assumes the identity of a necromancer and is followed by legions of the undead. This does not seem healthy. I watch him play, wondering why I am here, why I'm in their home. Who am I to them? I find out.

"You a drinking man?" Pam asks.

"Sure," I say.

"I don't drink much," Pam says. "My ex did, and well, that kind of turned me off of it. But tonight, tonight I need a drink, and maybe you could join me. If you don't want to, I understand. I think it's important to listen to yourself, do what your inner self tells you, not what's been imposed on you by others." She pauses, pours two generous jiggers of rum into a glass and adds a little Coke. "What do you want? I think there's a beer in the fridge, though it's pretty old. Men like beer, especially In Wisconsin. That doesn't mean they don't drink other things, but, men, they like their beer."

"That's fine, the old beer," I say, more to shut her down than to acquire an old beer.

She takes long pull on her drink.

"Okay," she says. "I'm turning in." She hasn't even sat down, just made the drink and now walks off. My old beer, if it's there, is still in the fridge. I find the beer and go downstairs.

A few minutes later, Pam says, "Knock, knock."

"Hi," I say, emerging from my massage lair.

Pam stands on the stairs. "There is one thing I wanted to tell you, I guess. Abut Dylan."

"Yes?"

"Have you noticed anything different abut him?"

"No," I say. "Well, he works a lot of hours."

"Anything else? Anything in the way he relates to people?"

"Nope," I say.

"Oh," she says. "Good night."

"What is it that you are trying to tell me?" I ask, mildly curious.

She sits on the stairs. "My ex abused him, but you probably already figured that out. We are so dysfunctional," Pam says. "This was my second ex, his step-dad. His real dad, well, that was a high school thing. I was Dylan's age when I had him, can you believe it? I was a lot different than Dylan, though, a lot more motivated and mature."

"He works pretty hard," I say.

"That marriage didn't last a year, and before you know it, I was married again. Then things got really bad." She falls silent, stirs her drink with her finger.

"You don't have to tell me anything more," I say.

"The thing is, he abused Dylan. It makes me sick even to say it. And he isn't out of our lives. He shows up and it gets pretty messed up around here. So when Dylan said you were a martial arts expert, and that you were basically living at the Motel 5, I thought about having you stay downstairs. Sort of everyone wins. You're a big kid. Though you aren't a kid. How old are you?"

"Twenty-five, twenty-five and a half."

"See, not a kid. I've said too much. You are probably going to move out now, and I wouldn't blame you. Really, you aren't a body guard. I just thought it would make us feel better and Dylan is so frightened of that man. That's what I mean by different. Dylan is so cautious, so withdrawn, and he should see a therapist but I don't have insurance for that, though he did see someone provided by the state when all this broke loose and the cops were involved, and now look where we are."

I don't know what to say, so I drink my beer, which is not all that old and the real problem is that there is only one.

"I've said too much," Pam says. "Sorry," and she goes up the stairs.

Doc's shop is a busy place and I learn quickly that I don't like standing in a pit, watching oil drain. But I do it. It kills time and I make a little money. I ask Dylan more about BOWS. He won't tell me much. I make a guess.

"Was it your step-dad that brought you to BOWS?" I ask.

Dylan nods. He's on the computer and doesn't talk much then.

"Is he still active in it?"

Dylan shrugs, says, "I think he was interested for the wrong reasons. He laughed at the stuff about saving humanity. I think it's kind of cool."

"What did he like about it?"

"The guns, and the war games," Dylan says.

"War games?"

"Training," Dylan says. "Look, I'm trying to concentrate. I could get killed real easy on this level, and I can't bring my undead until I find the portal."

"Hardly seems fair," I say.

"I don't make the rules," Dylan says.

I'm off work by 2 PM. I work four days a week. This schedule is not great for hitting the bars, but it does give me some time during the day. Though I don't feel much like it after work, I keep running. Lots of nice country roads around Winter Lake. I run, and sometimes I take out Roger's bike. I go explore, get a feel for the area. It's beautiful, really, with state forests all over, lots of trees and lakes, neat cottages, small motels, small towns that look a little worn.

"I like it here, "I tell the guy at Dairy Queen, my main source of food.

"You haven't been here for the winter," he says.

It's already cooling off. Nights are chilly. Pam is yet to turn on the heat, to save money, and the basement is freezing cold. I've moved my bed to the floor and folded up the massage table. It's hard as hell on the concrete, but I can't roll into space. Now I'm really vulnerable to Raccoon, who has taken to sleeping with me, and every once in awhile during the night, he sits up and swats me. I don't get it.

"Pam," I say. "Do you mind if I buy a mattress for downstairs?"

"Oh, I'm sorry," she says.

That is her answer to many things. It strikes me that Dylan, though quiet, is pretty solid and Pam is the wreck. I don't know what went on here, but Pam bears the burden.

"Pete," Pam says. "This is our boarder, Jason. He's an expert in martial arts."

"Pete is the ex, the latest one, the one who brought the trouble. He's got gray hair, which I didn't expect. His narrow face is heavily lined and he's built like a gorilla. Pete looks at me appraisingly. I know that look. It's the I can kick your ass look. I try not to answer with the oh yeah, you can kiss my ass look. Something about Pete makes me feel belligerent. It's hard to hide.

"Hey," I say to Pete. He ignores me.

"I'm here to take Dylan over to Turpid," Pete says.

"I've got work," Dylan says. It's a Saturday, about noon. I've already been changing oil. Doc's closes early on Saturday because Doc likes time more than money.

"I'll go," I say. Everyone stares at me. "Seriously," I say.

"You don't even know where I'm going," Pete says.

"BOWS," I say.

"What has this little jackass told you?" Pete asks, looking at Dylan.

"Nothing," I say. "I'm from the Coalition."

"The fuck you are," Pete says. "They don't have anything to do with us."

"I'm supposed to spy on you," I say.

"The fuck you are," Pete says.

"Seriously," I say. "Just take me along. I'll explain."

Pam is reddening. I don't know why.

Pete considers for a moment, takes out his cell. "I've got some asshole here who says he's from the Coalition," he says. He listens for awhile. "How the fuck should I know?" Pete says, then "No way," and finally, "Alright, but..." and then he hangs up. "Get in the truck," he tells me.

Pete doesn't say anything for a long time. He drives his truck hard. He growls at slow drivers and tailgates. I see that Pete is not a happy man.

"So," Pete says finally. "Are you banging Pam?"

"No," I say. "Not my type," I add, to be reassuring.

"Not good enough for you, asshole? Not hot enough?" Pete says.

"Not that," I say. "I'm just renting a room. Don't want things complicated."

Pete says nothing. After another twenty minutes, we turn on a gravel road that says "Mud Lake Boat Access" and then onto a dirt track. We end up in front of a couple of pole barns and the remains of a wood barn. There's an overgrown windbreak of poplar trees running down one side and a weedy field on the other. The first track continues between the buildings and disappears down a hill. Pete stops. "Out," he says.

I get out. Pete drives away. It's very quiet here. I can hear the breeze in the poplars and a couple of arguing blue jays. I walk around. The pole barns are empty and smell of manure and diesel. I hear a motor and then an ATV appears on the dirt road. It pulls up to me. A man is driving.

"Hop in," he says. The ATV seats two. He shakes my hand. "Beck," he says.

"Jason," I say, shaking his hand. The motor idles quietly.

"From the Coalition?" he says, smiling at me. "Who's on the Executive Committee these days?"

I list the names. Beck nods, revs the ATV into a U-turn and we head down the hill, bouncing and pitching. We arrive at the shore of a lake, with a dock, a boathouse, another pole barn, and couple of log-built cabins.

"Used to be a hunting and fishing camp," Beck says. He turns off the motor, looks at me.

"What is it that you want to know?" he asks.

We get out of the ATV and walk onto the dock and I ask him about BOWS. Beck doesn't tell me much, though he talks a lot. He's friendly, self-deprecating, and I like him. BOWS is a kind of boys club, with a few meetings, a few outings, a few paintball matches, and a gun range. The members learn a little about survival techniques, but it's mostly social. They have a few women members, but the culture is masculine, Beck says. He asks me how I know Pete. I tell him.

"I'll be honest," Beck says. "Pete's an asshole and I wish he'd quit. We don't see him much, thank God." Beck asks me what brings me to Winter Lake, how long I'll be around. I'm vague in my answers, but mostly honest. Beck nods. He's a nice looking man, with a trim beard, baseball cap, and a long sleeve shirt with the sleeves rolled up. He looks fit.

"Ever do paintball?" he asks. I shake my head. "Well, if you are around in a couple of weeks, let me know. We have a day of paintball out here, divide into teams, throw a few creative rules into the mix, and then have a pig roast. Might even drink a little beer. Here," he says, handing me a card. "Give me a call if you are interested." The card lists a phone number and says BOWS in big, blue letters.

When I get back, Pam is in the kitchen. "What happened?" she asks me. I tell her.

"Oh," she says. "I'm making spaghetti. Want some?"

"Sure," I say. "Want some help?"

There's not much to do. Pam heats sauce. I boil spaghetti. She reaches high into the cupboard to get something down. "Can I get that for you?" I ask and take half a step her direction. Pam flinches, actually flinches. I freeze.

"Sorry," she says. "I'm sorry. It's the oregano. I don't know why I have it on the top shelf, or why they put these cabinets so high up. I don't really need it. There's probably plenty in the sauce already." She backs up to the sink. "This food is probably pretty awful, isn't it? I know I cook kind of odd food most of the time. At least that's what Dylan thinks. But I try to have healthy food and this sauce is from the co-op in Superior. I go up there once a month and buy what I can afford. This organic stuff is not cheap. Did you know that Dylan's uncle, my ex-brother-in-law, runs the co-op? Called Lake Harvest Cooperative. I should have married him, though I didn't know him when I married his little brother. That was my first husband, not Pete. No, not Pete..." Pam trails off. "You go to the bars, right? Are you going tonight? Can I tag along? A woman can't go by herself around here. I think you know why. Maybe you don't. Sends the wrong message, like I'm looking for something. But I'd just like to get out around people, have a good time. I'm not big on TV. Dylan probably told you that. How weird I am." Pam starts wiping off the counters. "How's that spaghetti? Do you know how to tell when it's done? I can tell by looking at the water. Don't even have to try it. It boils different and you can smell that it's cooked. Here, let me drain it."

We eat in silence.

What I've noticed about Pam is that she has very dark brown eyes, like an animal's. She has downy sideburns that most women would get rid of. She's sturdy, probably overweight by magazine standards, and she has an earth mother figure that is hard for me to ignore, the bust of a fertility goddess, and wide hips. She moves likes she talks, in bursts and darts. She has small wrinkles around her eyes, which might be from worry or squinting, but not laughing. She wears readers half way down her nose when she is working on earrings, which she does every evening, at the kitchen table. She does yoga and some kind of workout by video. I hear it over my head in the morning, the cooing announcer, the awful sound-track, and Pam's movements in synchrony.

Now that I know where to look, and have a plan, I feel a strange reluctance to talk to Phaedra or Davey. I tell myself a lot of things, like what business do I have interrupting their lives, whatever they've become. Or that they both may be less than enthusiastic about seeing me. Or worse, that one or both might panic at being uncovered and bolt into some oblivion more obscure than Winter Lake. But the truth is, I don't know if I want them in my life, and I've grown quickly and disturbingly comfortable in this new routine, in my living arrangement, and in the fact that I know I can contact Davey and Phaedra but they can't contact me, that I have the initiative, the potential energy rather than the kinetic. I am in control, and that was difficult for me to keep when I was around them, in what seems like an alternate universe.

I am even drumming again. Not all the time, but a few nights each week, I drum a set or two with the Black Mambas, who give me absurd drum solos in rockabilly songs, like we are a jazz band, or Iron Butterfly. Their drummer has carpel tunnel in both arms. Drumming is an agony for him, but he can't stop, and I offer a low maintenance alternative. They even pay me a little, and I still have the truck, and the Coalition is happy with the reports. Delirious, in fact, and stunned that I've made contact.

It's all potential. Maybe I could sleep with Pam. Maybe not. But it's possible, and it has crossed my mind. I can track down Phaedra and Davey. It's up to me. I could go back to college. I can quit Doc's in a heartbeat. I can always go back and live with Anna Bella. I'm in control.

A few days and many oil changes later, I track down Dylan and get him to take me out on Winter Lake. I rent a fishing boat from the marina, just an aluminum bass boat with a 25 hp motor. A stiff breeze blows from the north and our little boat bobs over white caps. I'm nervous when we get out in deep water, but Dylan seems unconcerned.

"Pretty big waves," I yell back to him. Dylan holds the steering handle of the motor and shrugs, maybe even looks a little amused.

"How far?" I ask, wiping spray from my face.

"About a mile," Dylan yells back.

I see it long before we arrive. Skaarenor Island, and the castle. The Winter Lake Library is one of my haunts. I use a computer there to send updates to the Coalition, Anna Bella, and, recently, my sister. They have this room, a small room, local resources—some file cabinets with old photographs, the local paper on microfiche and CD, and a few area histories put together by local residents. One profiles Adolphus Skaarenor, a Swede who immigrated to the area in 1869. Somehow he worked his way up from lumberjack and drover to owner of a lumber and sawmill business. The remains of his mill are on the Marinette River, east of Winter Lake where it has some current before it slows down and enters the Lake. He made a lot of money from white pine and was shrewd at land acquisition, especially land that might contain iron ore. Once he'd clear cut a parcel, it was practically worthless, unless he could convince others that iron ore lay beneath the surface, and in those days, there was an iron ore boom in northern Wisconsin. He sold a lot of that land to east coast speculators.

But he was active in other ways. He fathered seven daughters with a local woman, reported to be part Indian, and died of pneumonia in 1915. He built the castle in 1899, to usher in a new century with the satisfaction of his longings from the old country, the peasant's desire to be an aristocrat, something he never forgot. A half mile timber bridge joined the island, his island, Skaarenor Island, to the mainland. It even had electric lights. He built his castle at the summit of this hump-backed island, a pine fringed heap of rock about half a mile square. In the old photos, Adolphus Skaarenor stands, stout and solid in front of the substantial stone building that was his castle. He has a Teddy Roosevelt mustache, and indeed, Teddy once visited the island and caught muskie, no easy feat.

A square tower sits at one end of the castle. Nothing balances it at the other end, giving it a lopsided look. The interior was built of thick white pine and in the photos, it looks more like a lodge at a dude ranch than a medieval castle. Animal heads line the walls and bright blurry lights hang from thick beams. In the photos I can see a walk-in fireplace, lots of heavy furniture, and daughters everywhere. They are striking women, taller than their father, with square jaws and steady eyes, and slim, athletic builds. It's hard to tell the birth order except for the youngest one or two. I see them with long skirts, tight bodices, and fishing poles. I see them on picnics with many bottles of wine, posing unsmiling around their father. I see them lined up on a dock, like roll call, in a picture taken from out on the lake. I never see Mrs. Skaarenor in any photo. Or maybe I do, and I don't recognize her as the mother.

I read that the castle stayed in the Skaarenor family until 1931, when it fell victim to the Depression. There's nothing about descendants or what happened to the family after that. Too bad. I would like to meet a Skaarenor, to see the echoes of the past in a daycare worker, or a podiatrist.

The castle no longer sits on a bald rock. Now it's surrounded by pines, buried, with just the tower and one angular corner visible from the lake. But it's still impressive. The timber bridge is long gone. Burned, according to Dylan, during a great forest fire in 1940's. We slowly circle the island, corkscrewing and nearly swamping when we take our nose out of the wind. Even on this sunny day, the castle's gray limestone seems to swallow the light.

When we get to quiet water, I ask Dylan, "So, you've been inside?"

"Yup," he says.

"Is it a wreck?"

"It sure is, though it still has rooms and such, if that's what you mean. People have stripped it of anything interesting and a lot is rotted, because people broke the windows. It's been abandoned since I was a little kid. Really don't know how long."

"But the realtor lady lives there?" I ask.

"Well, there's some cabins, too. She probably lives in one of those, if she lives on the island at all. No electricity."

"Why don't we land and take a look?" I ask.

"Nope," Dylan says. "Promised my mom I'd stay off the island."

"Oh, for god's sake, Dylan. Just land and I'll get out. You don't have to come."

"There's only one place I can go in and the waves are too big today. I'll show you."

We continue to circle the island. It has abrupt, rock edges and dense woods behind the rock. The only thing that resembles beach faces dead north and the white caps tumble on the crumbled rock.

"Jesus, Dylan, those waves are like one foot tall," I say. "You can land in that."

"Can't get in that close. Really shallow. Can't use the motor to get back out unless I drop you off in four feet of water. You want to swim?"

"No dock?" I say.

"Long gone," Dylan says. "We can come back on a calmer day."

I watch the island shrink as we head back to the marina. I wanted to see the castle up close. But part of me is also relieved. I don't know if I'm ready for Phaedra. And somehow, I knew she was there.

"I'm promoting you," Doc says. "You can thank Hammie for that. He thinks you just about walk on water. Anyways, radiator flushing."

"Great," I say.

"Maybe fuel filters. We'll see. You got to prove yourself. One step at a time," Doc says.

"Okay," I say. "I'll be patient. I'm sure there's a lot to learn about coolants. And life."

I hear Hammie laugh in the pit.

"Smartass," Doc says. "Okay, I'll leave it up to Hammie, but it's his ass if you screw up."

Wow, I think, a promotion. I have not had many of these. At Miller construction, I worked my way from demolition to general laborer. But this advancement fits well into my new plan of self-improvement. I visit the library at least twice a week. I am trying to read up on the Middle Ages. The Winter Lake Library does not have an extensive collection on this topic. In fact, it has two books, Barbara Tuchman's A Distant Mirror and one kids' picture book called I am a Serf. I order some other titles through interlibrary loan, with the library card I've acquired, thanks to Pam. And I'm working on the physical me. I run, I do push-ups, I eat healthy food. Strangely, I don't feel any different. My outlook is not more optimistic. I don't sleep any better. My mind does not seem razor sharp. In fact, I find self-improvement is quite tiring and after two weeks, I'm ready to give it up, but I think I'll give it another few days. I can't expect miracles overnight.

Chapter 20

On a dreary afternoon, I don't feel like running or reading or doing much of anything. Dylan is at work. So is Pam. I watch a Kung Fu movie I rented at the gas station. This is my training to become an expert in martial arts, only I fall sleep to the drone of Chinese dialog, body blows, and shrill screams. Raccoon is on my lap and drizzle spots the picture window. I don't know how long I've been asleep when the door bell rings. It's really, really loud, so Pam could hear it in the massage studio. I jump a foot off the couch and launch Raccoon across the room. I stagger into consciousness and to the door.

"Hello?" I say.

"Can I come in?" a woman says. She's middle height, very blond hair, wearing a skirt and a bright blue blazer. The blazer says "JJ Realty" with the J's overlapping.

I step aside. "Sure, come on in. Pam isn't here, if that's who you are looking for."

"Jason, it's me," the woman says. "Phaedra."

"Jesus," I say. It does not look like Phaedra. It looks like a soccer mom, or a minister's wife, or a TV weather lady.

She smiles broadly at me. I recognize the little gap between her front teeth, the general lines of her face.

"Hi," I say.

She looks me over, still smiling. "You look good, Jason. Older."

"I am older," I say, ridiculously.

"If you would like me to come back some other time..." Phaedra says.

"You are Jasmine, right?" I say.

"Jasmine Jones," she says.

"Jasmine Jones," I repeat. "How did you know where I was?"

"Davey called me. We don't talk much, but I suspect you've heard something about that. He called to say that you were around. Couldn't believe it, frankly," Phaedra says. "But I guess it was predictable."

"Predictable?" I say. "It wasn't predictable to me."

"Predictable in the sense of who you are, Jason," Phaedra says. "Or at least the Jason I knew."

"Do you want to sit down?" I ask. "Want some tea or something?"

"No," she says. "No thank you. Look Jason, I'm here for a simple reason, for a once and only once visit. Davey and I, we aren't with each other anymore, but we do agree on one thing. We want our privacy. We don't see anything positive that can result from renewing our relationship. After all, you refused to come with us. You made your decision."

"I don't think it is that simple," I say.

Phaedra sits on the very edge of the couch, pushes away Raccoon. She opens her purse and takes out a floral billfold.

"Are you going to college? Or have you been? Do you owe money?" Phaedra says. She begins to scribble a check. "Here," she says.

"I don't want it," I say.

"Take it," Phaedra says.

I take the check from her hand. It's for $10,000.

"You were so bright, Jason. You deserve an education. Here's a contribution. You don't have to do anything for this. You don't have to pay me back. All I ask is that you respect my privacy, and Davey's privacy. The part of our life that we shared is gone, Jason. It's gone, and you know the past is, well, just what's happened and gone. It has no other meaning."

I put the check down on the coffee table. "You bought a castle," I say.

"I'm not going to talk about that," Phaedra says.

"Where does Davey live? How do I know you speak for him? Do the Miller's know where he is?"

Phaedra shakes her head. "Oh, Jason, listen to you. You sound like an old woman. That was always what was most distasteful about you, wanting to be in control, to hide your fear."

"You're just making that up."

"Okay," Phaedra says. "I'm making things up." She stands, moves to the door. "Leave us alone. Both of us."

"Or?" I say.

"I'm late for the Chamber of Commerce meeting," Phaedra says. "So nice to see you again, Jason. Say hi to Pam. You could do worse."

"I'm just renting a room," I say.

"Bye," she says, and leaves.

I go to the window and watch her drive away in a white SUV. She accelerates slowly, like nothing unusual has happened. I stare after her a long time.

When I come back from the bars that night, Pam is waiting up for me. She hands me Phaedra's check.

"What's this?" she says. "What's going on? Why did you leave this on the coffee table? Why would you even have this? Jasmine wrote you this check. You didn't tell me you knew her. Why did she write a check to you? For $10,000. $10,000! I grossed like $26,000 all last year, and you leave a check like this just lying around. Are you showing off? What's going on? Why are you playing with Dylan and me? You think that's funny?"

I just walk past her and go down the stairs. I have no idea why she is so upset. But then, I clearly don't know anything. I didn't know I had so much fear, and wanted to be in control. I didn't know I came across as a person who could be bought. Admittedly, it's not a bad price. But I loathe the idea. I feel anger towards Pam now. This is none of her business, and I owe her no explanation. I owe her and Dylan nothing. I don't owe anyone anything. Like Ned said, I'm no one. And I don't look all that bright. Hammie the mechanic is a wiz at chess. He can kill me in half a dozen moves. He sees the future. I only see the past, and the past is just what happened, nothing more.

I had a terrible time at the bar. It was nearly empty all night at the Winter Lake Pub, and I couldn't drag myself anywhere else. The background music was too loud and it irritated the hell out of me. Awful playlist. I only had five bucks to last me the whole night. Forgot to cash my check from Doc. The Coalition money is gone. Couldn't afford food and I nursed a couple of cheap beers for the whole time I was there. Like Lark said, I'm a loser. A loser's loser, a paragon of loserhood. The zenith, the epitome, the archetype, embodiment, the corporeal expression of an ideal. In this I excel. In this, I am somebody.

I go back upstairs. "Pam?" I say.

"What?" comes her voice from the living room.

'Sorry."

"Sorry? What do you mean?"

I don't know what I mean. I guess I'm a loser at apologies.

"I don't know," I say, honestly.

"Apology accepted," Pam says.

Things look up the next day. For one thing, I do an automatic transmission flush. Who wouldn't find that fulfilling? I also figure I'm not going to accept Phaedra's word that she speaks for Davey. I'm going to find him and ask him myself. It's not like I take any immediate action toward this end. It just feels good to be contrary and restore some of my sense of purpose.

I didn't like Phaedra. She smelled like a plastic flower. I didn't like how she looked, certainly not what she said, and I didn't like her pre-emptive strike. In three short minutes, she jilted, thwarted, and embarrassed me. I guess I helped with the embarrassment part. I did not exactly shine in my repartee, my insightful and devastating verbal counter punches. I could blame the King Fu movie for that, or the nap. But she took me by surprise. And I envy her initiative.

"Hello, Anna Bella," I say on the phone.

"Jason, you are still alive. What a pleasant surprise," Anna Bella says.

"How's the poetry business?" I ask politely.

"Why, it's wonderful, Jason. Do you need money? Have you been shot?"

"No," I say. "No new holes and I'm working at an oil change place."

"An oil change place?"

"Yes," I say. "I've been promoted to radiator and transmission flushes."

"I don't know what to say, Jason. I'm so proud."

"If you drive up here, I can get you 15% off a Get Your Car Ready for Winter service."

"You amaze me."

"Thanks," I say. "When I finish up here, can I go to your college?"

Anna Bella hesitates. "You'd have to take out some big loans. A community college might be a better idea until you know what you want to do."

"I have no fear," I say.

"I do," Anna Bella says. "Don't expect me to co-sign your loans."

"But could I get in?"

"My school? Yes, I think I could help you with that, as long as you wanted to go into the liberal arts."

So, college is as good as done. That also brightens my day. Also, I call BOWS, get a mechanical voice telling me to leave a message.

I say that Dylan and I want to show up for paintball. Dylan doesn't know that yet, but I'll get him to agree.

And Pete showed up at Pam's, demanding custody of Raccoon. Pam refused. Pete called her names, called Dylan names because he stood in the door with Pam. I tried to loom menacingly in the background. Pete cussed us all out, then left. That night, raccoon didn't punch me.

I ask Pam the next morning, "How long have you been divorced from Pete?"

"Well, actually, we aren't divorced. I threw him out in July."

"That's like ten weeks ago. I thought it had been years."

"Nope. Sorry."

I hear back from Beck. Dylan and I are welcome. He'll have some equipment we can rent. We need to be there at 8 AM. I tell Dylan.

"So, next Saturday, we are going to BOWS for paintball," I say.

"Not me," Dylan says.

I convince him to change his mind, though it isn't easy. "You are a necromancer," I say. "Controlling legions of the undead. Paintball should be easy."

"It's not on a computer. I don't like real things," he says.

"I command you, in the name of portals and undead and all those things," I say.

"You can't command a necromancer. That takes a level 16 spell."

"Level 16 is for children. Babies. I invoke a level 48."

"You don't even know what that is," Dylan says.

"Don't make me go level 49," I say.

We ride out in Carmen. Dylan is pale and silent. I keep my foot on the gas pedal. I think that if I slow down too much, he'll bolt.

A bunch of men mill around a grassy field behind the cabins. Many have padded bags that they open, take out paintball guns, face masks, padded jerseys and pants, gloves, and lots of other stuff.

"Here," Beck says, handing us each a bag. "$10 each and sign these forms."

The guns look like little automatic weapons. They are lightweight and have attachments that Beck needs to explain. "These are not fully automatic," he says, "though you can get a three-shot burst. You don't have as many markers as some people here, so don't waste shots."

"Markers?" I say.

"Paintballs," Beck says.

The paintballs are round. "They are biodegradable," Beck says. "You each have one CO2 tank. That should be enough. Works like an air pistol."

A guy gathers everyone. He explains that we'll be playing capture the flag, two teams, several heats. Each game has a one-hour limit. Ten people per team. He explains that any hit knocks out a player. Each team has a squad leader. Do what they say. The man goes on and on about discipline, tactics, communication, trust, and the brotherhood of war. He talks about the boundaries, how they are marked on the field, and how you are disqualified for the whole match if you leave the field. I begin to tune out and find myself with Dylan, put on a team with yellow arm bands. We are in the second heat.

Pete spots us.

"What are you pussies doing here?" he says, very loudly. "You aren't going to last thirty seconds, either of you. I should just shoot you now and get it over with." He raises his paintball gun and makes tat-tat-tat sounds, which I find out is really a very good imitation of how they actually sound. So Pete has at least one talent.

Dylan is more pale than on the ride over. Even his lips are pale. He won't look at Pete. When Pete finally walks away, I pull Dylan away from the others.

"Do you understand the rules?" he asks me in a faint voice.

"Not really" I say.

A man walks over to join us.

"Welcome to yellow squad," he says, shakes our hands. "I'm Jim. I'm the squad leader. I take it you are new to this.

Whatever I say, you do. You don't think, you do. I'll get you through this, and God willing, we'll take that flag."

"I sure hope so," I say.

Jim nods. "Good. Good to hear you have motivation. Practice is real, did you know that? If you don't practice like it's real, when it is real, you fail. This is war, guys. We don't win here, we don't win anywhere. You follow?"

Dylan nods.

"Let me at 'em," I say.

Jim smiles. "Only thing is, you two have tee shirts on. The camo is good. Someone should have told you. You should have another layer. These markers sting like a son of a bitch on bare skin."

"That just motivates me," I say.

Jim looks a little doubtful. "Well, okay. The trick is to not get shot. I think you know that. I'm going to put you two on flag defense. The honor of Yellow Squad is on your shoulders."

We meet the rest of Yellow Squad. They all know each other, talk a lot about their guns and paintballs and previous games. We are supposed to memorize the names, to communicate with names on the field, and to communicate a lot. It seems like only a few minutes and the first match is done. I've heard the tat-tatting of the paintball guns, people yell, people cuss. I gather that one team wasted the other. We start walking to the patch of woods where this will all take place.

"Rough terrain," Jim tells us. "Perfect. Lots of trees, a couple of ravines." He turns and smiles as we walk. "You are going to love this."

I see that Pete is on the opposing team. Dylan sees that, too. "Oh, no," he says.

The men put on their goggles, check their weapons, start high-fiving.

"I'll place a rear guard in our attack," Jim says. "You are the last resort. Stay concealed as long as you can. Don't shoot until anyone from Blue Squad is close, very close. No one should get this far. We are pretty good at this. But if they do, if they do, you have to hold your ground. Look, listen, keep your heads."

Jim places us, flanking the yellow flag, but out in front, quite a ways from each other.

A whistle sounds, and the match begins. Yellow Squad, except for Dylan and me, slinks away.

I immediately leave my spot and join Dylan.

"Do you know how to fire this thing?" he asks me. No one showed us. We fool around with the guns and get them to shoot. We pick off some trees. It's really kind of fun.

"You should go back to your spot," Dylan says.

I think about this, then take off my yellow arm band.

"What are you doing," Dylan says.

"Take yours off," I say. "Welcome to Team Vengeance."

Dylan doesn't move. I tug at his arm band. He pulls away. "Don't!" he says.

"We'll put them back on," I say. "But for now, lose it. Trust me. You heard that guy talk about trust."

Dylan looks at me, then slowly takes off his armband.

"C'mon," I say.

"We can't leave the flag," Dylan says.

"We'll come back," I say.

"Where are we going?"

"On a mission," I say.

"To get the blue flag?" Dylan asks.
"No. We are going to hunt Pete."

Chapter 21

This sounds like such a good idea, to bag Pete. But it turns out to be complicated. For one thing, they all look alike with face masks or goggles.

"What was Pete's gun like?" I ask Dylan.

"It had blue on it and a lumpy thing over the barrel," he says. It's something to go on, but not much.

And everyone is slinking around in one's or two's and jumping up and shooting, and running, and rolling, and shooting some more. It's very confusing.

We edge away from the Yellow Team base, follow the right hand boundary. The boundary is marked by blue ropes tied to trees every so often. We see a guy on the other side. I think he watches for rule breakers. We quickly discover we are not the only ones taking the boundary route. Paintballs splat on a tree trunk next Dylan.

"On my god," he says and hits the dirt.

I join him. "Let's crawl forward," I say.

We pull ourselves along on our elbows. We come up on two guys with yellow armbands, our teammates. Dylan shoots, hits them both.

"What the fuck!" one says. They both yell at us but stalk off the field.

"They were on our team," I tell Dylan.

"I know," Dylan says. "I guess I panicked."

"Well, at least we have a kill," I say. "It should get easier now, like Henry the 8th. He didn't execute anyone for quite a long time, but once he started, he kind of got used to it, started having everyone's head chopped off."

Dylan looks at me. "I guess," he says.

We stay on our bellies, crawl forward, looking for Pete. I think. Where would I place Pete if I were Blue Team? An attacker seems to be a natural choice. But Pete's a jerk, probably is not well-liked, maybe isn't good at coordinating with others. He might be fierce on defense, though.

"I bet Pete is guarding the blue flag," I say.

We crawl into a ravine. Dylan rolls and rises to his knees, shoots another yellow armband.

"Jesus, Dylan," I say. "Blue, shoot the blue ones."

Then we see a blue armband. He's hiding awkwardly behind a sapling. He shoots at us. Paintballs pepper the leaf litter in front of us. I take careful aim at a shoulder that sticks out from the tree. I shoot, just as the guy steps out. I get him right in the crotch.

"You asshole," he says. "That hurt!" He stomps off to the boundary.

"These guys really follow the rules," Dylan says.

"Lucky for us," I say.

We stay in our ravine. It's mucky at the bottom, and quiet. I hear the tat-tats in the distance, some yells, but no one seems to be near us. We scramble forward. I'm not sure where we are going. I've lost my bearings. But I do enjoy the yellow leaves on the maples above us. Everyone in a while, we are showered with falling leaves.

There's a stir behind us and Jim bursts through the undergrowth.

"What the hell are you guys doing here!" he says. "Where are your arms bands?"

Then paintballs zip through the air. One almost brushes my nose.

"Sniper!" Jim yells. "Bravo 3!"

"What's that?" I say.

We are crouched behind tree trunks. Paintballs whiz past.

"Oh, never mind," Jim says. "You don't know any of the tactics."

"I'll be a decoy," I offer.

"Good man," Jim says. "Go! Go! Go!"

I run.

There's an exchange of tat-tats, hoarse yells. Dylan follows me. We hear a voice near us and we drop to our bellies again.

Through a gap in the trees, we see Pete. He's been hit and is walking toward the boundary, muttering.

Dylan shoots him.

Pete whirls around. "Hey, asshole, I'm already hit!" he yells.

I shoot, a three ball burst up his leg.

"Goddam it!" he bellows.

We start giggling. "Get him again," I whisper.

Pete is turning in circles now. His face is bright red. He pulls off his goggles, cursing.

"Maybe we got him enough," I say. "Let's head back. Put your armband back on. Vengeance is done."

Pete has charged off in the wrong direction, away from us.

"Follow me," I say.

I head away from the boundary, into the middle of the game field, into an area less wooded.

"Let's see if we can get some blue guys..." I start to say.

Tat—tat. We are both hit. It stings. Three blue guys have popped up, right in front of us. But a second later, they're hit, too. Jim and another yellow armband run up, yelling.

"That's all ten!" Jim yells. "We got 'em! Praise God, we won!"

"Jim says he doesn't want you back on Yellow Team," Beck tells us. We are eating bratwursts and drinking Pabst. Dylan doesn't like beer, but holds a can.

I nod. "Our tactics were a bit unorthodox," I say.

"Yes," Beck says. "You could say that."

"But we won," Dylan says, hurt by rejection.

"True," Beck says. "Want some sauerkraut?"

I love sauerkraut. We didn't eat it much. Tom, my dad, cooked pork chops in a big pot with sauerkraut and beer. It was my favorite meal, with the bonus being that Lydia despised it, the smell, the taste, the texture. She wouldn't even come in the kitchen.

I slather my brat with kraut and spicy mustard and chopped onions. This, and the venison jerky, and the baked beans that someone actually made from scratch, this is the best meal I've had in years.

"Jason," Beck says. "Let's talk."

He leads me away. We walk past the cabins, along the lake for a short while, then up a steep hill. At the top is a clearing, and in the middle of the field, a tall tower.

"Fire tower," Beck says. "Decommissioned."

It's a steel framed structure, maybe 70 feet tall, with an unprotected ladder up the side and a platform on top.

"Let's go up," Beck says.

I don't mind heights. I actually kind of like the feeling of hanging out over the edge of oblivion. But it's a long, wobbly climb. The ladder rungs are angular, like brackets, and uncomfortable to grip. The ladder narrows as we near the top and I can feel the vibration of Beck's movements running through the metal.

The ladder simply stops at the platform and you have to crawl onto it. I wonder about reversing this process, legs hanging out over the edge, searching for rungs.

The platform is weathered wood, rough to the touch, with a laughable two-foot railing around its edges, except on the side with the ladder, where there is nothing. It's bouncy when we walk and I can feel the tower sway in the breeze.

But it's an amazing view, the fall colors against blue sky, the rolling hills, and the very blue Mud Lake. I stand with knees bent and arms out. I can't help it. It feels precarious.

Beck looks totally relaxed. He turns to me.

"This is where I saw it," he says. "Last March. Clear stretch of weather. Came up here and I saw it."

"What?" I say.

"Near Earth Object," Beck says.

"Like an asteroid?" I say.

Beck smiles. "Good," he says.

Beck tells me that he is an amateur astronomer. Amateur, but a serious amateur. He gives a long explanation about his stellar photography project, how he uses this tower, how he compensates for the tower's wobble, how he took a series of photos that caught his eye.

"The thing is," Beck says, "I don't really hunt for NEO's. Not at all. I just happened to catch this image, just a speck, moving across the area I've been scanning. I didn't think much about it at first. You know, Jason, that there are a lot of objects out there."

"Billions and billions," I say.

"Well, not in the earth's vicinity, but that's the general idea. Asteroids, comets, even space junk. Any of these could impact the earth with the right trajectory. Or should I say the wrong trajectory. It's happened before, you know."

"The dinosaurs," I say.

"Right," Beck says. "Massive extinction, most likely due to an asteroid impact in the Yucatan. It's inevitable, really. Just a matter of time."

"And you found one?"

Beck nods. "I've contacted various authorities. Not much interest. But I'm no fool, Jason. I'm an engineer. I know how to do certain things. By my calculations, it will intersect earth's orbit, or come very near."

"When?"

"Soon, Jason, soon."

We climb back down the ladder. The wind has picked up and the tower twists as well as sways. I'm happy to touch ground.

"You showed some leadership today. Some real initiative," Beck looks at me earnestly as we walk. "Out of the box thinking. I'm not good at that. I know my limits."

"I'm not much of a leader," I say modestly.

"Listen, Jason. I'm talking about something very serious now," Beck stops walking. Pulls off his baseball cap, smoothes his hair, puts it back on. Seems to be considering.

"You were sent by the Coalition," Beck says. "They want to know what's up with BOWS, right?"

"Yes," I say.

"What have you told them?"

"Nothing much," I say. "There hasn't been much to say."

"I have nothing against the Coalition," Beck says. "They are good men. We share a common cause. I'm not sure why there is… well, suspicion between us. A lot of that happened before my time, before I got involved with BOWS, and certainly before I became commander."

"I didn't know you were the commander," I say, though I was pretty sure.

He considers again.

"Here's the deal, Jason," he says. "We want that castle."

I didn't expect that.

"The one out on the lake?" I ask.

"Skaarenor's castle, yes," Beck says. "We need it. Humanity needs it."

On the way back to Winter Lake, Dylan babbles about his victory, his marksmanship, our great adventure.

"Most of those guys you shot were on our team," I remind him.

"Does it matter? War is hell," Dylan says. "I didn't know I could do things in the real world. You know, hero things."

I think this maybe wasn't such a good idea, bringing Dylan.

Dylan goes on about "wasting" Pete. I guess I understand this, but the light in Dylan's eyes is alarming.

"Oh, we nailed that sucker," Dylan says.

"He was already out," I remind Dylan.

Dylan shrugs. "The important thing is that we got him," he says.

Pam looks at me a lot when Dylan recounts the day. The story has grown. Dylan has an imagination. Nothing I would know about.

"Has he been drinking?" Pam asks me.

"Only the sweet nectar of victory," I say. I don't think Pabst counts as drinking.

"Well, he looks a little wild," Pam says.

Dylan has retired to his online world, to share his adventures I assume.

"Did you eat?" Pam says.

"Bratwurst," I say.

"Were they organic?" she asks.

"Is there any other kind?" I say.

Sunday. No work. I drive Carmen to the little marshy park by the lake, sit at a picnic table. It's chilly. Not too bad when the sun is out, but it gets cloudy and I end up back in the truck. I'm going to need to buy some cold weather gear.

So, BOWS wants the castle. I assume that the scenario is Near Earth Object strikes earth. Chaos ensues, brave men and a few women of BOWS sustain their version of civilization on the island redoubt. It's a compelling image. Good marketing for BOWS.

Later, I try to call Bill. No answer. So I try Ned.

"Jason here," I tell him.

"Glad you called. Chess Chalmers is looking for you. Want his number? We've crossed paths a lot in the past three or four weeks. An interesting guy. I have his Christmas album. Must be twenty or thirty years old. Kind of fun to meet the guy. Good voice."

"Yes, well, sure give me the number," I say.

"What's up? Why'd you call?" Ned asks.

"BOWS predicts an impending astronomical collision. They are trying to acquire a castle."

"Oh, Ned says, then pauses. "That's a lot to take in."

"Wanted to let you know," I say.

"Are you writing something up?" he asks.

"Sure."

"One more thing," Ned says. "Our two casino robbers are claiming insanity."

"I hope it works," I say.

I drive to Superior, watch an action movie at a new big box theater. I eat an enormous tub of popcorn. I feel sick all the way back to Winter Lake.

When I return to Pam's, Dylan stops me.

"Someone called the Motel 5, looking for you."

"Who?"

"Jefferson Davis," Dylan says.

"When did he call?"

Dylan thinks. "About two weeks ago. Forgot to tell you."

Davey. He tried to reach me after I left the number at the nursing home. Looks like I've ignored him.

"Did he leave a message?"

"He said something," Dylan says. "But I don't remember what."

"Great," I tell Dylan. He smiles and pantomimes a gun. "You've been paintballed," he says.

I drive to the nursing home. There are only a few cars in the parking lot. It's 9:15 PM and it's dark. But I wait, hoping Davey will appear. I don't know if he still works there, or if he works on Sunday night. This is not a great plan, but I want to do something.

There's a tap on my window.

"Hello, officer," I say.

The cop shines a flashlight in my face.

"What are you doing here?" he says. "We got a call that someone was hanging around. I'll need to see your license and registration."

I pull out my driver's license, hand it over. I have no idea about the registration part. I lean over, open the glove box. There's an envelope stuffed with paper. I hand it to him. He gives it a cursory look and hands it back, then takes my license back to his squad car. I wait.

"Okay," he says, handing it back. It's like a miracle. I actually didn't get arrested. Or shot. "But why are you here?"

I tell him the truth, more or less.

"I think you'd better move on," he says.

I drive away, thinking, wow, I'm like a normal person. What a strange feeling.

"I hear you have an opening for a janitor," I tell the lady at the front desk of the nursing home. I just got off work at Doc's.

"No, we don't," she says.

"What are the hours?" I ask. "Is it night shift? What time would that start?"

"We don't have an opening," she says again.

"But if you did, when would I need to be here?"

"You would need to be here by 10 PM," she says. "But we don't' have an opening."

"Oh, that wouldn't work for me," I say. "I've got custody of the kids. Little Barnie has the night terrors. I could never leave him alone at night. Poor kid would climb the walls. And his sister, Colorado, she sleepwalks. Found her at the shopping mall once, stiff as a board, standing in a planter. Kids, right?"

Chapter 22

I have to be at work at 5:30 AM and here I sit at the Winter Lake Club, with, of all people, Pete. He's drunk.

"I just love her too much," he says.

I make a noncommittal noise.

"Hate that frickin' kid, though," Pete says. "You know," he says, putting his hand on my arm, "I'm just too much man. I'm all man, like Brett Favre or Rambo. And a man is just—manly."

"How true," I say.

"And Pam, sure she's a bitch and she's crazy, but she's all woman, know what I mean? You better not know what I mean, you son of a bitch!"

"I don't know what you mean," I say.

"Well, that's good. That's so good, my friend, or you would see a Man. All man. Like a tidal wave of balls, know what I mean?"

"Sort of," I say.

"Balls to the walls. Buy me a drink," Pete says.

"A man drink?" I say.

"Fuckin' got that right," Pete says.

"How did paintball go?" I ask.

Pete shrugs, theatrically. "Okay, I guess," he says.

"Did you take a bullet?" I ask.

"Hell, no. I like wasted a ton of guys. Tat-tat-tat." He imitates a gun, and looks a lot like Dylan doing the same thing. "Yeah, but my team. Fuckers. They didn't listen to me. You know, I'm like an expert on war," Pete says.

"Like strategy and stuff?"

"Like the whole thing. Hell, I could run the whole frickin' war. Both sides. I could do it."

"Wow."

"Hey, I told you to buy me a drink," Pete says.

"I have to head out. Work tomorrow," I say.

Pete waves his hand. "Fuck tomorrow. This is now, with two men talking. I thought you were a prick. You are, but not so bad as I thought. Tell me you aren't screwing Pam. Swear."

"I swear."

"On what?"

"On my honor as a man."

Pete punches my shoulder. "Fuck yeah," he says.

Pete stands. "Okay, then. I'll let you go just this once. Go then to your little work. Just keep away from Pam or you know what."

"A tidal wave of balls," I say.

"Fuck yeah," Pete says.

I wasn't planning to go to a bar. I was going to intercept Davey if I could. So I sat, again, in the nursing home parking lot, just before 10 PM.

About 10:15, with me already half asleep, there's a tap on the passenger window. I lean over and roll it down. Davey is there, smoking a cigarette.

"They are going to call the cops," he says, and blows smoke away from the window.

"Hi," I say.

"Hey," he says.

I get out of the truck. "Been a long time."

"It has," Davey says.

He's changed a lot. His blond hair is shoulder length, but the hairline is higher than I remember. I see a bit of gut against his tee shirt and his jeans ride below it. He smokes calmly and watches me.

"So," I say. "How are you doing?"

"Pretty good," Davey says.

"You are Jefferson Davis these days?" I say.

He snorts, drops his cigarette butt, grinds it out, and lights another. "It's as good a name as any," he says.

"You into the Confederacy?" I ask. "Gone all Johnny Reb?"

"What do you mean?" he asks.

"Jefferson Davis, president of the Confederacy."

"No shit?" he says. "Phaedra picked the name."

"She's changed," I say.

He pauses mid-inhalation. "You've seen her?"

"Yeah, she found me. She's gone all realtor."

Davey continues smoking, says nothing.

"So, you live in Winter Lake?" I ask.

"Yeah," he says.

"Where?"

"Apartment," he says. "I've got to get back to work."

"Can I get your phone number or something?" I ask.

"You want a date? Don't know if you are my type" he says, with some amusement around his eyes.

"Just want to catch up."

"No phone," he says.

"Well, can we meet somewhere when you aren't at work?"

"Not what you expected, am I," he says. "Janitor. Gone to fat."

I shrug. "Doesn't matter at all," I say. "I didn't expect anything. Look at me. I'm a total loser," I say.

Davey laughs. "We've done real good," he says.

"I'll buy you supper tomorrow," I offer.

He looks at me for a moment, then says, "Okay."

We work out a few details, then he turns and walks back to the building. He sort of ambles, with slumped shoulders. I think about the Miller's, their prosperous, loving family. I think about Davey in high school, popular, smart, even a kind of football star. That's when I decide to go to a bar.

The next day we eat at the diner on Main Street. It's called the Main Street Diner. It has a very simple menu, mostly burgers and breakfast, all day long.

Davey orders quietly. Eats slowly. Stares at me while he eats. Dismisses my small talk with shrugs and grunts.

"More ice tea?" the waitress asks.

"No, thanks," Davey says.

"I'll take some," I say.

"Want dessert?" I ask Davey.

He shakes his head. "Too many calories," he says.

"So," I say. "Do your parents know you're here?"

Davey's eyes narrow. "Not really your business," he says.

"Sorry. Just wondered. I knew them, too, you know. After you guys left, I worked for your Dad for quite a while."

"Good for you," Davey says.

"They talked about you all the time. Hired people to try to find you. It was in the papers…"

"Enough," Davey says, cutting me off. "You talk to them recently?"

"No," I say.

"Don't," he says. "Look, I don't know why you're here, of all places. Or why you felt you had to track me down. Or Phaedra. And I guess it's fine. Hello and all that. We're both losers, etc. But that's it. We didn't look for you, you notice that?"

"I figured you weren't looking for anyone," I say.

"You don't know anything about us or what we did or didn't do. Life goes on. What's gone is gone. And you're, like, gone."

"Gone," I say. "I seem to be sitting here."

"I need a cigarette," Davey says and stands up.

He walks outside while I pay the bill. When I go outside, Davey is standing on the sidewalk, smoking, running his hand through his hair.

"Want a beer?" I ask.

"If you're buying," Davey says.

We go to the Club. The Black Mambas are setting up.

"Jason," the guitar player says, "hey, man, we were looking for you. Want to drum tonight?"

"Later, maybe," I say.

"You play drums?" Davey says.

"Yeah," I say. "I've been touring most of the summer."

"No shit," Davey says and smiles. He looks like Davey when he smiles.

"Did you go to college?" Davey asks me.

"A little," I say. "I don't have a ton of credits, but I've got plans to finish a degree."

Davey nods. "Good," he says. "I haven't done shit."

"Look, I have to ask. Don't you want to see your folks? For all they know, you're dead."

"No, no," Davey says. "Not like this. When I get my life together a bit, then, maybe. Everything is too fucked up now."

"Do you mind if I keep asking some questions?"

"Go ahead. Might not answer, though."

"Phaedra seems to be made of money all of a sudden," I say.

Davey laughs. "You don't know anything about that, do you?" He shakes his head. "I don't know if I even want to tell you."

"She bought an island and a castle. How'd she do that?" I ask.

"She's a poser," Davey says.

"What do you mean?"

"Go ask her yourself. Tell her Jeff says she's a poser. See what she says." Davey laughs again.

"I forget that you are Jeff," I say.

"I'm not anybody. Call me whatever you like," he says, and drinks half a beer in two quick gulps. "Doesn't life just totally suck?"

Jasmine Jones Realty occupies an office suite in a new building on the highway, just before you enter Winter Lake. I have to make an appointment to see Jasmine.

"What do you want, Jason?" she asks me. I sit in a fake leather chair. Her office overlooks a little pond, one of those man-made puddles designed to make property more expensive. The kind that breed mosquitoes for three or four years, then dry up.

"I want to be a realtor," I tell her. "Jasmine Jones and Jason." I trace three J's in the air as I speak.

"Very funny," she says.

"I talked to Davey."

"Look, Jason, I'm at work. I have a lot to do. A showing in half an hour. A closing after that. If you aren't here to talk about property, then..." She spreads her hands.

"I want to buy a cabin," I say.

"You do not," she says. "But let's see what you qualify for. What's your income, Jason? Zero? What do your assets look like, your equity in another property? Could that be zero, too? That won't buy much of a cabin, will it?"

"I have ten thousand dollars. Came to me from a total stranger."

She reddens, just a little.

"You don't know anything about me," she says.

"I know all about you, "You're a consummate poser."

"Poser," she repeats. "You did talk to Davey. He says that a lot. Are you best friends again? All wounds healed?"

"He's a wreck," I say.

"And what are you?" she asks.

"A drummer," I say. "And a student of human nature."

She smiles, just a touch. I can't tell if it's real or sardonic. There's too much make-up.

"You bought a castle," I say. "How did you do that?"

"None of your business," she says.

"Other people want it, did you know that?"

"I am well aware of that," Phaedra says. "I think that's enough." She pushes back her chair, like she's going to get up, but she doesn't.

"I hear from a very reliable source that the world is going to end as we know it, and that castle will make a great retreat to secure the new world order."

"Oh brother," she says. "Not that crap."

"You could be a queen," I say.

"What do you want, Jason?" she asks. "More money? Why don't you just go away. I bet Davey told you the same thing."

"He didn't quite put it that way," I say. "Can I visit the castle? I'd really like to see it."

Phaedra sighs, a big, deep sigh. "Okay, maybe sometime, when you are on your way out of town," she says. "But I need to get back to work now."

When I return to Pam's, she is waiting for me.

"There you are," she says glumly.

"Here I am," I say. "What's up?"

"Oh, nothing," she says, walks away.

I follow. "Is something wrong?" I ask.

"Never mind," Pam says. She goes into her bedroom and shuts the door.

I go downstairs. I'm re-reading A World Lit Only by Fire by William Manchester. A little on the sensational side when he talks about the Middle Ages, but I like his realistic view of Martin Luther.

Pam comes partway down the stairs. "Thanks a lot!" she says, and goes back up.

I look up from my book and wait.

Pam comes back down. "Why?" she says. "Why, Jason?"

"I guess I just don't know," I respond.

"What did we do to you?" she asks and goes back upstairs.

I follow.

"Pam" I announce to the air, since I don't see her. "What's wrong?"

"I'm in the bathroom," she says. "I just might stay here. For all you care."

"How about if I make some dinner?" I say. "Tacos?"

"Okay," comes the muffled reply.

I make tacos with organic beans, organic lettuce, and organic cheese. No meat. I put organic jalapenos on mine. Pam demurs. The shells are brittle and disintegrate as we try to eat them. My stuffing falls with a plop on my plate and I am left with a taco shard.

"You have beans in your moustache," Pam says.

I am tempted to say, so do you. "Thanks," I say.

"I was hungry," she says.

"Feeling better?" I ask.

She shrugs, wipes her fingers on her socks. I've never seen a woman do this before, but Pam does it unconsciously. She is wearing capri's, black tennies, and little white socks. Her shirt strains across the bust.

"Jason," she says, "I know you aren't totally bad."

"Thanks. That means a lot," I say.

"But I get some real mixed energy from you, and several things are bothering me. First, Dylan wants to join the Army and shoot people. That's your fault. Second, you leave your hair in the drain in the shower downstairs, which is really gross. Third, I am almost totally out of money. Do you know how much health insurance costs? I could massage every person in Winter Lake, massage them 'til the cows come home, and I still couldn't afford it."

"I know how that goes," I say. "I owe some big money..."

"Fourth, you hung out with Pete, which is so totally Judas to my Jesus, that I just don't know what to say. Fifth, why don't you offer to cut the grass? You see me slaving out there, sweating like a stuck pig, and you just sit there, reading like there's no tomorrow. I can see you through the basement window. Don't deny it."

"I don't," I say. "Though I have to point out that it's fall and you have only cut the grass once since I moved here."

"You could rake the leaves," she says. "Anyway, sixth," she pauses. "Oh, yeah. Oh, yeah, and this is the biggie. Are you selling drugs at the nursing home? This is a small town, Jason. A small town. Words gets out when you hang around and people need to call the police and you meet with unsavory characters, people who have reputations."

"Do the seniors buy drugs?" I say.

"They are vulnerable adults, Jason," Pam says. "Vulnerable. Just like Dylan, who now wants to be GI Joe. Join the Army and shoot people."

"Sorry," I say.

"Apology accepted, if you really mean it," Pam says. "What number am I on?"

"The last was six," I say.

"Seventh," Pam says. "Your running clothes stink. They smell up the whole basement. Why don't you wash them?"

"What's the point?" I say. "I'll just sweat them up again."

"That's gross," Pam says. "I think that's it."

"That's quite a list," I say.

"You made me tell you," Pam says. "I was just going to keep quiet about it. And now you'll probably move out, and I will lose the rent money, and I'll have to do who knows what."

"What?" I say.

"You know."

"No, I don't," I say.

"Sell my body just to put food on the table. What do you think of that?"

"That would not be good," I say. "I guess I am totally bad."

"No, you aren't. There's hope. You just have to think of other people once in a while."

I nod. "Okay, I'll work on that. Do you want the rest of the cheese?" I ask.

"No, help yourself," Pam says, passing me the grated cheddar. "I like a man with a healthy appetite."

I almost meet my match with windshield wipers. I know they are really easy to install, but I can't seem to get the hang of it. I know I am disappointing Hammie, who explains it over and over with bovine patience. I do have a knack for opening hood latches. They are so various, so diabolical, so knuckle-stripping that they are the bane of oil changers. But I approach each with a clear head and open mind, expecting nothing, but observing everything. I'm the one who figures out how to unlatch the hood of the '87 Mercedes. Otherwise, my job gives me plenty of time for reflection.

Where did Phaedra get all that money? I thought she was like a hobo. $10,000, just giving it away. It's an amazing amount of money.

I think about BOWS. An asteroid. Really? That no one else has noticed? Are they really interested in wresting the castle away from Phaedra?

What does Davey do besides clean the nursing home? Who is he?

Should I contact Chess? I have some strongly mixed feelings about this. The Black Mambas are really good, so I get my drumming fix. I can't get rid of the feeling that somehow Chess is partly responsible for the casino debacle, but I can't say why.

How much longer should I stay in Winter Lake? What is my plan? I've told the Coalition about BOWS. I've located Davey and Phaedra, something I didn't really expect that I'd do. It's getting chilly, the days are shorter. Do I want to be here for winter? I don't think so. I decide I should start making my plans to leave, though this doesn't feel quite right either. As usual, I'm indecisive. I wonder if I will ever outgrow this. Or is this who I am, unchangeable, unfixable, and adrift.

Chapter 23

"Happy birthday, Lydia," I tell my sister. It's October 4.

"Hi, Jason. You remembered. This is a first," Lydia says.

"No present," I say. "Just my call. How's medical school?"

"Grueling. I'm doing a pediatric oncology rotation. Interesting, but depressing. I couldn't face this every day."

"I'm changing oil," I say. "It's kind of rewarding. You take out this dirty oil and replace it with clean oil."

"How interesting," Lydia says. "Have you talked to Dad?"

"No."

"Cherry is pregnant," Lydia says.

"You're kidding. I guess we've been demoted again," I say.

"Yeah," Lydia says. "I think you're right. You might call them and say congratulations or something."

"Not very likely," I say.

"Don't be petty."

Lydia sounds tired, tired enough to be almost friendly.

"I know," I say. "Aren't they a little old for this?"

"Not Cherry. You know that. Dad? Well, let's face it. He was a strange dad. Maybe he'll get better with age."

"Maybe we were adopted," I say.

"Maybe," Lydia says. "You can't help but wonder."

"You look like Mom."

"You look like Dad," Lydia says.

"That could happen," I say. "Like dogs and masters looking alike. We get adopted and slowly morph into our physical environment. It's my new revolutionary theory of instant evolution."

Lydia ignores me. "What are your plans?" she says.

"I plan to drift on the river of life."

"Your life is slipping away from you," Lydia says. "You need to be somebody."

Adrift, but that doesn't mean I can't stick my head up once in a while and see where I'm going. I decide I need a few conversations.

I talk to Beck.

"So" I say. "You want Skaarenor Island as your retreat, your fort, when the asteroid hits."

"In a nutshell," Beck says, "yes."

"And this will be soon, you said. How soon?"

Beck shrugs. "Join the Brotherhood and I'll tell you," he says.

"Maybe," I say. "But I have another question. What will you do for women?"

"Women? What do you mean?"

"It takes these two distinct, antagonistic species to make a human culture."

"Oh," Beck says. "Well, some of the men are married. They'd bring their wives. We have a few women members. Really, our problem would be holding people back, including women of course, once things start to happen and word gets out that BOWS has a refuge."

"This will be good for membership."

"This will be great," Beck admits. "But that's not the point. The point is that survivalism is a mental exercise unless there is something to survive. I think I have the evidence of an impending catastrophe."

"You're sure about this?" I say. "How big a catastrophe?"

"Well, I can only estimate that. Mind you, I'm an amateur and my technology is limited. But I've done some rough calculations, and I'm guesstimating that the asteroid is somewhere in the vicinity of two kilometers in diameter."

"And that would cause a lot of damage?"

"It would end civilization as we know it, no matter where it hits," Beck says gravely.

Beck and I sit outside at a Hardees. I am buying him lunch. It's really too cold to sit outside, but it's a pretty day and our conversation is too private to share with teens, toddlers, moms, construction workers, and lots and lots of old people.

"Isn't this all kind of secret? Why are you telling me?" I ask.

Beck shrugs. "I've told the authorities about my find. I think I told you that. They continue to ignore me, either through incompetence or possibly a cover up. It's an old story, as old as government. But as far as it being a secret and BOWS, well, there are certain—strategies—that I would only share with members, but nothing I've told you is secret. Not really."

"The Coalition didn't know," I say.

"Yes, I'm aware of that," Beck says. "Look, Jason. I don't know what exactly you are up to, or where you intend to take your life, or really much of anything about you. But I trust my gut. My gut says you could be part of the Brotherhood." Beck looks away from me. "I wasn't kidding when I said join BOWS. We need young people, especially those who show some ability to lead, to think creatively. I know that some might think I'm a nut, and easy to dismiss, but I can tell you that I take this seriously, and I hope you will, too."

"What would that mean, being in the Brotherhood?" I ask.

Beck looks back at me, smiles. "You would need to agree first. There's a preliminary pledge," he says.

"Dylan mentioned that," I say. "But what you mean is trust. Not always my strong suit."

"Trust," Beck says, "is the basis of all successful human relationships."

I talk to Davey.

I find him at the only place I know where to look, Our Savior's Assisted Living and Nursing Care Center. I know enough now to catch him before he clocks in.

"Hey," I say. "Supposed to be nice tomorrow. I'm going to take the morning off. What to go on a hike?"

"A hike?" Davey says. He's smoking, getting in his last few puffs before we go into the building and can't smoke again until break. "What do you mean," he says.

"You know, a walk. In the woods. There are parks all over here. There's a state forest just down the highway. I copied a trail map at the library. We could do this 4 mile loop. It goes past some Indian mounds."

"No thanks," Davey says and begins to walk away.

"Wait," I say. "I brought you something." I thought and thought about this. I wanted to bring Davey a book, something entertaining but not condescending, something enlightening, yet approachable. I hand Davey Will Durant's Guide to Plato.

Davey looks at it and laughs.

"It's from my personal collection," I say.

"You are such a nerd," Davey says, hands the book back.

"Seriously, a hike. Wouldn't have to be that long, just a chance to get into the woods."

Davey frowns. "I'm late," he says.

"I can pick you up. What time would be good?"

"Jesus, Audley," he says.

"I'll pick you up at 10 AM," I say. "Where?"

He hesitates. "In front of the drug store, the one on Main," he says and walks away.

I call Phaedra.

I leave a phone message, as she apparently is not eager to talk to me.

"Hi, Phaedra," I say. "It's Jason. Say, I just wanted to take you up on your offer to tour the castle. I'm thinking of Saturday morning, or if that doesn't work, you pick a time." I give her Pam's number.

I call Ned the judge.

"Hey, Ned. A couple of things, I say. "Can you give me Chess Chalmers' number again? I'll give him a call. And then there's a legal thing. Can you see who owns Skaarenor Island? It's in Winter Lake."

"You'd better spell that," Ned says. "But, yes, I could probably take a look into that. What about this asteroid business? Did you talk to the commander?"

"Beck," I say. "He's a pretty reasonable guy. That's how he comes across anyway. What if he's right?"

"We've been wondering the same thing. Bill did some checking around. I have to say we are pretty convinced that a Near Earth Object would be detected by more established astronomy. NASA has a program devoted to tracking NEO's. I don't think BOWS can outdo NASA. No, this is a membership ploy, and it's damned effective."

I talk to Doc.
"Tire rotation," I say. "I'm ready."
"Hammie says you're ready for everything except you suck at wipers," Doc says.
"I'll figure them out," I say. "And I want a raise."
Doc's beard is so thick I can't tell if he's scowling or smiling or just crinkling up his forehead for no reason.
"You've been here like a month. Too soon. You'll just get lazy on me," Doc says.
"Carmen needs work. I've got expenses."
"Who is she?" Doc says.
"My truck. She's become unmuffled."
"Give you a discount, same as always," Doc says. "I'll think about the raise."

I talk to Pam.
"Pam," I say. "I will start buying some groceries." Since I seem to be eating more and more meals with Pam and then sometimes the elusive Dylan, I need to take on my share.
"Thanks," she says. She's making earrings and not paying much attention.
"I could run up to Superior to the co-op."
"Great," she says. "Shit." A wire with beads drops to the table. "Oh," Pam says, looking up. "I washed your running clothes. I think you will find they smell better."
"You didn't have to do that."

Pam smiles a little. "I know." She leans back. "I have an awful kink in my neck and here I am the massage therapist. It's this hunching over when I do earrings. I know better. I could use a little back rub. I'll tell you what to do. Mostly in the shoulder blades."

"Um, okay," I say.

She turns her back toward me, points. "Press here with your thumbs."

I press, gingerly. Her back is a bit fleshy. There's bulge around her bra strap, which must be 3 inches wide. God knows how many hooks are on it. I do what she says, pressing, rubbing, over her tee shirt. After a maybe five minutes, I say, "Okay, I bet that will do it."

"I do hour-long massages," Pam says. "Sometimes I spend the entire time on the rhomboids and trapezius muscles."

"You know your anatomy," I say, dropping my hands from her back.

"I'm certified," Pam says. She turns. "I think I owe you a massage. That was part of the deal."

I take Davey to the Brule River State Forest. It's further than I thought it would be and we ride in Carmen mostly in awkward silence. At least I think it's awkward. Davey looks out the window, his head turned away from me.

"I brought some lunch," I tell Davey, shouldering a small pack I borrowed from Dylan's room.

"Aren't you the boy scout," Davey says.

We choose a trail and walk. More silence. Finally Davey says, "Okay, what is it that you want to know? I assume that's why we are here. Either that or you plan to push me off a cliff or something."

255

"I don't suppose I'm an insurance beneficiary?" I ask.

"No," Davey says.

"Okay, scratch the cliff idea," I say.

We come to a narrow plank bridge over a trickle in a ravine. Davy sits, dangles his legs. "I'm not in shape for this," he says, and lights a cigarette. We've been walking maybe ten minutes.

"Pretty," he says, looking up the ravine. Some of the trees are bare now, but the oaks glow with red in the bright overcast. We can hear the breeze high in the trees but it's otherwise quiet. No birds. No bugs, just a soft gurgle from the steam.

Davey tosses his butt into a little pool under the bridge, where it turns in lazy circles. I have an overwhelming urge to go fish it out. Davey lights another. He blows smoke straight up, watches it.

"I bet you want to know what we did after you checked out," Davey says.

"I am curious," I say.

Davey's Story

We worked our way east after we left you. Took freight trains most of the time, but also did some hitching and a lot of walking. It took a long time and we got wet and hungry a few times, but nothing bad happened. We ended up in Maryland. Phaedra was going home, though I didn't know that. She took me to this humongous house. It was white, three stories, had columns like in Gone with the Wind. It was on a small river that emptied into Chesapeake Bay. We canoed to the Bay once. The house could've used a little work here and there. Most of it was built in like 1820 or something. The people who built it had slaves, and there are a few remains of what looked like a line of chicken coops but Phaedra said they were slave quarters. Don't know if that's true.

We took a few trips, but always ended up going back to Maryland, to that old house. Her mom lived there. They had this strange relationship, nothing like I'd ever seen. They didn't joke around or show any affection or, well, you know, nothing like our families. Well, at least my family. They talked in this formal way. May I suggest the eggs this morning? Shall we visit the garden today? Her mother never used Phaedra's name, hardly looked at her. Phaedra did the same. Her mother had this pinched look. Sour. Kind of miserable.

But that house. I got to know it. Amazing. Elegant. Very airy and spare and with windows with wavy glass, and it all smelled of just old, like old wood and old fires and old furniture. We stayed in a building on the property, not even in the house, a kind of apartment above what used to be a stable. This was also a very cool building, with lots of brick and a little tower on top with a weather vane, and a courtyard in the middle. Phaedra was real quiet then. I was bored to death half the time and really wanted to go home, but every time it came right down to it, to my actually leaving, Phaedra would kind of wake up and we'd do something cool and she'd want me to stay. It went on like this for a year, through a humid, hot summer, through a nice fall, with a near miss from a hurricane, through the winter and a warm, wet spring. I watched a lot of TV. Got good at Jeopardy.

But my brain was dying. I could feel it. I finally convinced Phaedra that I was serious about moving on.

That's when she bought the bike, the Harley Sportster. She just went out and bought it.

Whole time I was there, her mom, she wouldn't say a word to me. Looked right past me, like I didn't exist. Didn't hear me any more than she saw me. I talked to the workers who came and went, fixing up the house and gardens, that sort of thing. They told me the family had been in the house since it was built. Not that it hadn't changed hands a lot, and into married-in families, not an unbroken string with the same last name. But there was a thread that connected everyone who'd ever lived there, and they still had a lot of acreage, and there was still money.

Phaedra, just like when she was with us—I don't know if you remember—just always seemed to have money. Cash. Well, all she had to do was get to a bank, anywhere, and she could walk out with money. I don't know how that works. I'm an idiot on that. Haven't had any money of my own to speak of, so don't know how rich people handle their money. I still don't.

So Phaedra had this fund, where the older she got, the more money she could get her hands on. She's over thirty now you know, and that's when she got her pot of gold, with that birthday.

But back to leaving. Then it was me that got cold feet. I got used to doing nothing, and I drank a lot. A lot. What else was there to do, I'd say. And as time went by, I just got more disconnected and less willing to go back to where I started and eventually didn't want to leave at all. In fact, I'd get these attacks if I went too far from the estate. Like I couldn't breathe and my heart would pound.

Phaedra wanted me to see someone. Like she was. Ever since we got there, she'd have these appointments with a therapist guy who come right out to the house. Sometimes I'd hear her shout or cry or go into a cussing rage. It would all come from a room in the big house. That's where she met the therapist. A study, with lots of books and big doors that opened onto a stone patio, with stone benches, and a trellis with vines over the top.

But I wouldn't talk to anyone. Figured I just needed to tough it out. Maybe drink it away. That actually did help, beer and lots of it.

You want a cigarette? You sure? Audley, you are such a, hell, I don't know, wimp isn't strong enough, or weird enough.

Anyway, Phaedra got this bike. I couldn't ride it worth shit because as soon as I got away from the estate, I'd get these attacks. So Phaedra bought the sidecar and I rode along, with my heart thumping and hanging on 'til my fingers went numb and I couldn't catch my breath, and we'd tear along these roads around the Bay.

I got a dog. Some kind of retriever, white and brown, long nose, straight back. He wasn't a pup, just found him on the road one day and I kept him. Didn't advertise or anything. Wondered whose dog I'd stolen, or if he was a stray. He was a great dog and when we finally left, it just broke my heart to leave him. Do you believe that? Broke my heart. Here I run off from home, do all this shit, and the only thing that really gets to me is leaving this dog. Shit.

We didn't get along so good, Phaedra and me, at the house. She was so bitchy there. Explosive. Either mad as hell or oozy with baby talk to me, like I was a stuffed animal. We kind of got into, well, I won't tell you about that.

So Phaedra has a roll of cash the size of a softball and she says we are off. Right now. So I pack a few things and we get into the bike and off we go. She's crying like a baby for two hours. Most of my stuff is back in the stables and it's still there if no one threw it away. Haven't been back there. That was five, six years ago.

What next. Jesus. We went all over the place. For like two years, we just went all over the place. To a lot of Harley rallies. Started to get to know some people. Phaedra and me, we got along great for a lot of that time. She had her meltdowns. So did I. We had our bad habits and that got us into trouble. But stupid as it sounds, we had each other and we had no boundaries between us. Nothing. We were like one person.

What, you saw us in a magazine? The Winter Lake rally? No shit. That is so funny. And you came looking? That is so fucked up. You know that, right? You are so fucked up.

That damn dog. I still think about him. If I had any money, I'd go find him. Probably long dead.

Christ. Whatever. Anyway, all this time we are just making up names, doing everything with cash. Phaedra just needs to get to a bank once in a while and reload. I didn't even have a driver's license. Did you know that? I left without my driver's license. Still don't have one. I ride my fricking bike to work or catch a ride with someone. Winter? I haven't worked in winter. I hibernate, like a bear. Watch a lot of movies. Do some odd jobs for the pharmacy. My room is right above them, where you picked me up. Got this room upstairs. Shared bath, which I totally hate. Good price though. Got one big radiator, it's like half my wall. Hotter than a motherfucker in winter in that room. Makes me sleepy. It all comes together.

Lived in Colorado in this cabin on and off for a couple of years. With Phaedra. 'Til she dumped me, never touched another woman. Never even touched one. Phaedra said the cabin belonged to her family. Near Buena Vista. Beautiful but high and cold. Don't know if that was her cabin or she just picked one out. No one showed up though. Never knew with her, what was bullshit and what wasn't. Still don't.

We had a car then. Rustbucket Corolla. Drove all around the southwest. Then Phaedra got bit by some poisonous bug and that was the end of that, the whole west. She was done with it. I think she got stung by a bee or a wasp and had a reaction but she was sure it was a scorpion or black widow or something. She did get pretty sick. She always is getting colds and such. Not me. Never get sick. I smoke and drink and whatever. Never get sick. It's when I say something like that, that's when like my mom or dad just flash in my head, like they would be proud that I never get sick. Think about them every day. Never going back, not until I get myself together. Got close, oh, ten thousand times. Close. Never called. Phaedra didn't care. She'd say call or don't call, didn't matter to her. But I didn't.

So, is this pathetic enough for you? Enjoying this? Is this what you hoped for? Jason stays and goes to school. Miller goes off and... Whatever.

Winter Lake? Phaedra liked it here. We wandered through Wisconsin like five times. Went to rallies.

Then we pretty much moved here, I don't know, a little over a year ago. Then she went off the deep end. Like she wanted a different life. But what a weird choice. I mean, I could see going back and being baroness of the manor or whatever, you know mistress of the estate. But this? She hit thirty. Told you that. She's got real money now. Doesn't need anyone or anything. Doesn't need to work. She can flip off the world. And what does she do? Dumps me. Just fucking dumps me, and then becomes like a Martha Stewart looking realtor. A realtor. I mean what the fuck.

Chapter 24

"You know what I'd like to do?" Davey stands up, stretches, starts walking back the way we came. "I'd like to toss a baseball around, or a football, or even a Frisbee. You up for that?"

"Sure," I say.

We drive back. Davey is more talkative, tells me about some of his favorite inmates at the nursing home, those who never sleep, those who think he's someone he's not, those who just want to fade away, says he'd rather be tossed in a bonfire than placed in a nursing home.

I drop him off in front of the pharmacy. He doesn't say a word, just gets out of the truck and walks away.

Davey never once asked about me, about my family. He's in his own world and I don't think I'd want to be in it.

I stand in front of the mirror. Don't do that much. It makes me start talking to myself, which I don't think is a good habit, psychologically. I say things like Jason, my man, you need to get your shit together. Or, what an attractive beard you have. But here I stand, not talking, wondering if that's me, this old man. I found a grey hair. Just one. Is it a harbinger? Am I going grey? I saw these pictures of a guy who survived the sinking of the Titanic. He was a steward. Comes off the lifeboat with dark hair. Six months later, he's totally white, even his moustache. I could just shave my head, even though I like that I have hair again. I'm done with buzz cuts. Shave it, grow a long, pointy goatee, the heavy metal look. Stick with the neat little beard, I tell myself. Gives the illusion of maturity. I think of many come-backs, but the phone rings and Pam yells that it's for me.

"Hello, Phaedra," I say.

"Jasmine," she says. "You really want to see the castle?"

Work is beginning to get in the way of things. It's hard to get up at 5 AM and still be alive at 10 PM. Likewise, it's hard to get anything done in the mornings when you are in an oil pit. This may not be my calling. Phaedra wants to go to Skaarenor Island in the morning, when the realty business is slow. She needs afternoons and evenings. And Saturdays and Sundays. We finally settle on a couple of hours over dinnertime, when potential customers are otherwise occupied. But that is a week away. She makes a point of telling me how busy she is, how hectic it all is.

After work, I take Carmen to the marshy park. It's not a popular spot. I bring a book and my take away from Dairy Queen. But I find it hard to read. For one thing, it's a warm, sunny day, with dry air and a smell of fall leaves, a hint of lake smell, that thick, froggy odor lakes get late in the season. I'm such an expert. This is my first fall near a lake. The day reminds me of the woods where I grew up. But we had more of a clover smell, and a corn in the field smell, and a whiff of pig. I grew up in a suburb that bordered the rural, an outpost of sprawl in a pastoral landscape. From the air, it probably looked like dandruff on an agricultural scalp.

So I absorb the day. It's nice to be off at 2 PM, to have a book, and to have a milkshake. I put down Carmen's tailgate and sit there, for the slightly elevated view of the swamp and the lake.

Can't read. I think about Davey. I have a dilemma. I want to call the Miller's, really badly. Tell them I know where they can find their son. Why wouldn't I? But then, why would I? Davey clearly does not want this, and I think he will contact them, someday. He needs to have more going on than now, something to show for his absence, something to help balance his choices.

I also think about Chess. I'd called him. It took a lot of willpower on my part.

"Jakers," Chess says. "Good to hear from you."

"How are things going?" I ask.

"Great, great," Chess says. "Tour's all over, but I guess you know that. Another big season for Chess Chalmers. I was back at the tree farm for a while, nailing things down. Good year, knock on wood. Get it?"

"Yeah, that's a good one," I say.

"Me, Miles and Bob, we been doing some club work. Lounge type stuff, over at some of the motels you see along I-94 and I-90. One nighters, mostly."

"What were you guys called?" I ask.

"Chess Chalmers," Chess says.

We talk about a few trivial things, like Chess lining things up for next year, even the weather.

"Say, I don't suppose you'd like to do some drumming next summer?" Chess asks. "I know you've gotten into this security guard thing, and that is probably a year-round gig."

"Not sure what I'm doing next summer," I say.

"Well, keep it in mind." Chess sounds ready to hang up.

"Hey," I say. "What about Lark and Rusty? How are things going?"

There's silence for a moment. Then Chess says, "Those are dark topics, Jack. Dark topics. Them kids lost their minds. It was Rusty's fault. Lark is so impressionable. Such a sweet girl. You probably noticed that. Such a simple kid. So easy to lead astray."

"Yeah," I say. "Real uncomplicated."

"Right-o," Chess says. "So Rusty makes all kinds of promises and off they go, and they end up with the daydream that they can get them some money and run off to god knows where, and I guess that's how it all started. And now this legal mess. The law is a jealous mistress, Jake. Once you're into her bosom, she don't let go. And blind lady justice, she's holding Lark close and tight. Her previous troubles aren't helping much."

I can't help but ask. "What previous troubles?"

"Oh, why I took Lark out on the road. She had this thing about her uncle. Some kind of deal. Mad as hell at him. Said she wanted to kill him. Told that to near everyone. Figured it was better to get her out of town."

"Why did she hate him?" I ask.

"Well, that's family business, Jack. Family business. He maybe done something stupid. Maybe he didn't. I'm not saying. He might've got a little out of line. He might not of. I'm not saying. Lark, she might have had a few, um, health problems afterwards. She might not of. Again, I'm not saying."

"But robbing a casino," I say. "That didn't seem like something they would do."

"Who knows what the darkness in the human heart can... heck, that's a good line. I'm going to write that down. You got a darkness in your human heart."

"Catchy," I say. "What do you think will happen to them?"

"Oh, I've been working with a lawyer. Real buckaroo barracuda. That's for Lark. Pleading something like insanity. Probably plea bargain. Getting close to that. She'll get a few years over at the women's farm."

"Rusty?"

"That pooch is screwed in my opinion. Though his parents, they got some bucks. Got a history though, some convictions. Burglary when he was kid. Who knows. Too bad. He's a hell of a guitar player."

"Ned said you wanted to talk to me," I say.

"Yeah, yeah. Wanted to shoot the shit. You know, bandmates," Chess says. "Oh, one other little thing. Now don't take this wrong, Jack-o, but we had a gentleman's agreement. I believe we did shake hands. And I believe you said you was going to play drums for the whole tour. And that isn't how it turned out. Now I know we had stormy water go under that bridge, and I don't want no darkness of the heart going between us, but you don't get any money."

"I don't? Nothing? After all I did?" I say, baiting him. I can't help it.

"Well, Jake, business is business, and there ain't no business like show business. Especially when it comes to not getting your money. I guess you got to learn that. I guess you can take this as a lesson, a lesson from Chess Chalmers about the music business."

"Gee, Chess," I say. "The music business is a jealous mistress."

"That she is," Chess says. "And look at it this way. I hear you might get a little something from the casino, for getting yourself shot. Well, Lark, she launched that bullet, fired as a warning. You had the bum luck to be in the path of the ricochet. So, in a way, the Chess Chalmer's band has supplied you with money, and you didn't even have to drum for it."

"I guess you're right," I say.

"Well, you just keep your nose clean and keep working on those drums, as you do need it. And think about next summer. Maybe you can follow through and get through a tour. I know they're hard. Oh hell, how I know. You learned a thing or two from Chess. Just so I don't see you acing me out on the marquee, Jake what's-his-name sitting up there above old Chess." Chess laughs. "Not likely," he adds.

"Nope," I say. "Not likely."

"Yeah, real not likely," Chess says. "Keep in touch there, Jake. You're a good kid. If I can do something for you, you let me know. Once Chess says you're a friend, you're always a friend. Then we say our goodbyes."

Chapter 25

It's 5 AM and chilly in the house. I'm getting my breakfast ready, a bowl of Fruit Loops, and making coffee. Dylan comes home.

"Wow," I say. "That was a long shift."

"Sixteen hours," he says and falls into a chair at the kitchen table.

"Can I get you something to eat? Like toast?"

"Sure," he says. "Frickin' Andrew is supposed to come at one o'clock. Didn't show up until quarter to five. I couldn't just leave the place," Dylan says.

"Jam?" I say. Dylan nods, puts his head down on the table. He tells me a bit about his shift. It's not very interesting. "I can't keep doing this for minimum wage," he mumbles.

Pam comes in, clutching her robe around her. It's short, like a kid's robe, and she's got pale legs from mid-thigh down.

"I heard the talking," she says blearily. "Is everything okay?"

"Making toast," I say.

Pam sits next to Dylan, slouches in the chair and closes her eyes. Dylan starts to snore softly.

"Want Dylan's toast?" I ask Pam.

"Sure," she says. I pour coffee. It overpowers the hint of morning breath in the air.

"What?" Dylan says, startling.

"Stay calm," I say. "Something's coming."

"What?" Dylan says, head still down.

"Tidal wave of balls," I say.

"Oh, god," Dylan says.

"That's gross," Pam says.

I go to work. Slowing down. I guess everyone has winterized their cars. Hammie and I have time to sit and drink coffee. Eagle Stouthammer, that's his full name.

"Are you Native American?" I ask him. He looks it, a little. Big, strong, dark hair in a ponytail.

"Nope," he says. "German. My mother named us all after birds. Could be worse. My brother is Osprey."

"Not true," I say.

"True," Hammie says. My little brother, he's called Chickenhawk."

"I knew a Lark," I say.

"Two sisters. Robin. She's the lucky one. And Swallow."

"No way."

"Way," Hammie says. "My mom's nuts. Runs in the family. My sister named her dog Blue Footed Booby."

"Don't believe you," I say.

Hammie laughs. "I'm part Menominee. Last name is German, though. I'm a hybrid."

I like this guy.

After work, I clean up and head for JJ Realty. Phaedra is going to show me the castle.

"I'll drive," she says, eyeing Carmen.

We get to the private dock. Phaedra has a canoe. She's in jeans, sweater and an anaorak. Looks expensive.

"You go in the bow," she says. "I'll steer."

It's a super lightweight canoe, very unsteady. I can see the shadow of the water right through the sides as I make my way forward. She hands me a paddle. It's got a bent, swept-back sort of design.

"Hold it the other way," she says, getting in quickly and easily.

"This thing is weird," I say, looking at the paddle.

"Paddle on your left," Phaedra says, and we push off from the dock.

It seems like a long way to the island.

"Don't paddle so hard," she says. "You're screwing up my steering."

"Okay," I say. There's a breeze, but the water remains calm. Above, a rapid mix of clouds and sun, like a light blinking on and off. We get to the island, turn into a small bay. Doesn't look like a place to land to me. The shore is rocky and steep, with branches hanging down.

Phaedra steers us into a narrow channel at the end of the bay, a sharp right turn. It brings us to a landing, tree-lined and sandy. The canoe glides in gently.

"Get out and pull us up," Phaedra says. It's so lightweight that I almost dump her. Phaedra steps on the sand, grabs the canoe and lifts it over her head.

"Grab the paddles," she says. I follow her up a path. She puts the canoe down gently in a grassy clearing. I can see the castle, straight ahead, up a steep slope.

What I read didn't do it justice. It doesn't look squat or unbalanced when you're next to it. It's impressive.

"Local limestone," Phaedra says, touching the rough stone walls. Big, grey blocks, neatly laid, with scarcely a need for mortar. The tower is at the opposite end. It's tall, square, massive, with crenellations at the top. The first floor windows are high above us, large, rectangular, with stone sills. The windows on the second floor are smaller, in pairs, with gothic arches. Winter Lake runs east to west. The island runs north to south, tapered on either end. We stand at the northeast corner of the building. The trees around us are younger than those by the lakeshore.

"All this was cleared," Phaedra says. "These pines grew up in the last twenty years or so. I like them."

The trees crowd the walls and we take a narrow path. Pine needles underfoot are soft and fragrant. We walk in the direction of the tower.

"I thought all the windows were broken," I say.

"I've had them repaired. I've been busy. You'll see," Phaedra says.

We stop in front of the main entrance, a deeply recessed archway, and a massive wood door, trimmed with wrought iron.

"Pretty cool, huh?" Phaedra says.

I agree. The stonework around the archway is impressive, with a vaulted space above us. Phaedra lifts a latch and pushes the wood door. Inside is a short, unlighted passage and another large door, with a more traditional lock.

"In a medieval castle, this passage would be long. There'd be murder holes above, where defenders could rain arrows or boiling oil on attackers," I say.

"I know," Phaedra says. She unlocks the inner door.

We enter a large entrance hall. Ahead of us is a wide wood staircase that splits at the first landing, with flights continuing up on both left and right. It's tall, this space, a full two stories. Very few windows, so it's dim and hard to see the details.

From what Dylan said, I expected devastation. I've read about what American robber barons did to European castles in the late 1800's and early 1900's. They bought them and stripped them clean, paneling, banisters, fireplaces, even the flooring, leaving stone shells, like skeletons. I expected to see the same.

"All the fixtures were gone," Phaedra says. "And most of the wiring. All the stained glass was gone or broken. Lots of water damage, and lots of animals making their homes. Lots of vandalism. Initials in the woodwork, broken up sinks and toilets. Holes in walls. A lot of beer cans."

"Bullet holes?" I ask.

"Yeah," she says, "here and there. Random pieces of clothing, moldy blankets, condoms. Very nice."

"You live here?" I ask.

"Sometimes," she says.

"Ghosts?" I ask.

"Probably," she says.

Phaedra points right. "Great hall," she says, then points left. "Drawing room, music room, library. Behind the stairway is the kitchen and pantries. Big cellars below us. Two stories above us."

"Two?" I say.

"Second floor with the pairs of windows. Then there's an attic level. You'll see."

No creaks as we walk across the wide boards of the floor. We enter the Great Hall. Windows run down the right side, and there are more windows at the far end. Half way down the left side is the giant fireplace I saw in the photo. The room is paneled in dark wood, has a beamed ceiling, but is otherwise empty. Our footsteps echo as we walk.

"Haven't done too much here. Just basic repairs," Phaedra says.

"How long have you owned this?" I say.

"Almost a year."

"No one is working on it now?"

"No," she says. "I'm thinking about what I want to do next."

We walk out of the hall.

"There used to be more woodwork in here. Some built-in cupboards, moldings, tracery. It's all gone, and probably decorates homes in Winter Lake."

It's dead quiet—the location, the walls, emptiness. An eerie feeling. It's stale, still air, smelling of musk and wood, and something else.

"What's that kind of sharp smell," I ask.

"Coal," Phaedra says. "The place was heated with coal. Even burned it in the fireplaces."

"Hot water heat? Radiators?" I ask.

"All gone," Phaedra says. "Even the boiler."

We walk to the left of the entrance hall, through a broad archway. The drawing and music rooms are just big, empty spaces. In the library, there are a few bookcases lining the walls, and lots of evidence where the others used to be. From the library, you can pass into the rear of the building, where we find a couple of stripped bathrooms, and a devastated kitchen, and lots of little rooms for storage.

"No dining room?" I ask.

"Great Hall," Phaedra says. "Watch this." She follows a passage from the kitchen area, opens a door at the end. We are in the Great Hall. The door blends perfectly with the paneling.

"Where's the tower?" I ask.

"You get to it from the second floor." We walk up narrow, squeaky back stairs that lead to a hallway that runs along the back of the building. It's lined with windows, and I can see the rear of the castle for the first time. I can see that it's a shallow "U" shape, with a courtyard in the middle, enclosed by a high stone wall. The basic footprint of the whole castle is a large rectangle. You can only see the courtyard from above. The courtyard looks dark and shaded and its stone paving seems clean and undamaged.

Phaedra stands next to me. "Too dark in there for most plants. It was easy to restore. Anything stone here, it's almost like new."

We wander among identical bedrooms, small by modern standards. Each has a narrow fireplace. Here and there are destroyed bathrooms, linen closets. At the south end is a much larger room, with windows on two sides, and in the corner, an entrance to the tower.

"Master suite," Phaedra stays. "The bathroom is in the tower, but it goes on from there."

No windows in this bathroom, but I can make out the remains of the sink and toilet.

"All the bathtubs are gone," Phaedra says.

"Bet they were big, clawfoot tubs," I say.

"Look," she says. In the corner is an iron spiral stairway. We go up.

"Private study, I suppose," Phaedra says. We are in the third floor of the tower. This has windows, with great views of the island and the lake. There's another spiral stair. It goes to the tower roof.

"This is amazing," I say. We stand high above the trees, looking through the gaps in the crenellations, at a 360 degree panorama of Winter Lake and Skaarenor Island. The water is flat, grey, empty.

The rest of the castle is beneath us. I see that you can walk along the perimeter of the roof, behind a parapet, and a sort of A-frame structure runs down the center of the roof, with a few dormer windows.

"Servant's quarters," Phaedra says.

"How do you get on the roof?" I ask.

She points to a door on the end of the servant's quarters. "You get up there from some back stairs."

It's cold on the tower, so we go back down to the study.

"Thanks," I say. "This place is awesome."

"You're welcome," she says and sits cross-legged under a window. "Parquet," she says, running her hand over the floor. I sit across from her.

"Why?" I ask. "What will you do with this?"

Phaedra shrugs. "I have some ideas for Castle Jones. That's what I call it. Thought I'd develop it into a hotel or a center or something. I might just live here."

"Not easy to buy groceries," I say.

"Too bad the bridge burned," she says. "Or maybe not. Who knows what would be left of this place if people could drive to it."

We sit in silence for a minute or two. I get up and look out the window.

"You talked to Jeff," she says.

"Davey? Yeah," I say.

"About our time together?"

"Yeah, among other things," I say.

"What did he say?"

I'm not sure what to say, so I don't say anything.

"He didn't want you to tell me?" she asks.

"I think not," I say.

"Want to hear my side of it?"

"I do," I say, and sit back down.

Phaedra's Story

After we left you, it was great. Just the two of us. What I always thought it should be like, travelling, wandering, but not alone. Someone I could talk to, someone who liked this life. That lasted for awhile, weeks. But he began to get quiet at some point, kind of go downhill. I couldn't figure it out. Kept asking him what he wanted to do, what was wrong, all that kind of thing. I thought maybe he needed a break from just bumming around.

But where to go? So I just headed us east and we went, well, we went home. To where I grew up.

I hate that place. Bad things happened there. My mother still lives there, an old dump of a place. We can barely talk to each other, my mother and I. There was this hovel of an outbuilding and Davey and I stayed there. At least it had electricity, which is more than I can say for this castle.

Davey got weirder and weirder. I actually got him into therapy, was worried about him. It was some guy my mother knew. Hated to go through her, but I didn't know what else to do. Davey and this guy would talk and I could hear the yelling and crying and all kinds of things, even across the yard. I'd sit in the hovel and block my ears, wondering what I'd gotten us into. Then Davey found this dog, and that really cheered him up. Could care less about me, but he loved that dog.

Then I got us a Harley. A Harley. Can you imagine me on a Harley? I didn't know a thing about them. Went to this shop and they sold me a used one, a Sportster. Turned out to be a great bike, like a friend. Thought it would kind of wake Davey up. But he got terribly agoraphobic. Couldn't leave the house without freaking out. I pictured us on this bike with Davey driving, me on the back, hair blowing in the wind, laughing, all that crap. Only way I could get him out was to buy a sidecar, do all the driving, while he sat petrified, with a death grip on the sides.

I told him to go home. Said I'd take him there. I really didn't know what to do with him. It was like I had a baby on my hands, one that drank a lot of beer and was afraid of almost everything.

Finally, he agreed, and we took off on the bike. And then, somehow, he began to loosen up, to unwind, and we began to have fun again. He did have his relapses. I found it hard to totally trust him, know what I mean? Didn't know each day who he'd be.

We stopped at a Harley rally in Arkansas. Davey just loved it, so we started hopping around from rally to rally. Made up silly names for ourselves, crazy stories about who we were and where we were going. We stayed in little motels, ate at diners, hiked some parks, kept south in the winter. It was great, I won't lie, even with his moods.

He kept talking about mountains, so I took him to Colorado. I knew one area there. My family has a cabin. Belongs to some relative, and she's old as time, so figured we could stay there. Very simple cabin. But very marketable, just outside of Buena Vista, and it had great views and a mountain stream twenty feet away. I could turn that over for a lot of money. Anyway, we stayed there for a long time. It went pretty well. I got a job in town, waiting tables. Davey started getting real attached to that location and his panic attacks began to return whenever he went to town. Again, I told him he had to go home, at least talk to his folks. He wouldn't hear of it.

I decided we needed to get out on the road again. That had worked so well before. Thought it was worth a chance. But it didn't work so well this time. I was trying to take him home, sort of indirectly. I was more or less going to go to Illinois by the back door, come from Wisconsin. We'd had some good times there. Some nice rallies, riding along Lake Michigan, cruising around Madison. But we didn't get too far. He totally fell apart right here, in Winter Lake. We both had liked this place. We were here for a rally.

What, you have our pictures in the magazine? How funny is that. I have it, too, you know. It's in the office.

But anyway, here we were in Winter Lake and I had had enough of Davey. Sorry. I know it sounds awful, but I'd had it. So I told him to get some help, go home, whatever. Gave him some money, and I still do from time to time. Stupid. I'm just enabling him.

Why'd I stay around here? I worry about him. I don't want to be with him. I just worry. I want him to go home, do something.

Realty? It's something to do, a new role for me. I took the classes and got a license. I don't know why. And then I saw this place, the inside. It came on the market and I snapped it up before it even made the listing. It's unique, so there's always a market.

Me? No, I'm totally fine. Eat well, plenty of fresh air and exercise. Never felt better.

You know, it really bothered me that you showed up. I kind of panicked. I'd gotten used how things are, with Davey and his issues, but suddenly I saw it through someone else's eyes. It looked ugly to me and I didn't want to be judged. I still don't know why you tracked us down. Really, it's a little creepy, I don't care what you say. So I gave you that money, just to go away. And also to do something. You could say I'm tired of wasted people. Keep it. Keep the money. Be something. Do something. I don't care what.

No, I'm not talking about that. My finances are my own business.

No, I don't know if I'll stay here, in Winter Lake. Probably not. It's not like me to stay, especially in a place like this where everyone knows everything about everybody. Or they think they do. They don't know me. Nobody does, not you, or Davey, or even my mother.

Yes, smartass, I know me, I know me quite well.

So that's the story. You could say it's just young love gone wrong.

Chapter 26

Two cold and rainy days later, I come home from work to find a note from Pam. Call Ned RIGHT AWAY. The last two words are underlined twice.

I call Ned.

"Glad you called," Ned says. "I have some interesting news. I took a look at your castle, from the legal side. In fact, that's about all I've been doing for the last week. You need a little history before I go into this."

"I've read about Adolphus Skaarenor," I say.

"That may be, but I doubt you know the whole story," Ned says. "Adolphus had seven daughters. Four married, two never did, and one ran away when she was 17. The black sheep of the family. She actually became one of the few female jazz musicians in New York, for that time anyway. When Adolphus died, he left all his worldly property to his wife, who died just a few years later. It all went to the daughters then. There wasn't much, other than the island and some stock. The two unmarried daughters stayed on the island until they lost everything in the 1929 market crash. They were able to hang on for a couple of years, but finally needed to sell the property to survive. Neither had a job, you see. The daughters who married followed their husbands to bigger cities. These Skaarenor girls were prize catches at the time. Educated, rich, very pretty. And they all left, all except one. She married one of the mill managers and stayed in Winter Lake. Her father built a house for her, was very close to this couple. Her descendants are still in the area, and we will get to that later.

"Great," I say. "I'd like to meet them."

"No, you don't," Ned says. "But let me continue. When the two unmarried sisters sold the property, it was a distress sale. New owners got it for a song. But there was a problem, one that no one caught at the time, and in fact, no one caught until very recently. Six daughters signed the deed after the sale, releasing their interest. One daughter did not, the one in Winter Lake. I don't know if it was sloppy work or some personal issue, but no one challenged it at the time, and the title has been clouded ever since. And the property has been sold several times since then, all with bad title. A year ago, more or less, an outfit called C'est La Vie LLC bought the property from the Winter Lake State Bank. The bank owned the property as a result of a loan forfeiture, a situation that dragged on for some time, before the bank finally decided to dispose of the island."

"The previous owner had some kind of home for vets, right?" I say.

"Sad cases. They started it after WWII. Not all vets who came back were ready for society. The ones who lived on Skaarenor Island had major issues, post-traumatic stress syndrome we'd say now. But these poor guys had it really bad. The place housed a few Korean War vets and even some Viet Nam vets and then it slowly went under. The bank, it's a local outfit, didn't want to displace the men living there, so that's why it dragged on so long, though I guess the property sat empty for quite a while."

"I've been out there," I say. "It pretty much got stripped of anything worth money, but it's still solid as a rock. Who is this C'est La Vie company?"

"An LLC, limited liability corporation, could be anything. An individual, a group. Probably some group that saw this as a business opportunity. You say your friend bought it? Why don't you ask her?"

"I will," I say.

"And here's where it gets interesting. Stay with me, now. You mentioned BOWS wants this property, wants to turn it into a stronghold for this supposed asteroid strike. Well, they may have found a way to get their hands on it, or at least take partial control."

"How?"

"They found a descendant, a grandchild of the daughter who never signed the deed. Right there in Winter Lake. In a lot of states, that interest in the property would have been extinguished. Sort of a statute of limitations. Not Wisconsin—the interest never dies. BOWS is working with the descendant and has filed motions to challenge the sale to the LLC, to give the descendant his minority interest, to give him some say in the use of the property."

"They can do that? It can't be much of a share, right?" I ask.

"I'm calculating that it's about 1/64, given the size of the families and three generations since the will. But that doesn't matter. An interest is an interest. And the person with the minority interest can cause all sorts of problems."

"Can't she just buy him out?"

"Not if he doesn't want to," Ned says. "Eventually, your friend could go to court and force a partition, meaning there'd be an appraisal and a forced buy out, but this could take a long time, and the appraisal could be controversial. She's got a big problem."

"So, who's this descendant?" I ask.

"His name is Peter Duncan," Ned says.

"Oh no," I say.

"You know him?"

"Yes," I say. "I live in his wife's house."

Ned and I talk this over for a long time. My ear gets tired, as Ned tends to talk very loudly on the phone. I don't like long phone calls. I get restless, even if I'm interested. I pace around Pam's small house, finally turn on the TV without the sound.

"I think I can speak for the Coalition when I say that we would prefer that BOWS not get the island," Ned says. "It would be an amazing recruitment tool. It would put us out of business."

"This Pete is a member of BOWS," I say.

"Not surprised," Ned says. "I don't know what kind of legal help your friend has, or what her financial situation is, but I think the Coalition could be of some help, quietly."

"Quietly?"

"We'd prefer not to be in a highly visible pitched battle over this property. But we are resourceful, as I think you know. And we know a lot of people, and I'm not the only lawyer in the group. We could be of some assistance."

"What would fix it, from my friend's point of view?"

"A buy out, and Peter Duncan signing a warranty deed. This would end his minority interest," Ned says. He laughs, "God, I used to love these kinds of cases when they came to my courtroom. The stories. The drama. Beats the hell out of third DWI's and check kiting."

Dylan makes a rare appearance for dinner, and I can't help but tell Pam and Dylan about the minority interest.

"Holy crap," Pam says. "You mean Pete might be rich?"

"Well, that's not exactly my point," I say. "I suppose he could end up with some money."

Pam beams. "That's great news," she says. "I can't wait to get divorced."

It takes me a while to track Phaedra down, but I do. I summarize what Ned told me.

"I know," she says.

"You heard from your lawyers?"

"Yeah," she says. "Big firm in Chicago. I think they are on this. Already tried to buy the guy out. He said no. He wants to share control of the island."

"Are you going to let him?"

"No," Phaedra says. "I don't want to do anything for him. I don't even want to give him money now, though my lawyers say I should just offer him more. I'm not made of money, you know."

"You seem to be."

"I'm not. I put almost everything into buying this island. Used cash," she laughs. "Because I used cash, I didn't need to buy title insurance, so I'm screwed over this title stuff. And here I'm a realtor."

"Can't you force a—something?" I say.

She sighs. "I guess so. Look, I just don't want to deal with this right now. What money I have needs to go into the castle, or I can't make any money off of this. I need to put money in to get money out. I can't afford to buy off this jerk. He's asking for a small fortune. And if we get an appraisal, after this work I've been doing on it, it'll probably come out his way. Especially since I'm an outsider here. A foreigner. You should see how they treat my Chicago lawyers."

"This is Wisconsin, not Illinois. Can they practice law here?"

"Oh, look how smart you are. No," she says with exaggeration, "Of course they can. They are licensed in Wisconsin as well. Give me a little credit."

"So, what happens next?" I say after a pause where Phaedra puts pens in her desk drawer and takes them back out.

"I don't know," she says. "I might just bolt. I'm getting tired of this gig."

I tell her about BOWS and the asteroid and the Coalition, and all that stuff. She listens without expression.

"You are like the plague," she says.

"Don't I know it."

Phaedra rubs her face. "I'm going to live on the island, full-time," she says. "Let them come and talk to me. Or maybe I won't talk to anyone. Be the crazy lady in the haunted castle. I don't know."

"You should get a lot of cats," I suggest. "Wear your clothes inside out."

"Great ideas, Jason," she says. "Thanks."

I invite Beck to dinner at Dairy Queen. He agrees.

"We are going to close for the season," says the young man behind the counter. "Next weekend is it. What are you going to do for food?"

"I don't know," I say. "This is hard news."

Beck and I sit at one of the three indoor tables. Too chilly to sit outside, and it gets dark now awfully early.

"I'd like to talk about the castle," I tell Beck.

"Sure," he says. "Shoot."

"I know the woman who owns it now," I say.

"I'm aware of that," Beck says. "Though I don't know the nature of your relationship."

"Old friends," I say. "So, you are trying to get the island from her?"

Beck slowly eats a couple of french fries. "Yes," he says finally.

"How?"

"It's very interesting. I've learned that you can find a flaw in anything if you look hard enough. Everything. No engineering solution is perfect. That's what I do, you know. I'm an engineering consultant. I review work by other engineers."

"I bet they love you," I say.

"The management does. I'm good at finding flaws. You see, flaws don't really bother me. It's the nature of the universe. As soon as anything comes into existence, it begins to fall apart. Entropy. Why should any human creation be different? Every object, every theory, every work of art, they all have flaws. And I knew there must be a flaw in this strange woman and her ownership of Skaarenor Island. And I was right."

"What kind of flaw?"

"Bad title. BOWS has its resources. A local attorney looked into it for us. A clever fellow. He did a title search. Quite the local historian as well. Very useful man. First he found a defect in the deed, a missing signature. Then he found a descendant of the missing signee. It was like manna from heaven."

"And the descendant...?"

"Pete Duncan. You know him, of course. Not my favorite person, I'll admit. I'm not going to go into details here, Jason, as you are not in the Brotherhood."

"She can just buy him off," I say.

"Not so simple," Beck says. "His minority interest gives him a lot of leverage. Gives BOWS a lot of power. We plan to visit that island, suggest some changes."

"Like what?"

"That castle will make an imposing fortification in a time of chaos, of anarchy. Enclose those first floor windows and you have a vertical rise of over 25 feet. That entrance needs serious attention, but I have ideas. And the tower. A commanding prospect of the entire island. Take down the trees around the site and you have something that is pretty much impregnable, except to more sophisticated weaponry than people are likely to have. That castle was built on a kind of whim, but ironically, it will serve the same purpose as a true medieval castle. The world will essentially return to the Middle Ages, with local lords and peasants. I think you can see that. And a privileged class, a small privileged class. You could be one of those, Jason."

"Intriguing," I say, and I am half serious.

"Pete Duncan gives us the keys to the castle, so to speak. With his interest in the property, and our assistance, we will, well, work with your friend to achieve the desired outcome."

"I think she wants to make it into a hotel, not a fort."

Beck smiles. "In a way, it could be both."

"I see the military potential," I say. "The lake is like a giant moat."

"Exactly," Beck says.

I think for a moment. I can see flaws in his plan and I suspect he can, too. Like what good is a moat that's frozen six months of the year, and daunting supply logistics, that kind of thing. I still don't think I have the whole story.

"I don't think you are telling me the whole story," I say.

Beck laughs. "You aren't in the Brotherhood," he says.

I talk to Ned again, tell him that BOWS is pretty serious about this, that they may make a move to occupy the island, even before the legal dust settles, if it ever does.

"Let me talk to the Executive Committee," Ned says. "But I think we may be taking a field trip."

"I know this motel," I tell him.

Afternoons are still warm, most of them, and that's when I run. I can do six miles at a pretty good clip. I can do forty push-ups without cheating on form. I'm reading two books a week. In this, I am awesome.

One night, Pam comes down the stairs.

"Jason?" she says. "Are you awake?"

Of course I'm not. It's the middle of the night. Pam comes into my room.

"I'm cold," she says.

I know why. She doesn't have any clothes on. Her white body seems to glow in the darkness.

"Can I join you?" she says.

My pulse beats in my head. "Um, Pam, you're still married, right?" I'm thinking of Nora. I should learn from my mistakes. Avoid married women, even if you don't know for sure.

She crosses her arms. "Are you telling me to go away?" she asks.

"No, I guess not," I say. "I don't know. I think I'm still asleep."

She just stands there.

"Well, come on in and warm up," I say.

She does, and after some quiet talk and snuggling, we make love, slowly, for the first and only time.

Chapter 27

Phaedra calls me at Doc's the next morning.

"They're here," she says.

That's how it starts, the siege of Castle Jones.

For two days, a lot of fishing boats buzz back and forth to Skaarenor Island. War is all about logistics, and both sides have their needs.

On the one side are the inhabitants of the castle. That would be me, Phaedra, and as of today, the Coalition Executive Committee, all of them except Tony who didn't want to leave work. It's damn cold in the castle, but we scrounge wood and try to heat a couple of the rooms. Most of us, not me, have sleeping bags and pads and very nice camping gear. I have two wool blankets and a puffy Batman bedcover from Pam, and also my pillow, and not nearly warm enough clothing. The Coalition guys are ready for anything. I think they dug into their stores and brought everything they could fit in their trucks. It took a dozen trips to get their stuff across the lake. It was ridiculous, but thankfully, it included some of Daniel's homegrown whiskey. Like a case of it.

On the other side is a bunch of BOWS guys. They've set up tents where they could find space, mostly near the lakeshore. It's hard to see how many there are, through the thick pines, but we think there are a lot of them. We hear them talking, chopping wood, smell their fires and their coffee and their bacon.

We and the BOWS guys haven't exchanged a word. We use the small landing at the end of the bay. I don't know where the BOWS guys are going ashore. We've literally passed each other, running supplies, and we do the northern Wisconsin one finger wave, which is always returned.

Phaedra is hopping mad. She sleeps in her own space, a little closet of a room. She tends to avoid us and mumbles a lot about trespassers and stupid boys' clubs. The guys are wary around her.

We do have some comforts. The Coalition brings a small Honda generator, we have some light and recharge the cell phones, at least as long as we have fuel. One bathroom by the kitchen works, thanks to Phaedra's restoration before she quit doing that. She says the septic system is crude but operational. I expect it is not very friendly to the lake's purity, but ask no questions. We get water from an old pump in the corner of the courtyard. It took Bill four hours to coax it back into operation. "I think the pipe follows a fissure in the rock," he tells us. "Or maybe it draws from a spring. Not real deep. Can't vouch for the potability." The Coalition guys treat the water with iodine pills. Phaedra and I just drink it. We drank worse when we were riding freight trains.

Using Phaedra's cell phone, I tell Doc that I have pleurisy. Can't make it to work.

"What the hell is that?" he says.

"Inflammation of the lung lining," I say, coughing vigorously. "Super contagious."

I also call Pam, so she knows I might not be around for a few days.

"Did we do something wrong?" she says.

"No, nothing like that."

"Where are you staying?"

I tell her.

"You're with Jasmine Jones." She sighs. "Well, I guess she's younger than me."

On the third day of the occupation. Pete and Beck approach the gate. Beck waves a white flag.

"Give up?" I say from the wall above them.

"Hell, no," Pete says. "Just didn't want you to shoot us. We know you got some paramilitary sorts in there."

"You never know," I say.

"You got to let me in," Pete says. "It's my…"

"Birthright," Beck says.

"It is," Pete says. "You have to give me control."

Beck says, "He has a legal right."

"This needs to go through the courts," I say. "I believe you are trespassing and the owner would like you to depart."

Pete reddens. "The owner? That's me. I've inherited this!"

"A tiny piece of it. Take a flagstone and go home," I say.

By now I've been joined by Ned, who's comes wheezing along the parapet. "My god, that's a lot of stairs," he says to me, then looks over the wall. "Mr. Thwaite," he says to Beck.

"Mr. Molson," Beck says. "How are you?"

"Doing well, doing well, thanks. So, what may I ask are you trying to accomplish with this invasion?"

"Just a friendly gathering to show our interest in supporting our colleague here." Beck puts his hand on Pete's shoulder, who shakes it off.

"We'll call the police," I say.

Both Beck and Ned look at me. "That's not necessary at this point," Ned says.

"I can just bust in here anytime I want," Pete says. "It's mine."

"He does have rights," Beck says. "A legitimate interest in the property. We'd like you to hear our proposal. Perhaps there's a way we can work this out."

"I've seen it," I say. Phaedra received it through her lawyers days ago. They offer to buy out Phaedra for a small amount of money and make Pete the full owner. "Your offer has been refused, I believe," I say.

"I'd like you two to take a look at a revised offer. We don't need lawyers. We can talk like men of good faith, reach an agreement. Then you can deal with that crazy woman."

"We'll take this under consideration," Ned says, and quietly to me, "that's enough—come away from the wall."

That afternoon, I find coal. Out of boredom, I've explored the place, top to bottom. The cellar is quite interesting. I guess they didn't want to bother with tearing out bedrock for a basement, so they just kind of leveled it and built it all higher. The cellar is dark and damp, but not really much underground. No pretense here. It's constructed of concrete. And has many little rooms. I suppose they needed a lot of columns to support the weight of the structure above, so these little rooms are really load bearing walls. At one far end, through a warped wooden door, I find coal. Didn't even recognize it at first. It's covered with dust and dirt, grey instead of black. But there's a lot in here and I suppose if coal can last millions of years in the ground, it can last 100 years or whatever in the basement.

It's messy to handle, hard to light, but it puts out a lot of heat and we colonize the Great Hall for the first time, putting a compact coal fire in the giant fireplace.

"Know any good ghost stories?" I ask. We're sitting and sipping whiskey after a long day of not doing much of anything.

"I heard about the tragic deaths of a Native American couple," Daniel says in his sonorous voice. "They are supposed to haunt the cliff where they jumped."

"Why did they jump?" I ask.

"I don't know," Daniel says, and that's the end of the ghost story.

We hear a thunderous knocking on the front door. We all start.

"Now what," Bill says.

Ned says, "Don't open the door. Let's go up to the wall. Someone get Jasmine."

It's Beck and a few followers. They have flashlights and shine them up at us.

"What is it?" Ned asks them.

It's nearly total darkness under the pines and Beck's disembodied voice comes from behind the flashlights.

"I just wanted to give you an update," he says. "Tell you about our latest research. I think you'll see that it changes the situation. Ms. Jasmine Jones, or whatever her name is, she, well, she is not being straight with you. She's not who she says she is."

"Are any of us?" Daniel says musingly.

"Let's just say the legal situation has changed and Mr. Duncan holds all the cards," Beck says. "So we have a change of policy here. We are going to take possession of the castle, very soon. Unless, of course, Ms. 'Whatever her name is' is ready to sign a newly revised agreement. I'm afraid that your bargaining position is eroding quickly."

"We'll involve the authorities," Bill says.

"Go right ahead. I hint there are grounds for fraud and other malfeasance here. Ms. Jasmine Jones could lose everything, even face some prison time. But if she signs the agreement, we can keep this between us, like gentlemen. In the meantime, I think it's fair to say you are our guests on the island."

Phaedra, who has been standing behind us, goes to the edge of the wall. "You don't know who you're messing with," she says.

"Oh, yes," Beck says. "I think we do, and that's the point."

We go back downstairs to total darkness.

"Generator must've shut down for some reason," Bill says. "Be right back."

We sit in front of the dim coals, Phaedra with us. She's cross-legged on the floor. The Coalition guys sit in camp chairs they brought with them. I'm sitting in Bill's.

"It's gone," Bill says when he returns. "While we were chatting, they came over the courtyard wall and stole the generator."

We all stare at the trouble light that sits up on the mantle, trailing an orange extension cord that exits the room through the door in the paneling. Now it doesn't look turned off. It looks dead.

Orwin, who doesn't say much, clears his throat. I think it's time we reconsider this," he say. "We don't want BOWS to have this place, for all kinds of reasons. But this is getting really complicated and it's going beyond what at least I care about. Sorry, Jasmine, but I think you might be on your own."

Phaedra sits with shoulders slumped, so that her hair falls alongside her face. She looks young again to me.

"I think about what this used to look like," she says quietly. "There were big chandeliers in this room, lights along the walls. It was full of people, and talk, and the smells of food and fireplace logs and polished wood. And there was movement, with kids and dogs and Teddy Roosevelt talking about his muskie, filling the room with his voice. It could be like that again, not exactly of course, but a place full of light and life and people." She sits up straight, looks at the men. "Or it could be a fort with walled up windows, full of people cowering behind the walls, waiting for disaster."

"There's nothing wrong with being prepared," Bill says.

"Oh, yes there is," Phaedra says. "When it becomes the center of your life, when the craving for catastrophe overpowers the life of the moment. I know about this. We live in the present, nowhere else. The past is gone and the future is crazy, far crazier than you can ever predict. All you have is now, and if your preparation for survival is the moment, is the life in the present, what do you have?"

"Nothing?" Daniel asks.

"A lot of carefully prepared supplies," Bill says.

"You don't smell the flowers," Orwin says, and they all look at him.

"So, what are you saying?" Ned asks Phaedra.

"Don't leave me," Phaedra says. "Not yet. I'll lose everything."

I've read too much about the Middle Ages. In the theater of my mind, I see Queen Phaedra, adorned in regal apparel, but not her most elaborate, just the kind reserved for private audiences in her own chambers. Anyway, the Queen rises from her chair. She's loosened the grip on the chair's arms, the arms richly carved with twisting vines and snarling lion's heads, the grip that tightened as she heard the devastating news of the enemy, that the wolf was at the gate. Anyway, the Queen slowly rises, her many attendants lost in shadow behind her, though the dancing lights of the torches clearly illume the Queen's pale but strong face. Anyway, she rises to address the men assembled before her.

"Noble knights," she says. "You have heard that the wolf stands at our very gate. That the savage beast howls for our blood. Noble knights, I need not remind you of your oaths and the fealty sworn to me, my father, and my late husband, the noble Adolphus, Earl of Skaarenor." The Queen looks at each man in turn, engaging their eyes so that they cannot but find their own nobility.

"And I need not remind you of the house you serve, the house of Harald Blood Axe, who founded this line, and how his knights swore their oaths to him and vanquished his enemy, Peter Tapeworm, and noble knights have sworn oaths to every seed of those loins since, down through the generations. I do not need to tell you that now is the time to forsake comfort, forget wives and the gentle laugh of children, forget the banquet table, the mead, the wench behind the barn whose eyes are as blue as the summer sea. Now is the time to sharpen weapons, clash shields, and thirst for the enemy's blood. Now is the time to befriend friendless Death, to embrace the gore of glory, that your deeds may be remembered in song by the sons of your sons. Now is the time to pile the heads of our enemies and feed their bloodless bodies to the crows, whilst their widows weep and wail and their castles fall to ruins and the very skies of their homelands burn with the shame of defeat. For they have invaded our lands, with fire and slaughter and wicked intent, and they must be destroyed, here, now, and forever, at our very gate." The Queen's voice rises to a crescendo. "And these dogs stole our generator!"

"Now witness my oath," I say loudly, "When the blood runs, I am the Berserker!"

Ned stares at me. "Let's turn it down a notch, eh, Jason?"

We sit in silence for a minute or two and I tame my adrenalin.

"They took our generator," Bill says. "That unit was not cheap."

"I take offense to that," Ned says.

"So do I," Daniel says.

We look at Orwin. He looks at the coals. "Okay," he says. "I'll go with it for a few more days."

The next day, Winter Lake is again buzzing with fishing boats. BOWS people are boating back and forth to the marina, maybe for supplies. But we have our share of traffic, too.

Now, kind of like Orwin, I am having second thoughts. "Ned," I say. "Don't you think this is all going to attract some attention, all these boats? And with the generator gone, aren't you guys going to want the authorities involved?"

"This is all on private property," he says. "For all anyone knows, it's a family reunion. And Jason, you are dealing with a bunch of guys who have been seriously preparing for something or a long time. This is a kind of something. This whole thing, it sort of validates the preparation. These guys are having fun."

We use our dwindling cell phone batteries to make a few calls.

Ned calls his legal colleagues. Orwin calls to tell his wife he's staying for a bit longer. Bill starts the Coalition calling tree. I call Pam and Doc and cautiously ask for a few favors. I don't know who else to call.

We talk a lot about what BOWS means by taking possession. We know we can't leave the castle unattended, but how many people does this require? And how exactly would they take possession? Storm the castle?

"Yes," Ned says. "I think they intend to more or less physically displace us."

"That is so illegal," Phaedra says.

"Do you have anything you'd like to tell us?" Daniel says gently.

"I change my name a lot," Phaedra says.

"Legal name changes?" Ned asks.

"Fake ID's," Phaedra says.

"What about the realtor's license?" Bill asks.

"Forged," Phaedra says. "I know these people in New York."

"You said you took the classes," I say.

"I took a few online," Phaedra says. "It seemed pretty straightforward."

"And your purchase of the island, where does that stand?" Ned asks.

"That should be totally legitimate," Phaedra says. "I went through my lawyers. They created the LLC. They know, well, a few things about me. I've been a good client."

"I bet you have," Ned says.

"But this doesn't mean I can't have a dream," Phaedra says, charming the men with a smile. "A person has to have a dream."

"Yes, well, that may be," Ned says. "But this is quite a pickle."

"We need more bodies here," Bill says. "That would be the best deterrent."

"Or we could just see this as a lost cause," Orwin says. "Sorry, but that seems like the outcome to me, that this is going to end up with Duncan owning some piece of it."

"Over my dead body," Phaedra says.

"Don't say that," Bill says sharply. "I've buried a wife and a son."

"We could man the wall with dummies," I suggest.

"Give them fake muskets?" Bill says. "I saw that movie. Didn't work."

"Well," Ned says. "Here is how I see it. First, we should find out what BOWS thinks they know that changes the situation. Jasmine—what should I call you?"

"I'm leaning toward Lucinda now, but Jasmine is fine," Phaedra says.

"Jasmine's past should not be a major issue, if the sale is legitimate, unless you did something fraudulent in the transaction."

"I didn't," Phaedra says.

"Second, we should see how they are playing this out. Maybe a couple of us visit them or even leave the island," Ned says.

"They might just take the castle then," I say.

"I think we could spare one or two of us," Orwin says. "I'll go."

"Third," Bill says. "I want that generator back."

"Agreed," Ned says.

"The phone tree should be working its magic soon," Bill says. "We should be getting more supplies, maybe even a few bodies."

I still think a lot about my conversation with Beck and the hint that there might be more to the story. Either he planted that with me as a distraction, or Beck made a mistake. Either way, it's interesting to ponder.

What else could be going on?

On the face of it, the asteroid paranoia seems pretty reasonable. If you look at that situation from a BOWS point of view, obtaining something more than their barn and two cabins makes good sense. I'll grant that. The asteroid, to me at least is a big if. Beck gains too much from this convenient impending doom for me to accept it without a healthy dose of skepticism.

But what else could be involved? Is there something else in the castle or on the island that BOWS wants? Or that Beck wants? That makes me pause for a moment, and something in my gut resonates to the idea of Beck wanting, gaining something. He's always seemed straight enough. Candid. Eminently reasonable. Disarming. Almost eager to share information.

I know that Cherry, my dad's wife, and once my friend, would see this differently. She worked as a waitress where I washed dishes and bused tables. She gave me rides home, and lots of advice. Most of it had to do with not trusting men. I have extended this, in a limited way, to women, but I've never fully embraced that world view. To her, the better things looked, the worse they really were. I wonder what it's like to be married to her.

I can even hear Rusty sounding a warning note, or Lark. Or Bob. Or Miles. Or Nora. Chess would be oblivious.

Still, I have to come back to one thing. What is in this for Beck, or for anyone, if not just possessing a castle, for whatever purpose?

I decide to investigate.

Chapter 28

The next morning, day six, Pam and Dylan arrive.

"I called in sick," Dylan says. "First time. It was easier than I thought."

Pam hands me a cardboard box. "Here's some food for you and the boys," she says. "Three loaves of whole grain bread. I baked them myself from that frozen dough you get at the grocery. Two packages of tofu. They are from my fridge. Date's expired, but they should be fine. And then some things that Dylan thought of. Beef sticks. Pepper cheese. What else? Raisins. Cheese crackers. And hot chocolate mix."

"That sounds great, Pam," I say. "Thanks."

Pam smiles but then her face clouds. "Sorry," she says.

"For what?" I ask.

"I think all of this is my fault," she says.

"I don't see how," I say.

"Pete, isn't he in the middle of this, says he really owns the castle?"

"Where did you hear that?" I ask.

"You told me, and it's all over town. Everyone knows that's there's this big standoff here, though no one quite understands why."

"Well, Pete does own a little piece of it," I say.

"Give it to him, the little piece. He will never let this go. God, anything I ever did, like talked to some guy or forgot to pay a bill, he would bring it up over and over."

"So how is this your fault?"

"He's doing this to get back at me, for wanting to divorce him, and for bringing you into the house, for having Dylan, or for giving him hell, which I did, because he deserved it."

"Pete is just a pawn in this," I say.

"Will he still get money?"

"I don't know," I say. "I hope not."

"I hope so. Oh, how I hope so."

My investigation gets off to a slow start. First, I make a list of possible things that could benefit Beck, and them I'm stuck. My list: buried treasure, in the house or somewhere on the island. Unlikely, but possible. Wants to create his own hotel. Possible but unlikely. Too much work, and he has a good job, or so he says. I don't know, maybe the guy is broke. Really likes the castle. Reject. Really wants this for BOWS and the benefit of humankind everywhere. I reluctantly reject this too.

I try a different strategy and search the castle for clues. Since I've wandered it from top to bottom at least a dozen times already, this yields little. Actually, nothing. I take a stroll outside the walls, for the first time. I don't know what to expect if I encounter a BOWS guy.

"Hey," I say to two men walking in the woods, along the same barely traceable path as me.

"Good morning," one says.

"Did you see the white pines on the west side of the island? I don't think those were ever timbered," the other man says.

"No," I say. "Haven't seen those yet. Thanks for the tip."

This is a very polite siege.

In the afternoon, Hammie and Doc show up. They bang on the door and I look down from the wall. I'm standing sentry, a two hour shift.

"Get your ass down here and help us," Doc says.

They've brought six cases of beer in bottles, like I requested.

"Thank God," I say. "Did you bring an opener?"

Hammie and Doc look at each other.

"Crap," Hammie says, but then shows me how to pop a bottle cap with his ring.

"I wish I had a ring," I say.

"It's the concept that matters," Hammie says. "You can find something."

"So, how's it going?" Doc says. We are up on the wall, with one of the cases. "Anyone get killed yet?"

"Not yet," I say. "Though we are missing a generator and there's a mysterious spray of paintballs on the side of the tower."

"I'll get the generator," Hammie says. "Give me another beer first."

"I'll go with you," I say.

"Naw," Hammie says. "I'll bring Doc. You'll just say something nerdy and piss everyone off."

It's starting to get dark when they leave. I tell the others about their plans.

I take the beer to the basement while they're gone. It will refrigerate it enough. I walk carefully over the uneven floor and find a place to stash the beer where no one will trip over it. The case wobbles on a floor bump and I shift around, trying to find a smoother spot. My flashlight shines against the wall, on the concrete. I think this must have been quite a job, pouring all this concrete, quite an engineering feat, just to design this place so it wouldn't fall in on itself.

Then why is the floor so bumpy?

I scuff away dirt. It's clearly rock, not concrete. Makes sense, I guess. They're on the top of a rock hill, so who needs to pour a floor? Just smooth it enough to place the walls. But why not smooth it more? It's got cracks as I begin to study it, big cracks. You hardly notice walking. The cracks don't gape to an abyss. But I can see them, all over, when you look closely. And the rock itself, it's greenish. The castle is gray limestone, and the rock I've seen all over the island looks like granite to me, rough and spotty grey. This rock is a lot smoother. Of course, they could have smoothed it. But why is it different?

I scuff away dirt in different parts of the cellar, actually finding a few things in the process, like an old nickel and two bobby pins. When were these invented, the bobby pins? Did these belong to the Skaarenor daughters? Did they play down here, hide and seek? Maybe tell terrifying stories?

Everywhere I scuff away dirt, there's greenish rock, and more cracks.

My musings are interrupted by the return of Doc and Hammie. We let them in the main entrance. They are splattered with paintballs.

"Did you get the generator?" Bill asks.

"No, but we kicked some ass," Doc says. "We go into their camp. Well, actually there are like four camps. We picked one. "Give me the goddam generator," Hammie says."

""These guys all look at us like we're crazy," Hammie says. "They start asking us if we are from the castle.""

"Hell, yes, we tell them," Doc says. "And give us the generator and no bullshit and no one gets hurt."

"They just stand there, looking stupid, and one guy says, what generator, and we're like the one from the castle, asshole. Give it up," Hammie says.

"They said they didn't have it, so we say go get the son of a bitch," Doc says. "And one guy, this little guy, says no."

"He said no, right to us," Hammie says.

"So what happened?" I say.

"We went apeshit," Doc says. "Started just kicking down their tents."

"Then it was like ants, all these guys come boiling out and there's all this yelling," Hammie says.

"That's when they opened fire," Doc says. "Those little suckers sting. Why would anyone want to shoot these at each other? Crazy motherfuckers."

"So we started laughing our asses off and ran back here," Hammie says.

"Our first sortie," Ned says. "Well, good try, men."

I ride back to Winter Lake with Hammie and Doc in their camo bass boat. The water is rough, and Doc has been downing beers, and he and Hammie whoop and holler every time the boat tips or we crash into a wave. It's also almost completely dark and I have no idea if they know where they are going.

They don't. "Hell, it's a lake," Doc says. "You can't get lost forever."

"Unless we run out of gas," Hammie says.

It's great to see Carmen, and it's great to sleep in my own bed, though it is no warmer in the basement than it is in the castle. Pam is happy to see me, doesn't seem surprised. Dylan has the night shift.

The next morning, I head for the library. I spend all day on the computer and in the reference section. I take a lot of notes. I do a lot of thinking.

When I get back to the castle—I hitch a ride with a couple of Coalition re-supply guys, dropping off goods and going home—Ned meets me at the gate.

"She's gone," he says. "Your friend Jasmine."

"Gone?"

"Yep. All her stuff is gone. We checked her room. Now what?"

"She might come back," I say, knowing she won't. This was getting a bit too real for her, and she was at risk of being held accountable for something. That's how I see it, anyway.

Phaedra might be gone, but I find Chess is in the castle.

"How'd you get here?" I ask him.

"Boat," Chess says. Bob and Miles are with Chess and I give them all beers. The supply is going fast.

"I'll be right back," I tell them.

I find Ned. "We need to have a meeting tonight. I might have something interesting to tell you."

Ned nods. "We can arrange that," he says.

Chess tells me they heard about this from Ned.

"We kind of stayed in touch," Chess says. "He's a fan, you know. I signed his Christmas album. Figured I'd better get the boys." Chess leans close to me. "Sounded like a military operation."

Bob and Miles drink their beer and, as usual, submerse themselves in brother talk. They could be anywhere, here, a café in Paris, a soccer game in Lima, the top of Everest, it wouldn't matter. They'd still have the same conversation.

"Brought my guitar," Chess says. "Thought you folks could use a little entertainment. Where's your little lady?"

"Run off," I say.

"They do that, bless their hearts," Chess says.

We meet in the Great Hall, with a blazing fire in the giant fireplace. There are 17 of us now, including Chess, Bob, and Miles. Most of us sit on the floor. Only the Executive Committee thought to bring chairs.

I stand. "I found some things that made me wonder when I was poking around in the basement," I say. So I went into town and did some research. First, bobby pins became popular in the 1920's, to hold the poplar 'bobbed' hairstyle in place."

"Who gives a shit," someone says.

"I think that's interesting," Daniel says.

"Okay, okay. Here's the more important stuff," I say. "Long, long ago..."

"In a galaxy far, far way," Miles says.

"Nope," I say. "Right here. Long ago there was this huge volcanic eruption, covered what would be a lot of Canada and the US in molten lava, which cooled. This sort of became our base rock, our bottom layer. Then mountains came and went. Did you know that Wisconsin once had mountains like the Alps? And when the mountains went away, there were oceans here. And there were the glaciers. All these things put rock on top of rock, and underneath it all is the basalt, that volcanic rock."

I pause. They all stare at me.

"Well, time passes," I say. "And erosion and more glaciers and whatever sometimes bury this old rock under miles of newer rock and sometimes they scrape it bare. The old rock is called a craton, this base layer..."

"Get on with it," Bill says.

"Okay," I say. "Up here in northwestern Wisconsin and over in Minnesota, you can find, in a few places, some of the oldest exposed rock in the world. It's the craton, this old, old basaltic rock. Isn't that kind of cool?"

"Guess so," someone says.

"Well, you're sitting on an outcropping of this old, old rock. It's called greenstone, and where it's exposed in an area, it called a greenstone belt. All the softer rock has eroded or worn away, leaving the fundamental rock, the layer that goes right to the mantle, way, way, down. Our Skaarenor Island is a hump of greenstone, with some granite chunks, as you may have noticed." Again, I pause. Again they stare.

"So here we are, on greenstone. And I was in the cellar, sorting beer..."

"Who wants another beer?" someone says and we wait while two guys go to fetch it.

"Anyway, I noticed when I was in the cellar that the floor is not concrete but just bedrock, and now I know it's the greenstone. The basement floor is greenstone, with lots of cracks. Now why would Adolphus Skaarenor leave this exposed, I asked myself."

"And what did you answer?" Ned says.

"That Adolphus not only gave his daughters this island, the castle, and some stock, which, by the way, turned out to be worthless, which is pretty sad. But he left them..."

"What?" someone says.

"A goldmine," I say.

"Like a figurative goldmine, or a real one? I'm an engineer. I don't like metaphors," Bill says.

"I think it's a real one. Or it could be silver. Or even diamonds. Or maybe just copper, but that's worth a lot of money now, too."

"I don't follow" Ned says. "Why does greenstone, if that's what it is, equate to precious metals and such?"

"Long ago," I say. "Like in the late 1700's, this area of Wisconsin was mined for copper and lead. The Native Americans collected hunks of copper. People even panned for gold around here back then and they still do now. These are base metals, formed in base layers. There were some rich deposits around here, and right now in Canada, they are mining greenstone for diamonds."

"So is the exposed greenstone that rare?" Ned asks.

"Not really, not around here. It is everywhere else," I say. "But I think Adolphus was a very smart man. He made a lot of money buying and selling property and he sold a lot of property to mining speculators. I think he knew what he was doing. I think he located his estate in this isolated place for a reason. I think he did some test drilling and built his castle on the best site he could find. If it was a rich vein of, say, gold, he could just about guarantee the Skaarenor's wealth for generations. And he had all these daughters. I think he wanted to take care of them."

"And they didn't know it?" Bill says. "He'd have told them."

"I don't know what happened with that," I say. "It doesn't fit, I admit. But for some reason, he never told his family, or if they knew, they didn't follow through on it.

Maybe they didn't believe him, maybe he died before he could tell anyone. Who knows?" I say.

"So, Jasmine, who is gone, might have herself quite a parcel of land," Ned says.

"And I think Beck knows the same thing," I say. "I don't know how. He solves engineering problems, a consultant. Maybe he heard something, maybe he just knows a lot. He's a smart man. I think he wants this island, not for BOWS, or well, maybe for BOWS and their fort, and all that, but also to get at the precious metal."

The guys look a little doubtful. "I'd need more evidence," Bill says.

"So would I," Orwin says.

"It's a wonderful story," Daniel says, with a kind smile.

"Well," says Chess, "that calls for a song." He retrieves his guitar. "Once I found out what was going on up here, I thought you could use some music to fit the bill."

Chess strums a mournful chord. "Long ago, there were these ministers that wandered the land, singing songs."

"Minstrels," says Bob.

"Ministers," Chess says. "Minstrels are black guys. And don't interrupt me. Anyway, there were these singing ministers and they wrote songs about, well, religion I suppose, but also about stuff that happened. And in the spirit of that, I give you The Ballad of the Castle." He strums another chord and begins to sing.

The Ballad of the Castle
By Chess Chalmers

It was a dark and stormy day
And the prairie dogs did play

On a field far way
From the castle on a hill

And like the wind that cruelly blows
More than your fingers and your toes
That's how many came the foes
To the castle on the hill

The good people got afeared
As the enemy, they neared
That their hides would all be seared
In the castle on the hill

But there were soldiers bold
Like in the days of old
The darkness in their hearts was cold
Up on that castle on a hill

Even with darkness in their hearts
They knew they'd do their parts
Because they knew the martial arts
On the castle on the hill

They defended it like hell
But things did not go well
And every soldier fell
From that castle on the hill

And the people they all cried
And every one of them died
And the wind so lonely sighed
On the castle on the hill

Now the prairie dogs still play
On those fields far away
And the ghosts, they moan all day
In that castle on the hill

"That's it?" I say. "Geez, Chess, that's not very encouraging."

"Them was tough times," Chess says. "Many a good man, and woman, fell along the wayside. You need to read some history, Jake."

"I like it," Daniel says. "Let's hear it again."

"Someone wrote their initials in paintballs, right by the front door," Orwin says. We are on the wall, drinking hot chocolate from my private stock.

"Barbarians," I say.

"He did a pretty neat job of it," Orwin says.

"So, what do you think about the precious metal thing?" I ask Orwin.

He's quiet for a long time. I think maybe he didn't hear me.

"Have you looked for anything from Adolphus? Like go to a historical society and see if they have journals or letters?" he says. "Something to confirm your story?"

The Winawan County Historical Society is located in Elmwood, the county seat. It's in an old house, and an hour's drive from Winter Lake.

An elderly lady sits behind a desk in what was once the living room.

"Can I help you?" she says. She has a giant mug of black coffee. It smells good. I'm tired, been basically up all night. I don't know if I need to sneak off of the island, but I did, in deep night, using a Coalition boat. I made my own slow and careful way to the marina, which was closed, and I had to convince a German Shepherd I meant no harm and climb over a fence, and then walk back to town, which was a lot longer than I thought. It goes so fast when you drive, you lose perspective.

"Yes," I say. "I am researching Adolphus Skaarenor…"

"The castle," the old woman says. "Sure, we have some materials. What kind or research are you doing?"

"I'm looking for primary sources. I'm a graduate student, or I should say, will be soon, if all goes well, and this is sort of a private quest, though I hope to develop this into a more comprehensive study in the future."

"Hmm," she says and drinks coffee. "I heard there's some kind of turmoil up there right now, that a bunch of people are camped out and who knows what. Are you involved with that?"

"That's terrible," I say. "You said you have materials?"

She slowly rises. She's a big old lady and the floor squeaks as she walks to a wall of file cabinets.

"We should really have better storage for these documents," she says as she looks through files. "We're getting some deterioration."

"Anyone else been interested in this?" I ask, on a whim.

"Sure," she says. "Lots of people over the years. That castle attracts a lot of attention. People get curious… let's see. Here's something you might find interesting. We have some letters from the Skaarenor girl who went to New York, letters back home."

She walks heavily back to me, hands me the file. "There's a desk in the dining room," she says.

Her name is Solveig, and she writes in a fancy round hand, with many exclamation points. The ink has faded, though the paper is surprisingly bright. There are just a handful of letters, all to sisters.

Dearest Lenora,

Thank you so much for your letter and all the news. You asked me so many questions!

Yes, it is very hard here, and without the aid of father's business associates, I'd soon be starving on the street! Yes, my apartment is safe, though it is very noisy and so very close. The air is so bad here, I fear for my health. Am I lonely? Of course! I miss you all terribly! But I do so love the action here, and I think I shall get my chance to play piano with a quite good band, very soon. I've been speaking with the bandleader, a friendly man, who has assured me I would be quite safe joining his musicians some night. He is, he says, waiting for the appropriate venue! Things are so very complicated here with the Prohibition, but I do not need to tell about that. You have always been one to pour over the newspaper. I wish I had the desire to read as you do! You are so very smart, and I must be satisfied with my poor skills on the piano!

No, I have not become a flapper! I dress much the same as in Wisconsin, as that is what I own, and I cannot picture myself in so short and straight a dress as some women here wear. I am by far too tall and too thin as it is and I feel quite awkward enough!

Of course, I do not drink or smoke, or if I did, would never tell you!

Are you well? Are you enjoying the spring? Tell me all about the sounds and smells, and the flowers and the water! I miss them all so terribly here…

The few letters I read say much the same things, yearning for home, vague plans for performing, many assurances of virtuous behavior. The letters are difficult to read and soon I am seeing spots for concentrating. I lean back in my chair many times, and suddenly and quite inadvertently, I fall sleep.

In my short nap, I dream intensely. I am running in the castle, though it is bigger and stranger and part of it looks like a Holiday Inn. I know there is a fire and that the stones are burning. I know that everyone is gone but me, and I am trying to find Pam's cat. I am racing from room to room, door to door, with an alarming sense of urgency, looking for the cat for whom I have very mixed feelings. I fling a door open and am confronted by a woman in Victorian clothing. She clasps her hands in front of her. Her face is troubled. She is tall and straight and looks right though me. Behind her I see flames. She opens her hands and speaks soundlessly, just her lips move, but I have no trouble understanding. "Father," she says.

I awake with a jerk and try to cover it with a cough, but no one is watching me.

"Do you have other letters?" I ask the woman behind the desk.

"Indeed we do." I hate to make her move. It looks so painful for her to push back from the desk, struggle to her feet, and lumber back to the files. She looks for some time.

"I don't see the ones…. maybe misfiled." She turns to me. "Letters from another sister, the one who stayed in Winter

Lake. They are quite interesting, and she is not at all happy with being one of those left behind. Most the sisters moved on, except her, and two who were rather helpless, you know. I can't recall her name. Married a Duncan... no, I don't see them."

"Do you remember what kinds of things she said?" I ask.

"I remember one letter, to another of the sisters, one in Chicago. I don't recall her name. The Winter Lake girl is quite upset, complains of being saddled with caring for their father."

"Caring for him? Was he ill?" I ask.

"I suppose we'd say it's Alzheimer's. She calls her father a lunatic, wait, not a lunatic... She talks about his lunacy, which is different. Talks about his dementia."

Now I think I understand.

Chapter 29

Without Phaedra, defending the castle seems somewhat pointless, and after a few meetings under a white flag, both armies crowd into the Great Hall.

There is little sense of animosity, as the men begin to compare hardware, fish stories, exaggerated exploits, and the rest of my beer.

"We have reached an agreement," Beck says to the group. He nods to Ned, who, not feeling well, points to Bill. Bill rises to speak.

"First, we want to express our admiration for the skill displayed in executing so many paintball designs on the castle walls. Some are truly works of art, like the giant boobs on the south wall." Laughter. "Second, we'd like to recognize Beck Thwaite and his negotiating team for their hard work in hammering out this agreement." Beck nods to Bill.

"Third," Bill says. "Here's the deal. None of us get the castle, which is really too bad."

"May I speak?" Beck says.

"I yield the floor to the commander of BOWS," Bill says formally.

"Peter Duncan has accepted a buy-out offer for his share in the castle and Skaarenor Island." There are a few groans.

"No, no, this is business and his free choice. This is America, and we must accept any man's desire to have a financially secure future, and as Mr. Duncan is not present, let me add that this may be his only road to such a future." Laughter.

Beck continues. "C'est La Vie LLC now has complete control of the property, and the lawyers tell us that the LLC is seeking designation with the National Registry of Historic Places, which would prevent any significant alterations to the castle. For me personally, I regret this turn of events."

"I guess we can all go home," Bill says.

"Agreed," Beck says. "But we have gained something important for all this. Bill?"

"The Executive Committee of the Coalition will begin talks with BOWS, to explore areas of collaboration and common interest." A few people applaud. "If there is an asteroid headed for earth, and…" Bill pauses. I can tell he's going to cast doubt on that claim. "Well, let's just say that who knows what could happen. I mean, what is a disaster but lack of preparation? We can find common ground."

I stand by the door of the Great Hall, waiting for Beck to pass.

"Greenstone," I say to him.

He stops, smiles, and wags his finger at me.

"So they bought Pete," Dylan says to me.

"Surprised?" I say.

"Yes," Dylan says. "I thought he'd take this as far as he could, until there was total war. Then he'd be in his element."

"I think it was a lot of money," I say.

Dylan shakes his head. "Well, I hope Mom gets a big chunk of it."

Me, I doubt it. Things don't work that way. But I say, "I hope so, too."

Pam makes a victory feast, as she calls it, of tofurky, a tofu rendition of turkey meat, which is probably the most vile thing I have ever actually swallowed, and acorn squash with brown sugar, which is great. I contribute an ice cream cake and two bottles of champagne.

"Maybe Jason would like to go to college with you," Pam says to Dylan.

"Mom, I don't want to go over that again," Dylan says.

"I think I need to go back to Illinois," I say, though I truly hate to say it. This feels kind of like a family, and I haven't had a lot of time in one of these vaunted units, these legendary wellsprings of character, values, and successful relationship skills, all things I lack. But Anna Bella says I can start at her college in January, with a grant and a student job, and live in her house, and try this whole thing over again, if I want to. Maybe I can make it work. I doubt it, but maybe.

"Hi," I say. "It's Jason Audley,"

"Jason!" Marlin Miller says, and then off the phone, "Tookie, it's Jason."

"How are things?" I ask.

"Can't complain," Marlin says. "The economy hasn't been too good. Not a lot of new build-outs for us, but we're keeping our heads above water."

"That's great," I say.

"Well, how are you?" Marlin asks. "It's so nice to hear from you. Wait, I think Mother is going to get on the other line. Not your mother! What am I saying?"

"Hi, Jason," Tookie says warmly. "So nice of you to call. I ran into your father at the grocery store. He's lost weight, you know. Got a hair implant or something. He looks younger with hair on his head."

"I bet," I say, trying to picture my Dad's balding head with hair and failing. All I can see is his hairy back and shoulders and that's all I can handle.

"I have some news for you," I say.

"Back in college?" Marlin asks.

"I found Davey," I say. For some reason I am having trouble getting these words out. "He's in Winter Lake, that's in Wisconsin. He's not doing so well. I can give you his address. He needs you."

I think what happened is this.

Adolphus Skaarenor is a lumberman, and when he sees this boom in iron ore mining, he senses money to be made. He doesn't know anything about mining or iron ore or geology. He doesn't know base metals and ore quality and ore markets. He doesn't care. He has land-hungry speculators out east, people always eager to turn profit from land they'll never see. Will they mine it? No. They'll sell it to those who'll try. And Adolphus is willing to forgo some money to these middlemen. But there are a few things Adolphus needs to do. He needs surveys, reports, something, anything, that makes his land look like a sure bet for iron ore.

Somewhere in one these surveys, they spot something real. Might be gold, just copper, could be silver, could be diamonds. It's Skaarenor Island. And Adolphus takes it for himself. He wants a castle. Probably his wife and daughters wanted to live somewhere by a city. Who knows? Maybe not. His wife was local. Those striking young women look very outdoorsy in the old photos. Adolphus builds his castle, just like I suggested to the BOWS folks, on top of his goldmine.

Does he tell anyone? I think he enjoyed his little secret, a poor teenager who came to the United States seeking a fortune and finding wealth as so very few did. He held the secret of the greenstone for a long time, and then, not even all that old, developed dementia. Who knows how bad he was, or what he put his wife and the Winter Lake daughter through. He probably talked about the goldmine, desperate to share the secret, but mixed with who knows what other broken tales of his hard life, or maybe ravings in Swedish-- no one believed him.

Or maybe he never intended to tell them anything. Maybe the basement greenstone is a clue. He was a self-made man. Maybe he thought his kids could show the same initiative.

It's hard to picture mining the basement of your own house. If it's a clue, that might just tell his descendants to look elsewhere on the island. Or maybe, just maybe, I should have looked more closely at those cracks and fissures in the floor. Maybe they were veins of precious metal, right there in the open.

But who knows, maybe I'm wrong. But to me, the wealth Adolphus meant for generations of his family lies there, nearly in plain sight, haunting the castle. It's the ghost of Adolphus Skaarenor.

And Phaedra, gone again. Apparently freedom, money, and a certain courage, these don't add up to being happy. I wonder what does.

Chapter 30

Houston, Texas. NASA today denied that a Near Earth Object had passed in the vicinity of our planet, responding to allegations of a cover up. What started as a buzz on blogs and websites made it into the news media two days ago when a Wisconsin congressman called for an investigation.

"Asteroid Thwaite might have been real, "said Congressman Elam Harvey. "And if it was, the public has a right to know." Astronomers at several universities, including the University of Wisconsin, echoed NASA's rejection. Still, a number of amateur astronomers back the near miss story.

"Oh, it was real enough. Not big, but, gosh, that was close," said Paul Baker of Kenosha, Wisconsin. "They just didn't want people to panic so they hid the truth..."

On a dull December day, I'm back in Anna Bella's basement, ever the troglodyte. I pick through the musty books that lie in heaps and piles. I'm going to get rid of a lot of them. I need room. I once had drums, but they are long gone, so I bought a dilapidated set from the Black Mambas. Maybe I can find a band.

On the way back to Illinois, I stopped at Bill's. We gave Roger's bike a thorough tuning. I left it in Roger and Mai's backyard, in the middle of the night.

And I bought Carmen, though Orwin offered to give her to me. I knew she would never want to be valued so cheaply.

So I do have these things to show, and a little money from the casino, and some savings from changing oil. And from Pam's, a few lingering cat scratches.

Phaedra's check for $10,000 didn't bounce. I can't believe it.

CPSIA information can be obtained at www.ICGtesting.com
Printed in the USA
BVOW020125121112

305264BV00007B/2/P